P9-CKX-551

EX LIBRIS

California Four O'Clock

FOR JUNICHI —
MY BROTHER IN DESIGN & INTERSHIP!
THANK You FOR Your SUPPORT.

California Four O'Clock

Martin McClellan

Copyright ©2015 Martin McClellan
All rights reserved

Illustrations by Vicki Nerino – VICKINERINO.COM
Cover lettering by Scott Boms – SCOTTBOMS.COM
Book design by the author

Limited Kickstarter edition of 500 copies

Printed by Sheridan Books, in CHELSEA MI, USA

This is a work of fiction. Names, characters, places, and events are fully the
product of the author's imagination, or are used fictitiously. Any resemblence
to real people, businesses, events, or locations is completely coincidental.

CALIFORNIAFOUROCLOCK.COM
MARTINMCCLELLAN.COM

Letters From the Hellbox Press
PO BOX 19871 SEATTLE, WA 98109

LETTERS FROM THE HELLBOX PRESS

For Marilyn, my mother, the sunburnt redhead on the bus home from the beach

Each day is divided for them into a hundred little sensual experiences — a passing look, a flirting smile, an accidental contact of the knees — and each year into a hundred such days, in which the sensual experience constitutes the ever-flowing, life-giving and quickening source of their existence.

- Stefan Zweig

Should we have stayed at home and thought of here?

- Elizabeth Bishop

1955 – Los Angeles

DELORES SARJEANT marched across
the great hall of Union Station, her heels sounding click-clack on
the Spanish tiles. Behind her, a red cap shuffled along with her suitcases, his lopping rhythm and her strident march combined to echo
the movement her three-day train journey, with its lurching staccato.
They advanced across the shadow-cast deco noir, the box leather chairs
bearing smoking men in slumped sun-kissed fedoras, fingering sports
pages.

She wore a slate-gray tweed pencil skirt to mid-calf, a matching
jacket with padded shoulders. Sable hair smoothed and pinned tight
to her scalp, the best she could manage with the trifling glass in her
compartment.

Delores was almost thirty, and to her this milestone came with a
bundle of rights she previously felt unattainable. The right to happiness, for one. If 1955 held anything for her, surely it was this.

Along the path they went, she with chin up, preparing herself for encountering Mother. The walkway's lines converged on those big brass cathedral doors; they opened and closed during her progress as people came and went, each cycle a radiant breath into the blackened lungs of this shadowy architecture.

They reached the doors and Delores leaned in until they gave on their pivot. She held one for the redcap, who gave her a nod of gratitude as he came through, sideways, with her bags.

She let the door close behind him, and then turned and paused; shut her lids behind her cat-eye glasses. She took in the air, the moisture of evening lawn watering, rubber, exhaust, and salt. Sunset approached, on this cool, humid day in Los Angeles.

She summoned two visions, two fancies. The first: Cora arriving home, finding her gone, then finding her note — breaking down in tears at the thought of losing Delores. Her body would slump into her Louis XIII chair, and she would weep for her loss. The second: Sammi, in one of Dad's paintings, slithering across a snarling polar bear hide. She, in her ebony slip, glossed and rippled. Blonde hair curled under at the end of its drape. A fingertip pressed to the end of an excessive fang.

It was this painting that had called to Delores. Come to Los Angeles and seek this creature. Commit the unspoken in a note to Cora, then emerge from hibernation and feast.

She opened her eyes and spotted Mother leaning against a new car: A midnight-blue 1955 Chevrolet 210. Mother's cheeks showed rouge by the flickering flame of the match she held at the end of an erect cigarette. Solidly in her fifties but dressed from a teenager's closet in a men's white button-down oxford with rolled sleeves, jeans pinned at the ankle, and tennis shoes without socks. A folded red scarf smoothed the black hair on her crown. Her French-Persian features but a universe that rotated around the gravity of her dimples.

She looked up from lighting her cigarette and caught her daughter's eye.

"Darling!" she called, and ran across the drive, stepping into the path of a squealing, honking cab, which she ignored apart from a dismissive hand wave.

Mother gave a vigorous, eager hug, which Delores returned, holding the warmth of the moment.

"We're going to that car over there," Delores said to the red cap, pointing to the 210.

"Yes, ma'am," he said.

"Oh, I think we can manage," Mother said.

"Why not have the man help us? The bags are heavy."

"You've gotten soft, living in luxury," Mother said, reaching for a suitcase.

Delores turned to the red cap. "Sir, is this job of yours, being a porter here at the station, is this a union position?"

The red cap, maybe unsure of the thrust of the question, moved his brown eyes between Delores and Mother. "Well, yes, ma'am."

"There you go," Delores said to Mother. "You wouldn't want to put a union man out of work, would you?"

Mother shrugged, and acquiesced. She lead the way across the drive. Delores tried to give a conspiratorial smile to the red cap, but he kept his eyes down as he walked, struggling with the weight of her bags.

After securing the suitcases in the trunk, and after Delores had tipped the man a few dollars and he took his leave, they took their places on the bench seat, an expanse of buoyant stitched indigo vinyl. The dash was rolled steel powder-coated in sky-blue metal flake. Delores ran her hand down the cold of it. She opened the glove box and closed it with a satisfying click.

"Where's Dad?" she said.

"You know where he is. On deadline."

"I had a vision of the two of you waiting for me."

"You don't know your past if you can't guess whether he'd show up or not." Mother placed her cigarette in the metal tangs of the ashtray. The orange-red of her lipstick covered the faux-cork filter. "You haven't said anything about the car."

Through the windshield a chromed jet ornament took air at the bow of the Chevy, the hood tapering up to it as if the airplane had stolen a runway from the ground when it took flight.

"How did you talk him into it?"

Mother turned the key and the car rumbled. "Well, there are no streetcars to Santa Monica anymore, and you know how I feel about the bus. And I convinced him that fixing jalopies was more expensive than a reliable new car. But, in the end, it's because we negotiated his new contract very well and it paid for this, and more. And we got a great deal from Pal."

"Who's Pal?"

"Sammi's fiancé."

"I didn't know she was planning to marry," Delores said.

"Yes, well. Who can predict the heart?"

"Certainly not me," Delores said, once again seeing Sammi in black, a brow raised, fingering a bear fang. She reached into her Mother's pocketbook and took a cigarette.

Mother reached over and grabbed Delores's hand by the wrist and pulled it flat until her palm was on the dash. Delores's cigarette stood like a little skyscraper between her fingers. "Now, leave it here," Mother said, and then let go and put both hands on the wheel.

And then Mother pushed the gas pedal down so hard that the car revved from a purr to a roar in an instant. It shuddered and shook as the engine unfolded into a high whine.

"I made him get the v8," Mother cried over the racket.

"Should you be doing this?" Delores shouted, feeling a cold streak of concern for the new car.

Mother lifted her small foot and everything calmed down to an idle. She smiled and shrugged her shoulders

They went down the drive toward Alameda, Mother moving with a slow, smooth precision that seemed counter to the impetuous revving stunt only a moment before. As they passed, a man in a red ascot stood, arms akimbo, shaking his head at them.

"This car is just like me," Mother said. "Demure and plain on the outside."

Delores pressed a button and her window shushed down its channel. The medicinal musk of eucalyptus perfumed the air, as Mother picked at random some combination of streets that would get them home.

Black exhaust belching from a flatbed produce truck prompted Delores to close the window some miles later. Cartoon vegetables danced on the truck's wooden tailgate. They headed west, along Olympic. Mother hated driving Wilshire.

"Cora Fournier rang long-distance for you."

"Are you sure?"

"Of course I'm sure. I spoke with her myself."

"But she's in Europe."

"Yes. She called from Paris. Said she got a cable that you had disappeared."

"Oh, god," Delores said.

"She was sick with worry that something bad had happened to you. I had to let her know you were only coming to L.A. for a visit."

"I'm sorry you had to be involved."

"Did you not give her notice that you were taking a vacation?"

"I did. Well, I left a letter. I just didn't expect her to get it for another week or so."

Now she'd have to talk to Cora on the telephone. Cora had a talent for turning conversations to her own favor.

"Who ratted me out?"

"The maid, I take it."

Of course. Selma would have seen the letter, but not opened it. When Delores hadn't shown her face for a few days, Selma would have gotten suspicious — oh, God, maybe even thinking the letter could have been a suicide note or some such thing. Why hadn't Delores just told her she was leaving? How could she have overlooked Selma?

"I told her you'd be back in no time," Mother said.

"You did? Well, we'll see."

"You have a very informal relationship with your employer."

"We're close. We understand each other."

"And so you just left her without warning? I can't believe you've put me in a position where I'm supporting management over a worker. It really seems you're being capricious here."

"If you must know, I'm considering leaving my current line of work."

"'I live for my job,' I believe were words you used the last time we spoke."

"I do. I did. I'm taking a sabbatical, with an option to not go back. New York can really wear on you."

Mother nodded, agreeing. She hated New York. But then the penny dropped and she thought through the implication.

"Wait, are you saying that you're here to stay? In Los Angeles?"

"I figured it wouldn't be a problem."

"Where will you be living?"

"In my room, was my hope."

"Oh, with us?"

"Until I find an apartment. For now. If it's okay with you and Dad."

During their drive, night fully gripped the city. Street lights illuminated the road in round pools, aided by the headlights of oncoming cars.

"I mean, I may decide to go back after all. It may only be a month or so."

"I'll talk to Dad. I doubt he would mind. He could use some help around the studio, to tell the truth." At a stoplight, Mother pursed her lips, scratched her nose, and looked out the window, away from Delores.

"Then it might work out, right?"

"I just wish you had told me. We have lives. And I don't understand how you could just leave your job without giving notice or telling Miss Fournier. This all seems very selfish of you."

Delores counted to herself. One. Two. Three. Four. Five. *Sigh.* And then she tacked: "I'm eager to meet Sammi in person. Dad obviously loves painting her."

"Really, Delores, I'd like to understand."

"Really, Lily," she said, aping Mother's tone. "The game of changing the topic only works if we leave the first one behind."

"I'm not playing a game here. Stop being so evasive." If Delores were Cora, here she might turn the attack around, say something like, I'm not evasive, why are you so curious? No, it would have to carry an implied insult: Why are you so nosy?

Instead, she went with the direct approach. "Please! Can we please talk about it later?"

Delores pressed the button again and took the cool wind on her face. She put her elbow out the window. There was a quality to the air here that was different than in New York, not a smell so much as the way the air moved around her. It felt more lethargic. It felt more intimate. Headier.

When they turned off of Olympic was when she felt in her gut that they had rolled out of an uncontainable city of massive scale and into the knowable village by the sea where the Sarjeants had bought land, built a home, and raised a family. The air took on the brine of the ocean. The cry of the gull. The roar of Douglas aircraft overhead.

It had been nearly ten years, but Delores was home. She took a deep breath and hoped that just maybe Santa Monica was as happy to have her as she was to be there.

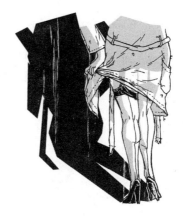

II

THE SARJEANT house sat on a southwest corner, as two wide streets intersected up the hill from the ocean. Mother parked in the driveway, the headlights splashing the raised diamonds on the two-car garage. The killed engine left a dripping tick under the hood as Delores emerged into a chill Pacific breeze.

Above her, under the eaves of the two-story garage, a trio of thin triangular clerestory windows hugged the gable. Bright, warm light from Dad's studio filled them, a soprano aria vague on the breeze.

Mother marched off to fix supper, leaving Delores to carry the suitcases. One of the two slipped as she pulled it from the trunk, and it fell to the concrete of the driveway, slapping flat on its side. Delores was sure she heard the muffled crack of glass.

Leaving the other suitcase, she hustled to the front door and inside, across the entry hall with the large flat river-stone flooring, a part of her registering the cool woody scent of her parents' home. Left, down the hallway past Mother's sewing room, and left again into Delores's old bedroom.

She slung the case onto the bed, relying on the light from the hallway to illuminate her action. She snapped the hasps and dug straight into a square leather case nestled at the center of her efficient pack. Opened a miniature belt loop in weathered brown leather, and unfolded the top of the box. Inside, a dense machined square riding in purple velvet.

She lifted it free and pushed a button. The top of the black and silver device clicked open like a trap door. She looked down into it, pointed its face toward the hall light, saw a ghostly image of her doorway upside down and floating behind a black grid. The camera was fine. She sighed, let the tension in her shoulders go.

She gingerly set the Hasselblad on the chest of drawers. Dug into her pack to find what broke: the glass on her silver gelatin edition of Irving Penn's *The Ballet Society*, and not just the glass. A jarring scar across the center of the print marked it as ruined. A slash across the face of Tanaquil Le Clercq, the dancer. A slash across her face and arm.

"Oh, damn," Delores said.

She put the frame face down, opened the back, and extracted the print, a gift from Cora a few years earlier. Signed, on the back, by Penn, Tanny, and George Balanchine. She looked to see if the damage could be repaired.

"Delores."

The booming voice came from the doorway behind her. For an instant she was a toddler hearing him call. Delores turned, and there he was, holding her other case with only a finger and thumb around the handle, as if the whole thing were made of paper and filled with air. He blocked most of the light with his wrestler's physique, thick and wide.

He stepped toward her and they embraced, and she had to stop herself from calling him "Daddy," a name Delores considered the mark of a little girl, or those who wished they were still.

He was crowded and muscular, made of denser stuff than most people, and his hug crushed the air from her. Safe. She should have been beyond it. He kissed her cheek. Stroked her hair with his hands, so wide, so fat, so dexterous, despite their meaty, clumsy appearance.

"Did you see?" he said.

"See what?"

He pulled away, turned on the light. Hanging salon style was nearly every portrait that Dad had ever painted of her. From a naked baby lying on a pile of rabbit furs to that awkward buck-toothed pony-tailed girl, and also the permanently mortified teenager. A dozen faces of Delores, all through the prism of Dad's brush, turning a glance into an advertisement, the eyes sparkling and happy, the emotional depth mere caricature, despite the technical prowess of the artist. Delores saw past the gloss into the truth of those faces, and that momentary sense of home and happiness faltered as every glance was met by the illusion of a younger, finer version of herself staring back.

"Oh, Dad."

"I knew you would love it."

Dad stirred gin and tonics with his index finger. One he handed to Delores, the other he put next to Mother, who was pushing a burger patty off a spatula onto a prepared bun. A line of plates sat in a row, garnished and ready. He opened a beer for himself.

Mother looked at Dad. "You think Sammi wants one?"

"She's here?" Delores said.

"Deadlines never sleep, so why should I?" Dad said.

Delores stood. "I'll fetch her."

She exited the front door, crossed to the studio stairs, and climbed the thickly painted slat steps to the landing. The over-lit interior shone through the inset glass panel of the door. She put her back to the wall beside it. Took a hit from her cocktail, then as slow as she could manage amid the plenty of her enthusiasm, she peered around the corner and looked through the glass.

There was Sammi on the model's dais. Perched on a high stool, one leg pulled up, foot over the opposite knee, inspecting a toe, a lit cigarette dangling from her lip. She was in her early twenties, maybe. Dirty blonde hair fell carelessly about her face. Done up in a salmon panty girdle and a matching bra whose cups were decorated by spirals that apexed at the nipple. Tan stockings attached to the girdle, the foot on the floor graced by one peachy mule, her whole outfit framed by a diaphanous lavender robe lined in faux fur. A chromed clip nailed to an upright two-by-four, which was in turn nailed to the dais, held the train of the robe, as if the model were a dog or a balloon in need of securing.

Oh, how Delores had imagined this. She was used to seeing Sammi in reproduction. There, it was many steps removed: printed on presses that took an image from a blanket, reversing the image from a stone, taking exposure from film, which in turn came from a photograph of a painting of an artist's take on the light bouncing off the flesh of the model.

And to hell with everything if Sammi wasn't about thirty times more alluring in person. Dad sweetened everything with his brush. He smoothed blemishes. He erased the bitter edges where authentic life settled.

Sammi looked up, and they locked eyes through the door. Delores retracted her peeking head, and leaned back against the wall, caught — then she leaned forward to look again. Sammi met her gaze. She lowered her leg, and slipped her stockinged foot into the other heel. She stood and stepped toward Delores, letting the robe drip from her and drape the stool. Once her hand was clear of the gossamer fabric, Sammi took the cigarette from her mouth.

She lowered her gaze as she walked closer to the door, her blue eye shadow and false lashes showing a modesty her tight smile belied. The click-clack-click of her heels on the worn wooden floors. She unlocked the door and opened it, inviting Delores in.

"I'm terribly embarrassed," Sammi said. "You caught me trying to find an itch on my foot that's been driving me mad. I scratch one place and it moves to another."

She walked to a rough-hewn wood side table, like one a carpenter might make in the middle of a job but dismantle afterward, that held an ashtray. She dabbed out her cigarette with a lethargic precision. Delores watched her tight waist, her sloping hips, her upside-down heart at the bottom of which her stocking supports began, black satin running across pallid paper skin.

She turned, pivoting on one foot, and once again looked right at Delores, who couldn't keep her gaze and looked down at her drink, cheeks flushing.

"Oh, is that for me?" Sammi said. "That is so sweet of you." She reached out, and Delores, mute and struck by the perfume of Sammi's presence, handed over her own cocktail. Sammi slugged back half of it in one go. "I've been waiting to meet you," Sammi said, leaning against the table and swirling ice. "It's like I know you already, what with your Dad's stories. He's just about talked of nothing else since he learned you were coming."

Delores spoke, but her voice caught and she realized it would be the first thing she was going to say to this woman, and in that moment all words seemed inadequate.

"I know you too, it's like. I have so many portraits of you. I keep them all." And that made her sound strange, like a collector or a pervert. Delores was a thick plank incapable of language or clear thought.

Sammi smiled. "Look at the mess I've gotten myself into this week." They walked to the easel in the middle of Dad's studio. It stood next to a chest of drawers with his palette, and with brushes in jars.

Delores caught the fishy, creamy scent of oil paint, the bitter stink of thinner. And then, when she stepped close, Sammi's faint aroma of rose water, felted smoke, and deeper, her voluptuous somatic nose. Delores breathed as deeply as she dared while trying not to seem like a sniffing dog.

On the canvas, nearly finished, Sammi was bent over to pick up a newspaper. Her robe caught in a doorway, a round-mouthed expression of surprise on her face, which showed to the viewer. Behind her, a lemon explosion of morning. The whole thing was beautiful, rendered in Dad's smooth grace, his healthy, fleshy pin-up girl in gaudy bright colors, all rouge and blue eyes, tensed muscles on extended legs, toes pointed just so to pull the shapely calf taut. It was flawless, like all of his work. And like all flawless painting, it was the advertisement of a dream.

"I'm locked out in my lingerie," Sammi said, her voice low and droll. "How embarrassing. Do you mind?" She held out the drink, and Delores took it back. Sammi ran her hands through her hair, wrapping it up into a bun that she secured by skewering it with a chopstick, and then took back the drink.

"Oh, dinner." Delores said. "That's why I came. Mother made some. Are you hungry?"

"Why, sure. Wait for me?"

Delores nodded. As Sammi entered the bathroom and closed the door, Delores realized that she'd been sucking in her belly, holding herself too stiff. She was tingly. She exhaled, moving her head to loosen her neck. Looked at the ceiling. Looked around the room. She came back to herself.

The studio was a mess. Not the kind of mess it usually was: the whitewashed walls covered with charcoal drawings and cartoons; the doors to the office, bathroom, and dressing room painted with trompe-l'œil vistas from Roman colonnade porches showing bodies of water and alpine forests; random text painted on the wall, such as "*Plus rien à retrancher*," which Dad sometimes added when he read a quote that moved him or found a line from an opera libretto that satisfied him; the floor, as Dad put it, "A readymade Jackson Pollack."

No, the mess Delores noticed was another kind of disorder: the stacks of canvases wrapped in paper, back from being shot for the publisher but not yet catalogued and sorted downstairs in racks that stood where most sane people kept their cars. Unsorted papers overflowed the desk in the office, 78s and LPs lay out of their sleeves by the console player. Sawdust and cardboard tubes from canvas rolls piled up under the table where Dad did his canvas stretching. Delores opened a drawer to see his stock of paint and materials ridiculously low. Mother was right. Dad needed help. He needed an assistant.

The bathroom door opened to reveal Sammi in a tattered baby blue terrycloth bathrobe with matching slippers. The robe, thick and luxurious, hung almost to her stocking-clad ankles. She had transformed herself into the ratty, and Delores thought Sammi possibly even more fetching than she'd been just a minute before.

Dad had finished his burger and was tipping into his second beer when they showed up. They scooted into the banquette — a u-shaped tuck-and-roll booth just like you might find in a restaurant — Dad at the bottom of the scoop, which he saw as the head of the table, arms spread on the booth back, bottle dangling from two fingers.

Sammi drained the remaining cocktail and put the tumbler down with a little dance of clinking ice.

"Fix yourself another, why don't you," Mother said.

"I'm fine," Delores said.

"I'd like another," Mother said, pushing her tumbler across the table. Sammi clinked the ice in her glass and lifted her brows, in lieu of placing a verbal order. Delores took the glasses and walked over to the counter to mix them all more drinks.

"What did you think of your surprise?" Mother said to Delores. She had a simple patty on her plate. A fried tomato. Some lettuce and dressing. She had moved the food around so that it looked well eaten.

"What surprise?" Delores said.

"The paintings, darling. The portraits he hung in your room."

"Oh, that. Right."

Delores decided to have a drink after all, then decided against it, and finally laid out the three glasses and poured in the gin and the sizzling tonic. Cut slivers off the already halved lime, and then found Mother had stocked the ice bucket, so she added that to each glass as well.

Sammi took a bite of her burger, and then while chewing reached across the table and took Mother's pack of cigarettes, spilling one out for herself and, when Delores nodded as she was sitting down and handing out the drinks, one for her, too.

"Lily?" Sammi said. "Be a doll and toss us a match."

"I'd like to know what you think as well," Dad said, leaning against the table and flicking a book of matches, which skittered over near Sammi. "We have a bet going."

"What bet? I don't understand," Delores said. Sammi struck a match, and Delores leaned into it. She cupped a hand around the flame, mostly to touch Sammi's hand.

"Your mother put down ten dollars that you'd have all of those paintings taken down inside of a week," Dad said. "I thought you'd keep them up. Remind you of some happy times in your life."

"Happy times," Mother snorted.

Delores sat back in the booth, smoked her cigarette and tried to read the expressions on her parents' faces. Sammi took a bite of her burger. Then, when she had mostly swallowed, a drag off her cigarette. Back and forth. Back and forth.

Delores knocked the table. A Formica top, decorated with a pattern of intersecting, multicolored, boomerang shapes, all ringed in ribbed chrome. "It was a difficult time for me. Happy sometimes. Hard others."

"Your whole childhood?" Dad said, incredulous. "Am I misremembering everything?"

"No. I was a good actress. Sometimes I wasn't acting."

"He won't be insulted if you take them down," Mother said.

"I think I gotta see these paintings," Sammi said. Then, to Delores, leaning in as if conspiratorially, "I will not let you get away with hiding these paintings from me."

"The hell I won't be insulted. I spent hours hanging those."

"Oh, dad. You can't expect me to look at myself all the time, can you?"

"Why not? I like looking at you. You're a pretty girl."

"It's not anything to do with that," Delores said. "Nobody wants to look at themselves all the time."

"We did not raise a narcissist, Gael," Mother said, reaching for her cigarettes and the matches. She pushed away her half-eaten dinner, leaned onto her elbows, and lit up. As she talked, she let the smoke exit her mouth in pulses of breath and sound. "She's a grown woman. You should have asked first. But what do I care? I just want to win the bet."

"Whoa, these are great," Sammi said, standing in Delores's room, looking at the wall of paintings.

Delores pointed to a cherubic young face, freckled, apple cheeked. "That one was used in a Coca-Cola advertisement. I was the face in the frosty window watching Santa. This one —" she motioned to a pigtails and pout portrait "— was used to sell breakfast cereal. 'Mothers: If this is the face you're used to, try Wheat Pops for breakfast.'"

"Are these all advertisements?"

"Everything he paints advertises something. But this one was for Mother on a birthday." Delores motioned to a gap-toothed girl with pigtails, laughing so hard her eyes were slits, a kelly green flare around her head faded to pure black at the edges of the canvas, an Irish halo.

Sammi sat on the bed. She leaned back onto her arms, and her robe parted, slipping down the sides of her legs. Delores's eye moved back and forth across the Maginot Line of her stocking tops, France cast in nylon, Germany in plump white flesh. But when she sensed she was being watched, she looked up to see Sammi throw a knowing smile and maybe, if she wasn't mistaken, part her legs just a bit.

Sammi lay flat on the bed, arms loose above her head, where a lover might pin them down. "I like your room. I'm trying to imagine it when you were teenager. I would have liked to be a fly on the wall to see what went on in here."

Delores lay on her side next to Sammi and propped her head on her hand. "You would have died from boredom. Seen me reading. Sleeping. Trying to take pictures." She had a notion to take the tie that kept that robe tight around Sammi's waist and pull it. She could feel how the terry would catch and feel as it let loose.

"Pictures? Are you a photographer?"

"I'm trying to be."

"Say, I need a new headshot. Maybe you could lend a hand, be a doll?"

"Sure. I'd be happy to."

A flashing from outside drew their attention through the window that overlooked the driveway and studio stairs. It was Dad, standing at the top of the staircase, turning on and off the studio porch light. When he saw he had their attention, he gestured to Sammi. Come, come, come and pose.

"Looks like I've got a date. Can you believe I get paid to stand around in fancy underwear?" She stood, adjusting her robe. On her way out she stopped, stooped, and grabbed the hem, pulled it up to show her legs. Sammi bent one knee slightly, brought that foot up on its toes, looked back over her shoulder to give a Betty Grable wink, and danced out of the room.

Delores woke to a pregnant shush in the near dark of her room. The kind of stillness that confused the newly awake, that seemed to suggest a loud sound had preceded it. She listened, trying to discern what brought her out of sleep.

Long shadows stretched across the paintings of her young faces, hiding eyes here, showing teeth there. Then: the sound of a car door closing. Maybe she woke when the car pulled into the driveway? She imagined a horn lingering in her memory. Did someone sound the horn?

She saw the figure of a tall man in a fedora walk the stairs to the studio. He took them two at a time, nearly falling back, once. He pounded the door.

"Sammi!" he bellowed, emphasizing the second syllable in her name, like Ricky Ricardo might call to Lucy. His voice low, out of place in the still neighborhood. Dad appeared, and immediately the man removed his hat. The men shook hands, laughed, and they went inside, Dad clapping him on his back.

Not long after, all three came out, Sammi dressed in Capri pants and a blue zippered coat. She descended with the man, her arm through his, and, as Dad locked the studio door, the couple appeared to bicker as they came around the staircase, up the walk, talking in tones so low that Delores couldn't make them out.

She slid from bed, and crawled to the window so she could see better. The couple approached a Chevy as new-looking as her parents'. When they reached it, Delores could hear Sammi talking.

"But I told you I was working late. I can't help it if you drank that memory away."

The man, facing away from her, answered sharply. Sammi tossed up her arms, and then ducked into the car. She slammed the door and crossed her arms.

"Everything okay, Pal?" Dad said, standing near the driveway.

The man waved. "Sure, Gael, sure. We'll see you tomorrow."

Dad nodded. Offered a small wave and waited until the car pulled away to walk inside and turn out the lights. A different set of shadows crossed the room.

Delores stayed at the window. She heard Dad come in, go into his bedroom across from hers. She sat on the edge of the bed. Heard water run through pipes.

She was all wound up. Tied tight to the dock of her tension, but she took some deep breaths and tried to cast off the lines so she could drift free. She walked around the bed, straightening the sheets, retucking them so that they were tight and firm. She slid in with slow care, trying not to pull them loose. She closed her eyes.

And then there was Sammi lying next to her — and Delores did pull that tie right off her robe, then she moved Sammi's chin over with a finger and told her, "Now, you just be a good girl and lay right like that, while I perform some experiments and figure out what makes you squirm the most."

And in the still of the room, the quiet midnight, Delores dipped her hand under the sheets and inside her pajamas, and remembered exactly how Sammi had smelled when Delores had leaned in close enough to inhale her.

III

THE PHONE sounded a trilling peal in the morning. Delores sat at the kitchen table, reading the paper with Mother, who wore a flowered robe over her nightgown, a green skin mask making a ghost of her face. She turned the page without looking up.

"Certainly not for me at this hour," she said, keeping her lips tight and still, the beauty ventriloquist.

Delores answered. "Please hold for an international call," said a woman's voice. "Go ahead New York."

And another, with a nasal upstate tinge. "Thank you. Go ahead, London."

Then a British one. "All right then, Paris."

Finally, "*Madame, votre appel est connecté.*"

Then, after a pause, Cora was there. "Hello? Hello? This is Cora Fournier calling from Paris again, trying to reach Delores. Is this Lily?"

"It's me," Delores said.

The line crackled. She wondered how many of the operators were still eavesdropping. How many miles spanned the wires that connected them?

"You need to speak up with these connections. Is that you, Delores?"

Delores cleared her throat. "Yes. Yes, it's me."

"Thank god I got through," Cora said. "I was worried sick by you."

"Nothing to fret over. I just took the train out to see my folks."

"But why didn't you tell me?"

"We've been talking about this vacation for years," Delores said, turning from Mother, but Mother stayed in her place, no matter how Delores attempted to use body language to communicate that she wanted privacy. "I was tired of waiting for it to actually transpire."

"But without telling me? Without taking me? I just don't understand it. It feels very emotional of you. Very impetuous."

"I left a note that explains everything. I can't talk now."

"Well, doesn't that just solve it then? A note, in New York. It's just my bad luck to be in Paris. Perhaps I could hire someone to re-enact it for me, like a radio play?"

Delores closed her eyes. Counted. "How's Paris, anyway?"

"Fine. Lovely, although I've been consumed with worry over you. And Mother is tremendously trying. She's very chatty. I'm getting no peace."

"She's probably just worried about your father."

"Oh, no doubt. We all are. But enough of you trying to change the topic. It may have taken me a few years, but I'm on to that neat little trick of yours."

"I'm not. I'm just...Mother is here. She says hello." Mother looked up, an arched brow showing question. Then, remembering her mask she composed her face.

"Ah. You can't speak freely."

"Yes."

"Well. Do I have to wait for this mythical note, then? I can't know what's going on."

"I'm sure you can guess."

"This feels like you're leaving me."

Delores paused. Tried to find something in the kitchen that might give her a word, something to offer. Not the copper bread box. Not the three round ceramic containers descending in size, one for flour, one for sugar, and what was the third for anyway? "The note explains everything."

"I take that as a yes."

"If you must." No answer came, and Delores wondered whether the connection had dropped. "I'm going to stay out in California for a while. Think about some things."

"What about your birthday party?"

"I sent notes canceling already. I was able to secure all the deposits."

"I wasn't concerned about the money."

"I was."

"As usual."

"What are you implying?"

"I'm really confused why you, who never lets any detail drop, failed to mention to our maid, who is in our house every day, that you were leaving. Who acted as if nothing were awry to me when I left just a few days previous. It certainly seems as if that was a deliberate choice so you wouldn't have to face me or talk to me."

"That's not true, in fact."

"I think it is. You are being very manipulative."

"I never found you receptive."

"To talking about us? Hah! I'm always trying to get you to talk about how you're feeling."

"Yes, to avoid talking about yourself," Delores said, her tone too stressed for a professional conversation, a little too ardent. Mother kept her eyes on the paper.

"Is that what you think? Here, let me state it plainly then. I love you. I want you with me always. I can't believe you have left me without facing me. It leaves me feeling bereft."

"God, I hate that word."

"Oh, to hell with you. Focus on the word and not my feelings. You are so cruel sometimes."

"Can we schedule a time to talk later?"

"Now that I know you are not dead or kidnapped and simply acting like a spoiled child, yes. Yes, we can."

"Thank you. I appreciate that."

"I'll be home on Monday."

"That early?"

"Yes, I booked an earlier crossing when I found you were missing. Now it's too late to move it back. I expect you to find a time to talk when you can speak freely."

"I will."

"God, Delores. I love you so much, and you make that so hard to do."

"I know."

"Do you know what my therapist says?"

"Yes. You tell me many things that he says."

"This is new. He says that my relationship with you is a sublimation of my adolescent desire to be like my mother. That my attraction to women is because of the weak role my father played in my upbringing. And he has suspicions that my nursemaid was taking liberties with me, although I think that is patently absurd. Anyway, he said that I picked you because you are like my mother. You fascinate me and frustrate me in equal measure. But I don't think you're very like my mother. Do you want to know why?"

"You'll tell me, whether I say yes or no."

"Because my mother never let me doubt for a single moment that she loved me. She stood by me in my darkest moments. And when it came to confrontation, she stood up and claimed me as her daughter and as her kin. I wish you had ten percent of what she had in this regard."

The line went dead, and Delores held the phone, listening to a series of clicks as the cable that connected Los Angeles to Paris, across a continent and ocean, that unique and particular connection that might never be made in that sequence again, was dismantled.

It was like a performance Delores saw by Tanny Le Clercq, in which the whole cast came together for a moment, fingertips just touching in a line across the stage, connecting every dancer, then a thunderclap and flashing lights caused them to flitter away from one another as the music swelled, most of the dancers flung off stage by the centrifugal force of their rotation, and left alone was Tanny turning like a screw as she deflated to the floor and the stage lights dimmed to black.

———————

A fragrant manure colored the air. To either side of the walk between the house and the garage studio, inset planters full of rich black soil sat optimistically awaiting Mother's hand.

"This gets a lot of shade, so not sure what I'm going to do here," Mother said. "I'd love to put in birds of paradise, but they need more morning sun." She and Delores walked along the path around the house, past the laundry room in the back of the garage, to the north side of the house where the kitchen windows found light. More planters ran along the pathway. "Boxwoods go here, so that they'll grow into a privacy screen" she said, waving at the stucco Spanish revival next door. Around the back a rectangle of smoothed concrete off the sliding glass doors acted as a sun porch, half covered by a roofed overhang. "Don't step on the grass, it's just sprouting," Mother said. It was a square of lawn, coming off the back of the porch. It stopped some fifteen feet before the property line, where shallow pits were lined with wooden planks to reinforce their edges. To one side, burlap bags of soil lay stacked.

"This is my project," Mother said, sighing. Arms akimbo.

"What are you going to plant here?"

"Not sure, yet, to be honest. I'm working with a girl who has quite the green thumb. She's trying to talk me into using mostly starts that are native to this area, but that seems horrible. Have you seen the plants native to this area? It's a desert. You can help me while you're staying here, yes?"

"I have a collection of desolate pots in my apartment to prove how bad I am with plants."

"Your father won't touch it, but he'll enjoy it. He comes out to grill and right now it's desolate. It's like a Berlin after the war or something. I want more life here, more color and vibrancy. I'd like him to be able to spend his leisure time enjoying it."

"He has leisure time?"

"He has slowed down a bit, you know."

"I don't know, no."

"He has that new contract that is quite good. You know that his kind of illustration isn't selling well anymore? Most young illustrators are getting turned away. No money in the pin-up industry. But your dad has a reputation and he delivers, so he'll always have a career, even if he's more bored with it all than he lets on."

"Sammi's a good model."

"Sammi is trouble, but your dad has a good rapport with her. I'd rather he just give it up and retire. I don't see what the big attraction is after all these years. You know he's just repeating himself, don't you? He's so stubborn."

"Ideas were always the hardest part. Remember he used to pay me for ideas?"

"I do remember. Somewhere I have your little scribbled notebook marking how much he paid for every pitch. You had quite the industry."

Delores walked along the edge of the grass, over to the pit where the plants would go. She looked back at the house, the morning sun dressing it. It seemed smaller than she remembered, somehow. More contained, less fancy. More boxy and simple compared to the molded cornices and picture rails of her New York apartment. Its clean lines seemed the opposite of the ornate business of a classic Manhattan building, which evoked an earlier time. Here it was modernism, the stripping of artifice to reveal simplicity.

"Are you in the same thing you wore yesterday?" Mother said, the lawn between them now, but Mother keeping even with her as Delores walked across the back of the yard.

"Well, it's clean."

"Darling, we don't change our clothes only to stay clean. We do it to stay fresh. Let's go shopping."

The boutique was one of Mother's favorites, and it was clear the shop girl knew her. A single storefront, uncluttered and open in the way that only upscale could afford to be.

"All of her clothes are too heavy. She needs a California wardrobe," Mother said to the girl, avian-like, and sporting heavy framed glasses, her hair swept back from her pointed fragile face.

Delores was accustomed to modern couture. She was not used to paying for it herself. So when they had pulled up in front of this boutique, with its expansive ebony tile front jutting up past the surrounding stores, and with silvered metal letters aslant, spelling out the name

Francois' in script as tall as a grown man, she knew she was out of her depths, financially.

"Can't we go to a department store?"

"Let's look here first," Mother said. "And if you're unhappy with the selection, we can."

The girl brought out a number of things at Mother's request, including a few nicer party dresses. After finding a casual ensemble she liked, Delores tried on one, a stiff sleeveless black cotton shift with a squared neckline that featured a small *V* divot in the middle of the breastbone.

"That is lovely," Mother said. "With pearls, it would be stunning."

"I don't like sleeveless," Delores said. She pulled her arms closer to her body.

"It suits you," Mother said. She had dressed herself in a belted calico print dress for the shopping. Delores wondered whether she had bought the dress in this very shop. She herself would be embarrassed, for some reason, to wear a dress you bought somewhere back to the place where you bought it. As if you were attempting to make a statement, but the statement was about desiring attention. It felt desperate. "You look lovely. Just because you have your father's physique doesn't mean you don't look feminine and lovely."

"You know what that sounds like, don't you? It sounds like you're saying I have a wrestler's body."

"Don't be dramatic. That's not what I mean."

"What did you mean?"

"Ask the girl, if you think I'm undermining you."

Delores turned to the girl.

"It's like it was created from a form of your figure," she said, a soft lilt to her high voice. "It's very flattering. And I feel like you do about sleeveless, I really do. But this silhouette is very appropriate and favorable to your figure."

"Fine," Delores said to Mother. "I don't want to argue." She stacked a few things on the counter. "But I can only afford to buy one outfit here."

"How can that be? You've been living rent free, drawing a salary."

"I didn't save much. And my salary didn't go so far in New York."

"How can you not have a large savings? You had a piggy bank full when you were five."

"It's complicated."

"Money is never complicated. You have it and you know where it is, or you don't and work to get more."

"I didn't draw a salary so much as an allowance."

"Well, how the hell does that work? You worked for one of the wealthiest women in the world, and she didn't pay you?"

"I lived a lavish lifestyle. I had season tickets to the opera, the ballet, any play I wanted. All free."

"That is no excuse for not paying you a regular salary. I mean, you did the work for her, and she drew no distinction. Your grandfather didn't get beat up and see his friends die just so you could ignore the forty-hour work week and labor laws."

"Back down, please. This is not a labor rights issue."

"If she wasn't paying you, it sure as hell is exactly that."

"I'm going to go take this dress off, and then we can leave."

Mother turned a tight smile toward the girl. "Put these all on my account." She looked again at Delores. "We'll settle between us later."

After throwing the shopping bags on her bed, Delores visited Dad in the studio. The finished portrait of Sammi, caught outside her morning door, leaned against a stack of canvases wrapped in paper. Dad, in a blue collared shirt and black chinos, was on the couch in the office, lying back and reading a sporting magazine. On the cover, an illustration of a muscular trout. It breached the water, a hook on a thin white painted line piercing its cheek, the thread leading back to a minuscule fisherman in waders.

"I brought you a beer," Delores said.

"A daughter who brings him beer unrequested? What more could a man ask?" Dad stretched. Tossed the magazine on the couch and sat up. Took the beer from Delores and held it out until she toasted with her own.

"Mother says you're bored."

"At this moment?"

"In general."

"There's the pot calling the kettle, all right."

"She said you're repeating yourself."

"Well, hell, of course I am. You try putting out a painting a week for twenty years without running out of exciting new poses. If you got some ideas, I'm all ears."

Delores leaned against the desk, a mess of mail, opened and stacked haphazardly. She put down her beer and started straightening piles, going through letters.

"Stop it. Don't do that."

"You won't. Why not? You need the help. I've done it before."

"Christ, just don't do it while I'm here. I'm going fishing tomorrow. Do it then."

"Fine. I'll do it then." But she kept sorting the mail she had in hand.

"Not for free, either. I'll pay you."

"Dad, this bill is overdue. By two months."

"It's just Frankie. He knows I'm good for it."

"Let's hope not all of his clients are like you, or he won't keep his doors open."

"I pay him as often as he makes me wait to get new paint in stock. Listen, while you're shuffling around tomorrow you want to shoot my most recent batch? Wouldn't mind having transparencies on hand."

Delores nodded. "Sure."

"Take some film money out of petty cash."

"Is there petty cash?"

"Go the bank and withdraw some money. Now you have petty cash. Use that petty cash to buy film."

She put the mail into three piles. Deal with immediately, soon, and whenever.

"You really think Mother is bored?" she said, picking up her beer and picking at the paper label.

Dad shrugged. Reached over and opened a wood humidor on his desk and extracted a cigar. He cut the tip with his pocketknife before returning it to his trousers. Cracked the lighter and lit the cigar, then settled back, rolling it between his thumb and index finger.

"She goes to church once a week or more. She has that garden project, which I think she has undertaken and finished three times in as many years. She reads a great deal at night. We've talked about getting a television, but it just doesn't seem necessary for us. She wants a boat."

Next to the couch, a stack of magazines. The one on top was curious. Two women were making a snowman, but the head of the snowman was a rabbit. The whole thing was tinted blue, except for a colorful scarf flapping about the snow rabbit's neck. One girl was putting a cigarette in a holder in the rabbit's mouth, the other was placing a button, but suggestively reaching down to who knows where? Flat slab letters spelled the title, knocked out in white: *Playboy. Entertainment for Men.* Delores picked it up. She flipped through, stopping on a full-page color cartoon of a woman and man playing cards. She was naked, her clothes sprawled around. He grinned like a Cheshire cat, shuffling the deck and saying, "Now what shall we play for?"

"That's the death of my industry," Dad said, motioning with his cigar. "Mark my words."

"Why support them by buying copies, then?"

"I don't. They gave me a free subscription. They want some pieces from me."

"You going to do it?"

"Hell, no. They have an attitude. They pay okay, but not what I'm used to. Besides, they have photographers do all the girly work. Call their models 'bunnies,' if you've ever heard anything like that. And they're all young, uneducated. Elvis girls, you know. Not appealing."

"Your models aren't exactly scientists, Dad."

"Well, no, but they're doing something. They're sailing, or walking their dog, or fighting a war, or painting a room. These girls just luxuriate around exotic locations, looking like they'll just let you come and take 'em. Like they won't even react to you. They're lifeless dolls.

"And worse, it's doing well, so lots of work for photographers, but if you want to get into my line...well, you're shit out of luck. That door has closed, unless you're top notch. Used to be hundreds of us pin-up men. Now? Maybe a few dozen. Now there'll be guys starting up girlie mags left and right, mostly in black and white so it'll be cheaper, and photos look better than paintings when you strip the color out. So the market's going to change, and soon an honest painter isn't going to be able to feed his family."

"You think it'll be that bad?"

Gael stood, took the magazine from Delores's hands, and dumped it in the wastebasket next to his desk.

"Doll face, it already is."

IV

THE SPUTTERING of an old engine woke
Delores before dawn. Outside of her window Dad laid his fishing gear
and tackle in the bed of a rusted red Dodge truck. He opened the passenger door, a throaty moan on hinges, and climbed in next to his red-
felt-cap-wearing friend, whom he greeted with a clasp on the back. The
engine skipped and caught, then backfired, echoing into the dark quiet
neighborhood.

Sleep evaded Delores. She lay with her eyes open, body still aligned
with a time three hours earlier and three thousand miles away. When
the birds started their soprano cacophony at first light she knew it was
a lost cause. Might as well get to work.

First order was a quick clean and straighten of the main studio
room, which she was done with by the time morning completely filled
the clerestory windows. She went to the office and wrote checks for the
most pressing of bills, and organized the rest so that keeping up on
them would be a simpler matter.

The copy of *Playboy* still sat in the garbage can. She rescued it, and put it with a stack of things she was to take downstairs, not sure why, but feeling that it was worth investigating.

Then back to the main room. Dad's publisher had a service pick up the paintings and shoot them for reproduction. Dad liked to keep the paintings on record, though, to have transparencies. Helped for insurance, and also gave him something to go through to remember the poses he'd painted.

There were canvases stacked all around, some from the disordered part of storage in the basement, others from the pile of unsorted work returned from the publisher. She put them in sequential order based on the date Dad scrawled in pen along the stretched edges. Nearly all were Sammi, but a few smiling executive portraits were mixed in, and three were of the brunette who had modeled previous to Sammi.

Delores set the easel on the model's dais and set her tripod a few yards back. Clip lights on the rails attached to the ceiling gave nice coverage to the paintings. A small mirror clipped to the leg of the easel at just the correct angle showed the handwritten date, albeit in reverse.

Her workflow: load the easel. Focus, shoot, move that canvas out, move the next canvas in. Repeat.

As she focused on Sammi's face, captured in mid-wink, Delores was reminded of the first time she set up a camera in this room. It was her father's old Leica II. He taught her the basics of photography when she was in junior high. It was he who ignited her love of taking pictures and taught her the fundamental skills. She often would shoot Mother for him, for reference when he didn't have a model. Occasionally, she'd pose herself, usually her hands, or facial expressions, that were tacked on to women of much different proportions than Delores. Women with thinner builds, less hippy, more busty. Delores saw that teenager, nervous about setting up the camera and getting poor results, and the adult who now moved through the job, finding it quite easy.

In fact, this task calmed the animal in Delores, like doing dishes sometimes would, or like some might find in a hobby like woodworking. That is, the work was complex enough to take her out of herself, but not so hard as to require intense continued concentration. It was mind-clearing to find pace and peace in repetition.

After a few hours' work she broke for a late breakfast. Mother, fully done up and even wearing perfume, was applying lipstick at the entry hall mirror. Ready for the day in a flower print dress with large black buttons. Heels. Seamed stockings. Delores, in dungarees and one of Dad's old undershirts, felt underdressed for the occasion of meeting in the entry hallway.

"You look nice," Delores said. "Big plans?"

"I'll be gone most of the day," Mother said. "Do you need anything?"

"Where are you off to?"

"Just errands. I'll see you before dinner."

Mother kissed the air next to Delores's cheek and left, the lingering of her powdered scent heavy, drifting in invisible eddies.

Around noon, back at it in the studio, Delores was focusing on a brunette model dressed as a cowgirl in a petite fringe vest riding a stick horse and holding a plastic gun, a tiny American flag–colored cowboy hat on her wavy brown locks, a calico blouse tied under her breasts, a Texas-sized wink on her face. And she talked. Or, at least, there was a voice.

"Oh, god, I hated her."

Delores jumped, nearly knocking down the camera. "Christ, you startled me."

Sammi stood in the doorway, white shorts, that blue zippered jacket with some orange thing peeking out from underneath. Her mouth moved, lips parted, smacking a piece of gum. The sunlight lit the edges of her from behind.

"I thought you would have heard me come up." She walked into the studio, looking around the way a tourist might inside a grand cathedral. "Say! Did you clean the place yourself?"

Delores shrugged. "You ever see him do it?"

"I really did hate her," Sammi said after making a full tour of the room, pointing to the brunette cowgirl. "She 'trained' me. Stuck-up bitch. Put on a fake British accent because she played Miranda in some community college *Tempest*. I hear she's putting out for producers now, trying to break into movies."

Sammi walked over and began leafing through the canvases like she might do with records at a phonograph store.

"How many models has he had?" she said. "I've never asked him. It's like asking somebody how many lovers they've had." She stopped, waited a moment then turned. "Not that I'm suggesting, you know...."

"Dad never sleeps with his models."

"Really? Never? I thought maybe it was just me."

"As a girl I was obsessed with Mata Hari. I acted out the spy and used to lurk around, hiding, climbing a ladder, and looking in the rear windows. Must have spent hours watching him over a year or so. He never did anything but work. Say what you will about my Dad, but he's not an artist who sleeps with his models. He's always very professional. No, that's not true. There was one model named Camille who was a dancer. They used to dance on breaks. Dad loves to dance."

"Bad enough he makes me listen to all that opera. If he tried to tango with me, I'd leave him with crushed feet."

"I think she was a special case."

Sammi went back to the paintings, spending a second or two on each before moving to the next.

"Can I ask you something? Why not work from pictures, then? Why have live models? I mean, I'm not complaining."

"Haven't figured it out yet?"

"I guess not."

"He hates being alone. He likes company around him all the time. Especially company that adores him and likes fawning over him. Especially pretty girls. He is the type of person who gets his juice from being around other people."

"Never thought about that. I just figured he had a thing for me and would sour pretty quick. Hasn't happened yet."

"He does have a thing for you or he wouldn't have hired you. He is picky about his models."

"Good thing I don't need to guard my virtue, I guess. Well, I mean, if I had any left to guard." She laughed at her own joke.

"Why are you here?" Delores said.

Sammi pushed the leaning group of canvases back against the wall, and walked to the dressing room.

"I'm guessing you haven't opened this door yet," she said. The door, painted with an armless Greek Aphrodite statue on the edge of a porch that overlooked a smoking Vesuvian mountain range. She turned the latch and pushed the door so that it swung into the room.

Delores came over and turned on the light to find a pile of clothing up to her waist. Corsets, stockings, dresses, shoes, fantasy wear and costumes, leather and feathers — a repository of feminine sexual shaping and primping. A still-musty laundry basket odor, rounded on the edges by sweet cosmetics and bottles of perfume. A many-lighted makeup mirror and table against one wall had a bent cane chair and small clearance around its feet, although on the countertop was a mess of cosmetics, a makeup Manhattan.

"Pal decided he needed to work today so, yeah, so I came to clean," Sammi said. "I figured it was about time. Just my luck to find you here, too!"

Delores pulled focus on a painting of Sammi. She was Little Bo Peep, by way of a Southern belle, splayed on the ground. Her hoop skirt rose from the soil like the Hollywood Bowl, lacy pantaloons tight on her legs, her bodice more clinging tissue-paper than humble peasant dress. A lamb sniffed at her hair, her mouth an *O* of surprise. Her cane, with its curved alabaster handle hooked over one thigh, pulled her leg askew.

"Now that one I remember like a dance move," Sammi said, from the dressing room doorway. She took the pose before the easel. She replicated it to a near-perfect degree, her expression, the limb positions. Delores took a step back, the effect was uncanny. She repositioned her tripod to get Sammi in the frame and tucked her head to the viewfinder to focus and capture the moment, a painting of a girl, a girl emulating the painting of herself.

She snapped. Refocused. Snapped again. A spirit ran through her. An instinct said that maybe this was a moment she should mark. This first capture of the muse in emulsion, frozen in a microsecond of emoting light, bouncing off a stray hair across the model's ear, off the fabric of her clothing, the skin of her arms, the glisten where she licked her lips before Delores pushed the release and engaged the mechanism that triggered the shutter and locked a certain fate in a certain fixative. And fixed Delores as well when this feeling went through her, this clarity and cleanliness of mind, this meditative presentness. She wanted it never to end.

"Hello? Help me up, would you?" Sammi said, a hand extended.

Delores offered an arm, and Sammi grasped it cross-palm. As Delores pulled, Sammi pivoted up on her, and once she was upright she slid her feet together and did a small bow. Delores applauded softly.

"Bravo," Delores said. "The audience is yours."

Larking over, Sammi went back to her tasks in the dressing room. Delores moved the tripod back in place to snap the canvas, but then she pulled the lever to loosen the camera, grabbed her light meter, and strode into the dressing room.

She took a few snaps of Sammi standing arms akimbo, and gazing into the pile of clothes at her feet. Sammi picked up a hideous corset and held it with two fingers, showing campy disgust. She moved through facial expressions like a dealer moved through cards, each look changing her countenance, her posture. Delores captured each one, moving around her to find an ideal angle.

Even if Sammi turned there was this draw and tension, a force that kept her awareness centered on the perfect middle of that curved glass. Her foot pointed, her brows raised a bit to enlarge her eyes, her lips parted in the slightest way.

"Well, if you're gonna shoot me, I gotta put a face on," Sammi said. She sat at the mirror. Delores moved in close, shot her in reflection, drew focus on her eyes. Sammi brushed her hair, pinned the front back and shook out the rest so it cascaded over her shoulders. The bulbs lining the mirror cast a bright shadowless light on her face and front. Delores caught sight of herself standing over the lambent girl, the lens throwing reflections, her own face obscured in shadow. She changed the aperture so she'd be lost in the blur, the shallow depth of field locked on the model.

Sammi laid color on her lids. She reached for a cardboard of false lashes, but Delores said "No," so she put them down and then did her eyes in mascara and liner. Did her lips and gave a hint of blush to her cheeks. And then, challenging the camera — eyelids leaden, brows high, mouth open as if breathing hard — she unzipped her jacket and unbuttoned her blouse until they hung loose, so that Delores could see the fabric make a stripe from her sternum to her belly button.

"You're not wearing a bra," Delores said. Sammi smiled.

"I don't really need one." And she pulled the coat aside with her left hand exposing a breast. She posed like that, her face settling into an inquiring tease, Delores felt a primal shudder move down her spine. Their look crackled with such energy that Delores was quite certain it could power all the lights in the house.

"Well," Sammi said. "Are you gonna take the picture or just gawk at it?"

Delores snapped. And kept snapping as Sammi stripped herself nude. Delores backed up, sat in the corner as Sammi stood slowly from the chair, turned toward the pile of lingerie, and began to clothe herself in the intimate fabrics, displaying herself for the lens, for Delores to capture. Lit first around the edges like a cloud with the sun behind it, and then from all sides as Delores ran and retrieved clamp lights to illuminate the dressing room.

No wonder Dad loved her. She needed almost no direction. Small corrections here and there: arch your back more; move your leg to the left; your hair is stuck on your lips (after getting a few shots with it stuck to her lips); get down on your knees; stand over me with your hands on your hips; point your toe. A perfect model who had a relationship with the eye of the artist, the lens of the camera.

She was wicked, and Delores, on a knee or standing above her, running out to pull lights into the room or change film, knew that there was an aliveness here.

Here was the epiphany for Delores, the awareness of her craft and what was wrong with nearly every mediocre picture she had ever taken, despite her years of studying and perfecting skill; the reason her photos were lifeless and uninteresting. Delores had a breakthrough that told her the one lesson she had left to learn before she could be considered an artist with her camera: you need a really fucking good model, and only a good photographer can capture a good model.

The dressing room was spotless after they cleaned and shot for a few hours. They sat smoking in cane-back chairs, a second one uncovered during the cleanup. Delores suspected the mess started with throwing one garment on the chair, then another, and suddenly a river, then a lake, of fabrics inhabited all space. Now the underwear hung on the rails that lined the room, neat and ordered.

Sammi was making up Delores despite her protestations that she preferred not to wear the stuff. Sammi concentrated, hovering over her in a semi-sheer bra and matching panties. Her cigarette dangled as she pushed Delores's eyebrow up with a finger to stretch the skin and apply sweet-smelling color. Delores watched Sammi's nipples through the black fabric, like a shadow behind a screen, mesmerizing, shifting, taunting, as it moved when Sammi's arms lifted and turned.

Cora had worn a bra like that once, on her more generous proportions that she viewed as a problem to be managed. Delores had bought it for her on the occasion of Delores's first gallery opening.

"This is very nearly obscene," Cora said when she opened the box, and parted the tissue paper to reveal what was hidden within.

"It's my night, and you promised," Delores said.

"It's embarrassing. What if there were an accident? What if that's what people think, that I'm the sort of woman who wears French lingerie?"

"Your obituary will talk more about your charitable works than your underwear."

Cora gave in. Delores, dressed and ready to leave already, sat in the armchair in Cora's dressing room, watching her in the mirror as she slid the brassiere on. That moment, still vivid. If she were a painter, that's what she would paint, Cora in a sheer bra, otherwise naked, both arms bent behind her back to fasten the clasps. Cora leaning forward and reaching in to settle the gravity of her breasts into the cups.

Once Cora was dressed, Delores moved to hold her — just that, to put her arms around her woman and to express affection. But Cora pushed her away. "Don't rumple me," she said.

The theme of Delores's show was formally dressed young girls in the lobbies of grand buildings. It started as a lark. She stumbled across a lovely girl in her yellow Easter best, waiting for her father in the modernist lobby of a skyscraper. The girl sat on a leather bench. Behind her, windows twenty feet high showed traffic in the wet city. Delores loitered until the child's father came down, and she asked his permission to capture his daughter. She took many, and one turned out marvelous.

Sure that the concept was sound, Delores hired other girls, dressed them, and placed them in lobbies. But these photos proved lifeless. Not nearly as nice as the first. At Cora's insistence she showed them to a gallery owner and was offered a show.

When they arrived that night, she learned the show had completely sold out. What a confidence booster, the beginning of a career, finally.

Then, a week before Delores decided to come to Los Angeles, straightening up the books before Cora took her trip to Paris, Delores found receipts in one of the private files. Cora had bought every photograph herself, through proxies. It was all a lie. Her art hadn't sold because it was good. Nobody had liked the work that much. Delores had failed, and that failure had been hidden from her.

"Shimmy shimmy shimmy," Sammi said. Delores, looking at her nipple, didn't react. Sammi moved her chest again. "Shimmy shimmy shimmy," she said.

"Oh, god, was I staring?"

"Yes, and I'm insulted. Because you were looking at me but your eyes were far away."

"Sorry, I was just reminded of something about Cora."

"Who is Cora?" Sami said. "Oh, wait, your Dad has talked about her. She's the lady you work for, right?" Sammi went back to her task of applying makeup.

"Yes. Cora Fournier."

"I've heard it implied that you two are very close."

Delores looked up, but Sammi wasn't meeting her gaze, focusing on her task. "What did you hear?"

Sammi shrugged. "Guess I can't be any clearer than the way I just said it."

A honk. Another. Shave and a haircut.

"Aw, darn," Sammi said. "That's Pal. I lost track of time."

She put the mascara on the table and stood up, leaning across Delores with a hand on her shoulder for support.

Delores turned and watched Sammi pull her shorts up with a sway of her hips. She tossed on her orange blouse and that blue windbreaker over the top. Underneath it all, Delores pictured that lingerie, and it seemed naughtier to have something like that under such casual clothes.

Sammi stepped toward Delores to give a hug, and then put a hand to Delores's cheek, and leaned in to deliver a soft open-eyed peck on the lips. A momentary kiss, warm, sweet, and perfectly breathtaking.

She paused on the way out. Didn't look back as she spoke, but very clearly enunciated, "I guess what I heard doesn't matter so much as that, when I heard it, I got really curious about you. I'm glad you're here." And then Sammi ran across the space and flew out of the studio, leaving Delores a lonely puddle on a dusty floor.

She turned to the mirror, one eye popping with dramatic sweep of color, the other plain and unadorned. Like this, like a vaudevillian half-man half-woman character, she could see her father on her unmade side, and her mother on the other. A perfect mix of the two, perhaps, but her father's broad face was the thing that defined her more steadily than the defined femininity of her mother.

She picked up a lipstick, a brilliant coral, and painted her lips, moving them together as if that could seal in the essence of Sammi's kiss beneath the pigment. She had a fleeting thought about addressing the unmade eye, but her hands were not as deft as Sammi's. She thought, instead, she would end up as a worse parody. She took a moment to turn her face this way and that, like a child opening only one eye, then the other, in rapid succession to see the difference in perspective. She reached for the cold cream and pulled the tissues closer, and began making herself authentic again.

V

DELORES TOOK a seat next to Mother on a hardwood pew in the San Diego Friend's church. It was a progressive congregation that came together in a meeting-hall style. Benches faced inward toward an empty center, illuminated by a skylight above. The space was just as Delores remembered: the woody smell of the pews rubbed by lemon polish, the newly vacuumed carpet runners, the industrial aspect of a church where the fixtures must be built to not only accommodate devotion to God, but also the wear and tear of constant use.

Service was underway when they arrived, thirty or so people sitting quietly as Mother and Delores chose their seats. Across from them, an Abe Lincoln character, his beard gone to ash, watched them enter and gave Delores a slow nod of acknowledgment. To his left, a clean-shaven young man held his eyes shut tight and swayed with his thoughts.

But apart from the human sounds of the room — the coughing, throat-clearing, occasional grunting, the pews creaking as people repositioned themselves — everyone was quiet and contemplative in the Quaker tradition. This was the main reason Delores accepted her mother's invitation to attend after she completed her day's labor in the studio.

Sitting quietly enhanced the vibration of that kiss on Delores's lips. She was flush with the heat of the day. She burned with an afterglow, both because she knew the photos were going to be great, and because this abstract desire for the model that helped her decide to come west had turned into true contact. A fluttering uncertainty took up residence in her stomach, which she hadn't felt since she had taken Tanny Le Clercq to dinner years before.

That kiss was impetuous. Sammi's hinting was so on the nose. It wasn't really teasing at all, in that she was clear with her intentions. But it was teasing in that it inspired confusion and excitement within Delores. Funny how new lust made you feel sick and well at the same time.

She closed her eyes and flipped through her mental canvases of Sammi, her energy electric in still paint, and now in light-sensitive emulsion. She felt the kiss again. She chased Sammi down the stairs. She pulled her by her arm back into the studio. She ripped the zipper on that windbreaker. She lifted that orange top to feel Sammi's summer sun skin beneath. Then Delores startled herself as a grunt came from her own mouth without her bidding, and she opened her eyes in the meeting house again.

When Delores had come down from the studio, Mother was redoing her hair, still in the flowered dress, though now bare-legged.

"You didn't spend all day in front of that mirror, did you?" she said.

Mother gave her a playful push, and Delores smelled her shampoo and newly applied perfume.

Here in church, Mother had a routine that Delores saw as feeding her spiritual self as opposed to her corporeal self. Sitting and drawing deep breaths, attempting, as she put it, to find the peace of God that would sweep over her and relax her shoulders. Allow her face to drop the public facade.

It was the way that she could see her Mother unbidden by awareness of eyes, unbidden by attention. At her most peaceful and open to the world. It was the place she dropped her carapace.

A moan from across the room. The rocking man moved with more animation, apparently agitated. With a crack of the floorboards, he rose. "We have now the power of ultimate destruction," he cried, his voice echoing. He pushed his hair away from his eyes, which he opened to look around the room. He closed them again and turned his face upward.

He drew a sharp breath, and said, with more reserve, more control. "We have now the power of ultimate destruction. Of weapons that could remove life from this planet. I pray to God that we can find the wisdom to banish this genie, if we cannot stuff him back in his vile bottle. I ask you to pray with me, so that we can affect the world. So that we can give wisdom to our leaders. So that we can guide our children to have the sight to banish these horrible tools. This hammer of the false gods."

The man sat in a sudden movement. His eyes clamped, his forehead knit as if he desired to bring his brows together, he rocked again, tears falling into his lap.

The man with the gray chinstrap beard approached Delores in the reception area. He took one of her hands in both of his, which were dry and hot, knobbed and cracked. A cabinet-makers hands. A warm smile split his broad face.

"And how is New York? I do miss the fall in New England. The leaves. The colors."

"Busy as always," Delores said. She forgot this man's name but keenly remembered the exchanges she'd had with him over the years. He was kind, an empath, a particular sort of man who has had any semblance of humor studiously replaced with earnest projected compassion. He made her extremely uncomfortable.

He nodded for a moment, perhaps waiting for her to continue. Giving her, at least, the time to continue if she wanted. Then he revealed the thing he had obviously been eager to say since seeing her enter the meeting hall.

"This may be a forward thing to say, to express to you, but as one who watched you grow, I feel that perhaps I have a license where it is likely I do not, so I will just say it and hope I am not overstepping a boundary, and if so, apologize for it.

"I think it is wonderful that you have found a partner such as you have and live a life as you are. I know your mother is worried about homosexuality in the eyes of God, but I cannot find faith in a Father who does not love in exact measure to how he has created. To put a fine point on it, child, you are loved and are not sinning insofar as I see the situation, and there are many, I daresay, who agree with me but yet are not quite brave enough to speak the words."

"My mother discussed this with you?"

"Worry, and divine spirit, drove her to speak out in a meeting, but we have not talked of it together. My brother, I'm sure you do not know, was a homosexual. He took his own life because of the rejection he experienced from our father and our family at large, and even from me. This is a pain beyond measure." The man's lower lip pulled in, and his chin quivered, but whatever emotion almost took him, he recovered from it.

"I'm so sorry," Delores said. "That's horrible."

"Yes. It quite changed my opinion on the matter, I daresay. He had one close friend. I try to see him quite often, and have even brought him to worship so that he might find peace amongst God's more accepting children. But there is something that happens to a man who is not allowed to love the ones he wants to love. I fear he finds more peace with liquor than with God."

"You say my mother discussed my relationship in a meeting?"

"Obliquely, once or twice, when moved to speak. She never used your name, of course, but it wasn't hard for those of us who know you to pull a sum from those mathematics."

Delores lit a cigarette and stared out the side window, turned away from Mother. She worked her leg, bouncing her knee, rubbing two fingers together. Mother had talked about her with strangers. That delicious fluttering, thanks to Sammi, was captured and sunk to the pit of her belly, with leaden weights tied to its wings.

"Can I tell you something?" Mother said.

"When have you ever needed my permission to yack at me?"

"I don't know what's going on with you. I really don't, and maybe that's okay. It's your life and your right to keep it to yourself. Light me a cigarette."

Delores did and handed it over to Mother, who held it in her right hand, at the top of the steering wheel. Her left elbow jutted out the open window.

"But here is the truth of it, I'm going to say in plain. It makes me happy that you're here."

"It does?"

"Do you doubt it?"

"You're very critical, you know. You're not very kind to me."

"Darling, I'd love to just dote on you, but then what kind of terrible mother would that make me? I need to prepare you for the world."

"I am thirty years old. I'm in that world, and have been for a decade or more."

"You're not thirty yet. And you're not exactly a normal girl, you know. Sure, you are very independent and I give you that. But dear, you're not married. You don't have children. You don't have a good income. You are frivolous with the very basic foundations of life. That terrifies me. I want you to be secure and safe and prosper."

"I am happy."

"Are you? You've left your life behind and you're happy?"

"I'm happier today than I was the day I left New York."

Mother looked over to her. Ashed her unsmoked cigarette.

"Then I'm glad for you." She tossed the cigarette out the window and put her hand on Delores's knee. "Look, here's what I'm trying to say. You're my daughter, and I love you. It turns out I'm enjoying you being around. Is that such a terrible thing to express?"

"No," Delores said. "Thank you for saying it." And feeling more obligated than inspired, she placed her hand on top of Mother's and gave it a squeeze.

They arrived home to find dad in an apron, on the back porch, perched beside a smoking grill, a cigar between his lips, a beer in hand. He turned as they came out onto the porch.

"Ah! My ladies!" He stepped toward them and stumbled, then regained himself. "I have hunted. I have gathered. I am providing for my family."

On a plate next to the grill, dressed in herbs and oil, were three gutted bass. "Vegetables are roasting inside. Allow me, if you don't find the role too feminine, to prepare our evening's repast. Perhaps you might set the table and we could eat on the porch in this evening's luxurious weather?"

He swept Lily into an arm, dipping her and planting a kiss on her lips. "And I shall be rewarded by this one in devilish and astounding ways," he said, and then he nibbled her ear.

Delores went to fetch the table dressing, as Mother laughed and turned her face so that Dad could take the nibbling to her neck. Delores looked in on the vegetables in the oven, finding them browned near to burning in a large cast-iron skillet. She put them on the cooktop and shook the pan so that they wouldn't stick. The steam fogged her glasses, blinding her.

She took them from her face, wiped them on a kitchen towel, which only streaked them. She washed them in the sink with dish detergent and dried them on a fresh towel. She looked outside to find Mother in Dad's strong arms, one of his hands cupping her behind, bending the drape of her dress. One of Mother's legs up, pressed against his hip. Delores pulled back so that they couldn't see her. She plated the roasted vegetables and fetched napkins and flatware. She peered around again to see whether they were still at it, but Mother was just coming inside.

"Do you need some help?" she said, her cheeks flushed. She cleared her throat and touched her hair.

"Why don't you get some wine?"

"Wake up. Wake up, goddamnit." Dad shook Delores awake.

"What is it?" she said, batting his hands away. "What's going on?"

"I can't find anything!" he cried. "You moved everything, and I can't work. It is a goddamn mess in my studio."

"Jesus, Dad, this can wait until morning."

"If it could wait I wouldn't have woken you. I thought you were supposed to clean, not fucking fuck everything around."

"What is wrong with you? You left it a mess. It'll take me more than a day to get your years of neglect straightened out."

"It's my studio. Mine. I keep it the way I want. Get your ass upstairs and fix it! Right now!" He stormed out of the room, scraping the hallway wall with his shoulder and knocking a small family photo to the carpeted floor with a thud. Delores rose. She pulled on the blue terry robe and matching slippers Sammi had worn the other night, pilfered earlier since they smelled of her, and followed to the studio.

Inside, on the chest next to the easel, a half-gone bottle of whiskey. He was in the bathroom, with the door open and, from the sound of it, some horse had snuck in and was urinating into the toilet.

A record spun impotently, the needle stuck on the inside groove. Delores lifted it and put it home. Cut the power.

"I think it's time you went to bed," she said, looking at the clock in the office. Small hand almost at the three.

The toilet flushed and Dad emerged, zipping up.

"I can't find anything in there." He pointed to the office.

"What exactly are you looking for?"

Dad stood swaying, his face blank. Like a kinetic statue, rotating on a base. Delores gave him almost a full minute to answer.

"Whatever it was, it can wait. Time for you to go to bed."

"I don't want to go to bed. She's down there."

"So what? What about her?"

"I got into the whiskey after dinner. She doesn't like it when I get into the whiskey. I go and sleep in your room. I snore too much, she says. I guess. That's what she says."

"Why don't you sleep on the couch in your office?"

Dad snapped his fingers. Tried to, anyway.

"You took the blanket! That's what it was. I couldn't find my nap blanket. I got mad, it wasn't there and I just want to sleep."

"I only washed it. It was a mess. Go lay down. I'll go get it from the line."

By the time she returned, Dad was down, eyes closed. Delores removed his boots, covered him. Gave his sweaty head a stroke, the overgrown toddler.

"Thanks," he said, not quite asleep, not quite awake anymore. "Your Mother won't do it. Clean up here."

"I know, Dad. It's okay. Get some sleep."

"She doesn't love me anymore," he said.

"Why do you say that?"

But he never answered. Whatever thought dragged him down took him all the way, and when his breath pivoted to deep draws through his nose Delores cut the lights and went downstairs. She wanted to heat some milk in a pan, but was faced with a counter and stovetop full of dishes. She set to cleaning them, and when she had at last sponged up the last of the soapy water from the counters and stove, she poured some cold milk into a pan and put a fire under it.

Shutting off the lights again to regain the feel of nighttime, she added some cocoa to the milk and stirred it so that no skin would form, and so the powder would melt into the mix. The house sighed, settled, ticked, and clicked. She poured the hot chocolate into a mug and sat at the banquette, closing her eyes and hoping that sleep would find her once the adrenaline calmed.

Through the living room she could see the glass porch doors, the patio where they dined only a few hours earlier drawn in varying chiaroscuro, barely legible. But then a shape, a shadow moving through shadows. Something up against the door. She felt that shiver of the spine, that human danger response, the raised hackles. Delores closed her eyes to let the dark claim them, to erase the light still echoing in her vision, and then looked again.

Yes, an animal — a possum? raccoon? — barely made out, walking against the glass, the length of the porch, trundling along that patio in the dark. Maybe called by the smells of their outdoor meal. It went one way, then the other, measuring the length of the doors. The clock in the kitchen, on the wall above Delores, keeping time for the creature, tick tick tick tick. Setting a pace that it appeared to keep, like a soldier to a marching call.

She drank and watched as it walked its beat, sometimes stopping for a measure or two before continuing. She saw echoes of it that she followed, thinking they were the creature, but that turned false once she caught its true movement. The dark was so overwhelming that the sight was more impression than definition.

She watched until her mug was empty, and then set it down. That hovering dread of uncertainty now colliding in her warm belly with the cocoa. And then the shadow was gone, just like that. It must have turned and moved away from the glass into a darker zone, unseen.

VI

THE FIRST LIE of Hollywood Film Developing was that it was not in Hollywood. It was downtown in what appeared to be a modest storefront. It had a simple counter and a white wall behind that, which had a single door marked private in hand-painted four-inch red letters. A sour odor hung in the place, half cleanser, half photographic chemical.

The second lie was that Hollywood Film Developing didn't develop motion picture film, it did only still work. Color and black and white, catering to a specialized market: it was the shop of choice for every cop and private eye in town.

Delores rang the bell on the counter. Every inch of wall was covered with framed celebrity photos. Movie stars, politicians, police officers, reporters, all signed to *Diego*. One was a picture of Gael Sarjeant standing next to a Sarjeant's Sergeants canvas, shaking hands with a tall gaunt man, Diego Peck, the proprietor of Hollywood Film Developing, carefree smiles on their faces.

The white door opened, and there he was. Hair black and slicked back, a lean face, as if a handsome man had been stretched a bit too thin. A William Powell mustache on a lip that curved into a smile when he saw her.

He put his hands on his hips and shook his head. "Can't say Gotham has put you out any, doll."

"The pleasure is all mine, Mr. Peck."

"I should get some snapshots of you. Put them in a file with any old ones I got. At the end of my days I can pull them out, have a single photo of you from every decade."

"I could do that too. I'd have fifty years of photos of Diego Peck, and you'd look the same in every one."

"Aren't you a flirt?" He leaned against the counter. "Say, you know your Pop doesn't work with me anymore, don't you?"

"Does that mean I can't?"

"Your choice, Doll. I always got room for you. You remember what I taught you?"

"Sure, but I'd rather the master do the work."

"Let's go toast to that."

"It's not even eleven."

"Sweetheart, cocktail hour is for businessmen and housewives. We're professionals."

The back of Hollywood Film was three adjacent retail spaces. A warehouse-sized location, with one large office framed in dark wood and glass. In a few hours that would be possessed by police detectives and private dicks having drinks and trading photos from clandestine collections. Delores preferred to work in the mornings, in Diego's quiet times, when they could be alone.

They marched past the office and into one of Diego's two darkrooms. Diego developed the rolls Delores shot of Sammi while she observed, and then he pulled proof sheets to examine at a light table.

Diego whistled, as he looked through a loupe at a shot of Sammi at her makeup table. "Rock-solid work here. You know I'm not one to lay on the praise, but you sure as hell found your muse, sister."

"I think I'm museless, Diego. And that's one *M* away from being useless." Delores laughed at her own joke, alone.

"Sweetheart, I'm talking about this skirt right here. Your muse ain't some high concept, it's this peach. I'd say she's your muse if you're shooting like this."

"Okay. She's my muse."

"I could sell these," Diego said.

"Not a chance."

"No, not like that. To legit channels. You can snap nudies all you want and be legit now."

"I don't buy it. I know what you trade in."

"Sweetheart, you'd have to be a lot more filthy for that clientele."

"That's never going to happen with this model."

"You could dress her in leather. Put a whip in her hand. I could sell those. You seen those photos coming out of Florida and New York? I move a ton of those. Don't even need to be naked."

"Now you're just teasing me."

"Oh, honey, you got no idea."

They did an edit together, picking the best shots, which Diego circled on the proof sheet in grease pencil. Delores picked up a small loupe, and started tapping it against the table.

"You really think these are good?"

"You suggesting I'm a liar?"

"I know for a fact you're a liar."

"Never about quality."

"You just want me to feel good so you can make a commission."

"Somebody inject you with some hot paranoia here? Give me some space. I command you to go into my office and wait while I pull these prints."

"Sure. Give me the archive keys."

Diego laughed. "Nice try, sister."

"Can't blame a girl." She walked away, angling toward the office.

"Bring us a drink!" Diego called after. "And one for yourself too, goddamnit."

Diego's office hadn't changed since Delores saw it last. It was lush, cluttered, comfortable, and smoke stained. A gentlemen's club, of sorts. A worn leather couch and matching arm chairs, all with heavy ornate deco wood accents, were the prominent furniture, complemented by a thick round table in glossy waxed burl, which served as his desk.

Along one side a governmental wall of file cabinets, all locked, held untold wonders. What Diego sneeringly called "The Pecker Archive." On the wall above the cabinets were certificates and commendations from the Los Angeles Police Department for his years of service as a photographer and lab technician. Diego worked for the city throughout the Depression, but left soon after to open his own store. His connection to the cops brought work his way, including overflow from the police labs when big crime was going down. Very few pictures of crime, naked people, compromised politicians, or celebrities passed without his seizing a print of them. He was the photographic Library of Alexandria for the midcentury Los Angeles underworld.

Delores opened the cabinet that held the booze and poured a finger of scotch into a tumbler. She swished it around and took a small drink so that she had it on her breath, then set it on the table.

She tried a random drawer in the file cabinet. Its paper label in a brass holder bore a perfectly centered, typewritten FD, which she recalled stood for "Female Domination." She went to her left until she found a drawer labeled *Busts*. Also locked.

One time it wasn't, though. She was fourteen, or so and Dad had brought her during one summer she was helping him around the studio. She was asked to wait in the office while Dad and Diego went into the darkroom.

"Look, brat," Diego had told her. "I don't care much what you do in here so long as you don't get into any of those file cabinets. We clear?"

But there it was, she noticed as soon as they left. One drawer, open about an inch. That hand label so enticing. What are *busts*? Are they pictures of ladies' bosoms? Of Roman statuary? Of empty mines?

She knew that Diego trafficked in police crime photos. Many of those she had seen, the murdered women, the car wrecks, the diner shootouts, the suicides, the bomb craters in the sides of buildings, the zoot suit beat to death by sailors in the street gutter, the body of a black man surrounded by very much alive police officers.

Mother didn't trust Diego. She heard he kept copies of photos the detectives got developed there. According to her there was an underground trade in this illicit material, and Peck was at the center of the commerce.

All this collided to evoke an unreasonable curiosity about that one unlocked drawer with that exciting title, *Busts*. Delores had to know. She went to the door of the office, saw the light on over the darkroom. They'd be at least a half hour, she knew from experience.

She pulled the drawer out on its rails. It slid, greased, smooth, quiet. Dividers bore labels with names of cities: *New York, Philadelphia, New Orleans, Chicago, Detroit, Austin, Seattle, San Francisco, Tampa, Los Angeles*. Within each were folders with dates on them.

Delores pulled one. Inside a black and white still from the thirties of five women against the wall outside a bar. Women, but one of them dressed as a man, a jacket and a button-down shirt. Wearing a poorly drawn mustache. The name of the place painted in a poor hand script over the door: *Ankles*.

A cop near the edge of the image walked by in a blur, but the girls were all clear. Only one, in a pretty flowered dress that was tattered and worn around the hem, hung her head. One looked downright tough, a wiry tomboy girl sticking out her jaw and giving the camera the bird with her expression. One — she must have been twenty-one or so and looked so old and mature to teenage Delores — had a round face and distrusting eyes, but she looked right into the camera with a soft intensity that Delores found irresistible.

She put that photo back and found another of men, a few dressed as women. Wiry men, tough-looking, squinting against the flashes of the police cameras. Mug shots. Interiors of bars designed never to see the bright flash of a bulb. People who were out for a private night and found themselves embroiled in the exact opposite.

A clipping, the paper and date cut off, rested in one file.

DEVIANT GATHERING DEN SHUTTERED BY COPS
Vice squad Detectives raided Tony's bar on 4th and Western Saturday night. Ten men were arrested and charged with indecent behavior. The club, known as a gathering for homosexuals and other perverts, has had its license revoked by the city.

And then it listed the names of the men who were arrested that night for their wives or their neighbors or their bosses to read.

Delores pulled the Ankles photo again, and just stared at in until she heard Diego laugh. She jammed it back into the folder and closed the cabinet as gently as her rising panic would allow, then dove for the couch and her comic book before the men opened the door.

And as she sat she wondered how in the hell was it that Diego Peck had recognized in her something that she had barely even recognized in herself.

It was remembering that photo, which Delores could recall with almost perfect detail even so many years later, that gave her an idea. It was that one woman with the tomboy face, her chin up to the camera. In that Playboy Delores had liberated from Dad's trash can there was an article on Gloria Pall, more popularly known as Voluptua, Goddess of Love and Romance, whose short-lived television show was cancelled after pressure from religious groups. In one shot, on page 45, her upturned face was in close-up, a heart-shaped mole on her cheek, her lips glossed, her eyes lazy and sensuous. Her jaw masculine, so that she almost read like a drag queen. Standing there in front of the Pecker Archive, Delores put it together, why that photo pulled at her so, why it fascinated her.

Because it looked like that girl in the Ankles photo.

Delores knocked on the darkroom door. The warning light outside the door was on, to signal light-sensitive work happening inside.

"Do not open it!" Diego called.

"How about *Playboy*? Could you sell these to *Playboy*?"

"That rag out of Chicago? I got no connection to them."

"Is that a no?"

"No. Not a no, just a long shot."

"Never mind, then."

"Whatever you say. You got my drink?"

"Can I open the door?"

"Leave it right outside. Be with you soon."

THEY WENT OUT, the lot of them, to celebrate the signing of Dad's new contract. It was a Friday night at Musso & Frank. A red-coated waiter with a towel over his arm worked the cork from a bottle of Dom Pérignon, a sweating ice-bucket on a stand delivered by a young man during the ceremony. Beyond him, the bar was half full, the dining room mostly packed. It was jovial in here, cigarette smoke and an occasional sharp laugh from an over-loud lady. The new room had just opened, but Dad wanted to sit "On the side where Cain and Hammett and Fitzgerald and Chandler used to drink."

The table was a half-circle, the flat edge facing the room, the booth following the curve. Delores sat at the apex, right in the center, with Mother between her and Dad on the edge. The other half was empty, waiting for Sammi and Pal. The arrangement was like a stage setup where the waiter and the other diners were the floorshow. Delores stole quick glances at each table as they had walked to their own, but she recognized no movie stars.

The rest of their party entered with flair, Sammi in a yellow number that was darker than Easter but brighter than mustard. It tied at the waist with a thin fabric belt. Pal was done up in blue seersucker with a red bow tie. Twirling a fedora on a couple of extended fingers.

"Looking fine, Pal," Dad said to him, rising to say hello, and they greeted each other with a handshake. Sammi got a kiss on the cheek and Delores was introduced to Pal, as this was the first time she had seen him not through a window at midnight.

Pal was a tall olive-skinned man, with the good looks of a movie star just beginning to go to seed. He was lean and towering, but his teeth showed a small gap in the front, and his Grecian nose had a slight pull to one side. For all that, it was a handsome face, masculine with a beard shadow. His eyes had a light and pleasure that warmed the table as he approached.

"Two more of those glasses, buddy," Pal said to the waiter with a pat on his shoulder.

"Of course, sir."

Sammi slid in next to Delores and gave her leg a squeeze. Pal was the one to offer the toast once the glasses were present and full, a second bottle opened and chilling in the bucket.

"To this man here who paints girls so beautiful that the world is made better just by turning your eye to them. Keep painting forever, and give me lots of memories of my lady when she's young so that when she's old and wrinkled I'll have something to think about when I've got her in bed."

"Pal!" Sammi said, and slapped his arm.

"Well, thanks, I guess," Dad said, with a chuckle.

All the glasses came together in pairs, arms reaching across the table in a scattered chaos, making sure that each of them found another before they drank.

"And here's to earning what you're worth," Mother said.

"I've always earned what I was worth," Dad said. "Provided a nice home for you."

"Well, then," Mother said. "Here's to earning what I'm worth. Finally."

They drank again, and before long both bottles were gone and they were on to cocktails, hors d'oeuvres, and, once dinner orders were in, a nice Beaujolais.

Later, Pal asked, "So, when you gonna buy a second car, now that you got all that new money coming in?"

Dad laughed. "Can't stop selling for just one night, can you?"

"Oh, no, it's not that. Buy a Ford for all I care. I'm just saying two cars give you freedom. The ability to be anywhere you want. Not having to coordinate. Let me tell you, with the rate they're tearing down those streetcar lines, you better have a way to get around. Way I see it, two cars are going to save you money. In a few years they're gonna put in that new freeway out to Santa Monica across that neighborhood where Sammi has her place. That's gonna cut travel time home for you down to nothing."

"Well, believe it or not, I'm thinking about buying a boat."

"I love to be on the water," Mother said. "You know, he promised me when we were married he'd buy me a boat. Round about time, I would say."

"Well, then," Pal said. "Now we have a topic here that has some legs. You know I have a boat, right? A thirty-foot sloop. I'm a lifelong sailor."

"My dad loved to sail," Mother said. "We used to sail down to Ensenada every summer. Stay in a resort. Hire these Mexican boys that would run down into the surf where they kept lobsters and run them back up the beach to pots already set to boil. It was the freshest, sweetest meat you'd ever have eaten. It was a big adventure."

"Well, aren't you in luck then, pretty lady. I was just telling Sammi I wanted sail out to Catalina tomorrow. That sounds like a fun thing. Tell you what, let's make it all of us. Let's all of us keep this party alive all day tomorrow and put it on the water and let the wind carry it to Catalina for a day trip."

Mother lit up at the suggestion. "Oh, yes, that would be just grand." She turned to Dad. "What do you say? Wouldn't that be just grand?"

Dad pressed his lips together as if he were about to turn it down, but then a smile broke through. "Sure, sure. Why not? Why not. Sounds like a day."

"God, the last thing I want to do is go to Catalina tomorrow," Sammi said. She stood at the mirror in the bathroom, dabbing the corner of her mouth where her fresh coat of lipstick overshot its mark. She moved her head left and right, checking her face, then brought her cigarette up to her thickly rouged lips. Delores sat on a chair behind her, looking at Sammi's burnt-orange pumps, her ankles, and the tensed muscles of her bare leg. Her skin was tan and young, broken only by a brown mole low on her left calf.

"Let's not go, then," Delores said, her legs crossed, one arm across her stomach, the other vertical, holding a cigarette. "Let's both complain of terrible hangovers. I'm sure the skipper wouldn't want us tossing up all over his precious yacht."

"You are a sly one, aren't you?" Sammi said. She kicked one foot back, and balanced it on the tip of her pump, a move that seemed shocking to Delores since it might scuff the toe. Underneath, in a cursive gold stamp, the name of the store that sold the heels laid against the blackened sole. Delores looked at the way it tensed the calf on her other leg as Sammi leaned into the mirror. When she glanced back up, Sammi was looking, and when their eyes were locked Sammi said, "But whatever would we do with our time?"

"I want to take you to the beach," Delores said. "We'll have a beach morning. I'll take your picture everywhere we go. We'll head back to the house for lunch."

"I want to do up your face again. Finish this time."

"Okay, then. We can pick up just where we stopped when you left the other day."

The stall doors were open. A water sound ran in the pipes, although they were alone. Delores pictured the bathroom like a crime photo from Diego's archive. All color removed. Contrast like from a flash bulb. Stalls knocked over. Sinks broken from the wall, cracked in two on the tile floors. Broken pipes spraying hot and cold water. Two women on the floor, splayed in each other's arms: two debased, drenched women full of destruction and desire. Only, in Delores's movie they flushed with life. They moved and writhed against each other, wet dresses going transparent and displaying undergarments, lingerie, moles, scars, thin fabric showing the hump of the mons veneris. A flush took Delores. She realized she was staring at Sammi's calf and darted her eyes up to catch Sammi's in the mirror.

"I like the way you look at me," Sammi said quietly, and neither looked away until the bathroom door opened and a woman came between them, excusing herself as she broke their gaze.

The plate that once held a crème brûlée and another that had held Bananas Foster were reduced to ridges of sugary trails and swipes. As they were finishing their sherry, Pal told a story.

"He'd been eyeing this little convertible, and I swear that damn hebe was making me crazy. He had this price he wanted, and damn if he was gonna budge. Well, I say always better to walk away from a deal than lose your pants. Plenty of car buyers in the world. Anyway, he wasn't moving and neither was I, and the both of us were plenty annoyed with the other. I'm sure he looked at me and saw some kind of rube, and I saw him like a cheap Jew, and that was all there was to it.

"Well, as a salesman I don't want to waste time, but I could see he really wanted this car, and I needed to find a way to free his pride from accepting a higher price after he set his limit so clearly with me. You know how proud they are. They don't want to feel ripped off. Taken advantage of, right? I mean, some folks do actually, they like knowing you got the better of them. They like it when you flirt with their wives and leave them thrilled and broke, but not those kosher types, right?

"So anyways, I drew an imaginary line with my hand and I said, 'Okay, friend, you and I need to sit down for a minute and stop talking numbers and get to know one another.' He looked about my age, even though he didn't have my luxurious hair line that drives the girls crazy." Pal laughed at his own joke, and Sammi ran her fingers through his hair and mocked fainting as she might on sight of a matinee idol.

Each bit of attention Sammi gave to her fiancé in front of Delores was a mark in her ledger of jealousy. But Sammi would erase the slate by occasionally swiping or laying a tender hand on Delores's leg in the most secretive of manners. The private language of their newly founded country, map lines drawn, not yet inhabited.

"So, I take him back into my office and I say, 'I was in the war. You?' and he nods. 'I was in Europe. Helped to free Auschwitz,' I said to him. 'Terrible things those Germans did. Most righteous fight of my life,' I said. Whatever he was thinking I was going to say, I very much doubt it was this. He just nodded at me, a moment of great solemnity. So, I add this last bit. 'It moved me so much that each year when I'm writing a check to my church I also write one to the Anti-Defamation League.'

"Well, that clinched it. Immediately, he told me my price was not as unreasonable as he figured on second thought, and in fact, if I came down just a little bit from that he would meet what I was asking. We shook hands, signed the paper, and he rolled off the lot in that new car."

"You are terrible," Mother said with a laugh.

Pal leaned back, put his arm on the booth behind her, and smiled the smile of the contest winner. Sammi lit him a cigarette, and he smoked with his free hand. "He's a terrible liar, is what he is," Sammi said. "Pal spent the whole war on a desk. He's got a bum knee." Pal shrugged, a little proud of himself.

"I'd feel bad about not donating to the Anti-Defamation League, but I don't have a church to donate to either, so that about balances the whole thing out. Anyway, who was hurt? He got a good deal off me, and a new car, and he got to feel good about the whole thing. I cleared some inventory, so I'm happy."

Dad was laughing, and so was Mother. A grand old time.

"I don't want this to end," Mother said. "Let's not let this end. Let's all go back to our place and keep on."

"Well, okay!" Pal said.

Dad and Delores took Fairfax to Wilshire. Sammi and Mother rode with Pal ("My lady stays with me," he said, then he elbowed Dad and said, "but I'll take yours too, if you don't mind"). Dad drove the 210, one hand draped over the big wheel. He managed to stay mostly in the lanes.

"You and Sammi seem to be hitting it off," Dad said.

"I see what you see in her," Delores said. "I took some photos of her the other day when we were cleaning up. They turned out. She knows how to pose."

"Glad you guys are having fun."

"You don't mind?"

"Mind what?"

"That I took some photos of her?"

"Should I?"

A carload of teenagers, in a souped-up 1940s Dodge, pulled up next to them at the red light, hooting and hollering. Leaning out of the windows, pounding the doors. The driver, freckled face and appearing to be all of twelve, looked at Dad. Raised his eyebrows. Gunned his engine. Pointed down Wilshire, straight and sparsely populated. Dad nodded. Gunned his engine back.

The light changed, and the kid hit the gas so hard that he spun out his tires before they gained purchase, and then he shot away from them in a second. Dad didn't even try. He did a slow start from his perch and kept his pace along the road, watching the kids take the easy win and, no doubt, jet off in search of another race.

"You really going to buy a boat?" Delores said.

"Your mother wants one. I learned how to sail a few years back. Something modest that we could take up to Santa Barbara or down to San Diego or Mexico."

"I went sailing with some of Cora's family once. Can't say I liked it very much. It was a very windy day. Too much chop. Guess I don't like losing my footing. Seemed unnecessarily risky."

"Almost got killed once myself," Dad said. "We were down near Balboa Island near Long Beach. I was in the harbor, learning how to sail in these little dinghy things, sabots, that they make you master before they give you something bigger. Here I am out on the water, all happy, and I have a cigar, so life is good, just drifting around and having a nice old time by myself. Singing a bit of this tenor piece from *Rigoletto* because nobody can hear me.

"But, comes time, I have to take a leak. So I get myself situated up and I do my business. Then I hear this blast of a horn, and I turn around just as I'm zipping up to see the Catalina Ferry bearing down on me. I mean, it was coming fast, and it was cutting some serious water. I pull the lanyard in and I grab the rudder, but I'm still standing and I yank up on it, the stupid thing comes right out of its braces. You know, it just sits in these little metal rounds. It's quite easy to yank out. Doesn't seem very safe.

"I look up and see the captain, or whoever, and he's moving his hands yelling, saying 'Go to the side! Go to the side!' or something. I look the decks, and they're full of people going out to the island for a nice day. I hold up my rudder over my head, and when that captain sees me he puts both hands to the sides of his face like a cartoon character and he's screaming something. I see another face in the window, all wide eyed, and then they're turning the ship as fast as they can. That thing came within ten feet of me. I got to ride its wake for a bit, rocking back and around, but I stayed upright. I got the rudder back in and made it back in one piece. Can't say my hand was steady for a few hours after that, if truth be told. But I made it back in one piece, and now I just stay the hell out of that big channel."

"Glad you didn't get clobbered."

"Painting is not a very active lifestyle, you know. Maybe it's not a bad thing to get out and try something new. Even something dangerous. Exciting. Anyway, people've been sailing for thousands of years. It's not all that risky, you know. We'd have a nice time on a boat, I think."

The teenager's car came back the other way, the boys in the backseat sitting on the sills of the open windows, each with one arm holding tight, the other pumping in the air, pistoning as they hollered, slapping the top of the car. Hair whipping in the current as they jetted past, their voices and the engine going Doppler, leaving tread on the road, fishtailing into the future.

"Idiots," Dad said.

"Yeah," Delores said. "Don't they know there are drunks on the road?"

Dad spit through his closed lips, and nearly swerved as he laughed. He slapped Delores on the knee, and she leaned against the door, giggling.

But Dad kept the ship steady as they entered the dark part of Wilshire, where it cut right through the country club, just as they left Beverly Hills.

Delores and Dad entered the house to a melody. Mother was at the piano, and Pal stood behind her with a hand on her shoulder. They harmonized on "I'm in the Mood for Love." A bottle of gin was open on a tray, beside a row of tumblers and an ice bucket. Sammi slumped on a couch reading *Sunset magazine.*

"They wasted no time," Dad said, collapsing next to Sammi. Delores took a chair across from them.

"They started in the car," Sammi said. "I should have come with you two." Delores pictured that, Dad driving them as she and Sammi were in the backseat, hands traveling where eyes in a rear view mirror couldn't see.

Delores rose and retrieved her camera, loaded it with fast film for the low light. She pointed it, and people reacted. Sammi leaned into Dad, who put his arm around her and took on a toothy smile. She captured Mother and Pal singing, faces upturned, mouths open on a held note. She stepped back and got Dad and Sammi leaning in to talk while Pal and Mother's voices attempted, and sometimes found, harmony. Something about those relationships seemed so natural, as if Sammi were the daughter who was bringing home her beau, and Mother and Dad having a normal night in, like they might with a son-in-law on deck, their daughter a blushing bride-to-be.

The song came to an end, the singers hamming it up and holding the last note until their breaths tapered off into gasps.

"Say!" Pal said after it was done. "Do you know 'Sunny Side of the Street'?" Mother started playing right off, and the two of them were harmonizing on the first line lickity-split.

But the drink had gone bad on Delores, and the whole scene rubbed against the grain of her. She gave Sammi a peck on the cheek.

"I'll wait for you in the morning, here," Delores said, close enough to her ear that her lips picked up Sammi's body heat. Sammi nodded. She waved her good nights and went to her room.

The light showed those portraits, an army of Delores, each gaze tracking her across the room. Each younger version of her whispering her impression of what their future would be. Each advertisement illustrating whatever mood would best bolster the brand name to be painted below. Pouty Delores, happy Delores, laughing Delores, all for the eyes of American mothers.

But it was after midnight, and now a full week that she had been in Los Angeles. That meant Dad had won the bet. She had sided with Mother in that she hated the pictures being up, but why make an ordeal out of it? Why embarrass Dad when his intentions were good?

But these portraits annoyed Delores. Each of them a reflection of her failures in some distinct over-sweetened way, a reflection of how her father couldn't see those failures. Of how he saw only the ideal. Wasn't he just the optimist?

Delores slapped the nearest canvas and it went sideways on its nail. She hit it again, and it bounced off the corner of the dresser on the way to the floor. Then she picked it up and examined it, worried that she had harmed the frame or scratched the paint.

She used both hands and took down the next, gingerly. She opened the closet and started a stack, leaning against the back wall, under the tails of plastic-covered coats.

In the living room Mother and Pal held the music steady, and it acted against Delores's mood exactly as if she was a character in a movie trying to say something. "Sunny Side of the Street," indeed. She closed the door to muffle them as much as possible. When that wasn't enough, she turned on the radio that she kept to the static of no station, and as the tubes warmed up the sound went from nothing to a toppling white noise that masked most of the amateur talent show in the other room.

Soon she faced an empty wall with nails sticking out. Little sentinels, casting little shadows from the overhead light as if sundials, the angle of each dark mark at a different inclination in relation to the hundred-watt sun at the center of the ceiling.

The torn picture of *The Ballet Society* still sat on the dresser. She hung it on a nail, right through the tear in Tanny Le Clercq's face.

The music continued, though to Delores it was a clanky far-off discord at the edges of her drunken reason. It melded into dreams abstract and bloodied, full of images she was both unable to parse and petrified by.

She woke to the quiet of the house, a low murmuring inarticulate at the edge of her perception. She switched off the radio and the murmuring resolved into voices outside, Pal and Sammi.

"Give me the goddamned keys," Pal said, sharp and low.

"You treat me like a child."

"I treat you how you act. Give me the goddamned keys, or so help me...."

Delores crawled to the window. Pal and Sammi stood by his car, on either side of the hood, Sammi with her hands behind her back.

"So help you what? What are you going to do?"

Then Pal, loud enough to wake the neighbors, and loud enough to scare Sammi: "Get in the goddamned car right now, or I'm going to throw you overboard and let you drown tomorrow."

Sammi turned on her heel and took her seat, slammed the door, and threw the keys across the car so that they hit Pal's window on the inside.

He opened the door. Fished about until he found the keys, then got in the car and pulled out of the driveway.

VIII

DELORES FLUSHED with a dull ache, and when she sat up the world split and tumbled, and then her head was back on the pillow. She lay with her eyes closed, taking stock. Nausea rolled across her. She cracked open her sticky lids and draped an arm over her brow to shade herself from offending brightness. The curtains were split wide, and the light had a dissipated quality that came only with a high, even cloud cover. She rolled onto her side, then ever so slowly brought her legs over until she sat over the side of the bed. A wave of sick. Well, at least the hangover would not have to be faked.

In the kitchen Mother packed a wicker basket lined with a checked red cloth. She added bottles of wine, meats, cheeses, sandwich bread, pickles, and hard-boiled eggs, all of which disgusted Delores.

"It's going to be freezing," Dad was saying.

"Wear a sweater," Mother said. "It's not like we'll be in a squall. Or stay home, for all I care."

"I'm not going to let my wife go alone with another man onto his boat."

"I won't be alone. Sammi and Delores will be with me."

Delores croaked, her throat mostly still closed by sleep. "Count me out."

"Why?" Mother said. "You're up in plenty of time." Delores looked at the wall clock to see it wasn't even seven yet. She watched the second hand tick tick tick and looked out to the patio, still and empty, shadowed in the desaturated daylight.

"My head is pounding. I'll be terrible company. Send my regrets."

"If you don't go, I have to go," Dad said.

Delores reached across Mother's basket of appalling smells and poured herself coffee from the percolator. Mother tried to bat her hand away. "That's for the thermos."

"Make more," Delores said, pulling the cup out of her mother's reach, unwilling to give it up.

"Come on Delores," Dad said. "You really should go. So I don't have to. I should work."

"You're the one who wanted to buy a boat. Get used to it." She paused on her way back to bed. "Besides," she called back. "I'm not so sure I want to spend all that much time with that Pal fellow."

Mother and Dad were rolling toward the marina in the 210, no doubt, when Delores climbed out of bed again and found her way to the bathroom. She turned the chromed handles in the shower. Hot water sputtered, then came true, the falling beads echoing around the foam-green tiled box. She made it hotter and let it sting and bring the blood to the surface of her skin. Aspirin and coffee had filed the sharpest edge of her hangover. The water washed away the shavings.

Sitting with a towel around her and wet hair touching her shoulders, she methodically chewed at toast slathered in butter. When that helped her general unease she found the wherewithal to fry an egg. She slid it onto another slice of buttered toast and let the warm semi-soft yolk bring her closer to the living. There was cold coffee in the unplugged pot. When that wasn't enough, she enhanced it with a cold Coca-Cola bottle from the fridge.

Then, feeling that her needle indicated normal operating tolerances, she stepped onto the back porch. She shivered, the cool of the morning pulling her scalp tight. It had to be in the low fifties. A terrible day for the beach.

She took a bulky belt-tie cotton cardigan from her father's camping closet. She pulled on an old pair of dungarees that she rolled at the cuffs and cinched tight with a belt. A pair of Mother's rubber gardening boots would do for shoes, though she also grabbed a pair of her sneakers while she had the closet open.

She took a moment to move through Mother's clothes. The block of hanging dresses, so neatly arranged. All of these beautiful things that didn't fit Delores. Shoe size was the only comparable number between their bodies, for one thing. But even more, when Delores imagined herself in a pretty dress cinched with a tight waist, with fine gloves and a chic Italian hat, holding a clutch, and wearing heels, she felt as if she were dressing as a caricature of a woman instead of being one. Or, rather, that the eyes that sought this sort of femaleness would find Delores a false note in its melody.

Sliding the closet closed, she turned to the dresser and opened the top drawer, the lingerie drawer. Mother's stockings neatly rolled. Her bras and panties grouped by match and folded, some tied off with little ribbons to keep them so.

She closed the drawer and glanced out the window, as if the clouds might have cleared in the past few minutes. Having a haze to diffuse the light might be a nice complement to what she was hoping to do. Bright sunlight meant hard shadows. The light would be even today. The beach would probably be less crowded, as well.

Into her camera bag Delores put film, a lens-cleaning brush, the camera itself, and Mother's folding tanning foil that she could use to bounce light, if need be.

She also put together a picnic, not quite as nice as Mother's, but it would do for the two of them. She added a couple of thin blankets to sit on the sand and a flask with whiskey to take the chill off. She brewed fresh coffee and poured it into Dad's spare camping thermos, and then fearing she'd forgotten something she unpacked her camera case methodically on her bed, then put it back together before feeling satisfied and piling all of it next to the front door.

———————

"God, Pal almost made me go," Sammi said when she arrived, keeping her dark glasses on, even inside the house. "I had to throw up to convince him I really was hung over."

"You're not faking it, either?"

Sammi groaned. "Not a great day for the beach."

"I know. It's ingenious. We'll have the place to ourselves."

"Maybe we should just take in a picture or something. I don't know if I can rouse myself to be presentable."

Delores stood, poured some coffee for Sammi, and gave her a pat on the head. "You want some food?"

"Blech. No." Sammi touched her stomach.

Delores offered a few aspirin tablets, setting them next to the coffee cup, and while Sammi drank her brew and swallowed her medicine, Delores retrieved the prints Diego had pulled for her.

She laid the 8 x 10 photographs on the table in front of Sammi. She took her time, putting down one and pausing for twenty seconds or so before placing the next. Sammi clutched her coffee with both hands. She pushed her sunglasses onto her head, her face clear and open with the hair pulled completely away, and studied each image in turn. When Delores was done she sat, lit a cigarette, and smoked while Sammi spent an eternity gazing into each picture.

One: Sammi sitting at the makeup table, Delores just discernible in the shadows of the mirror and looking down into the stacked circles and boxes of the fuzzy camera front, Sammi's face turned slightly down, big eyes looking in reflection straight into the lens, one of her hands perched in midair as if about to pick something from the table, her rounded nails a crimson that read black in the print.

Two: from the side, Sammi with a foot on the cane chair, pulling a stocking over her calf, her hair pinned back on that side, falling down the other, her haunch and behind forming a half circle echoed in the curve of the chair.

Three: Sammi in an elaborate bustier, stretched atop the pile of lingerie, one arm extended above her head like Esther Williams swimming out of fabric.

Four: in the main studio Sammi, fully naked, stood arms akimbo, one brow raised as if wondering whether the viewer were brave enough to break the gaze of her eye and look down, her vulva just visible beneath her pubic hair in an almost shocking nakedness.

Five: from behind, knee on the cane chair, other leg extended, clad in black seamed stockings, Sammi looking over her shoulder to the floor. The keyhole on the back of her thigh capped in the seam that led over the taper and hill of her leg to the pumps with the Cuban heel, the shoe on the other foot dangling and ready to drop to the floor.

Sammi looked up. She wiped her eyes with the back of her hand.

"That's really me," she said, her voice small.

Delores nodded. Tapped her cigarette in the ashtray. Let Sammi talk.

Sammi cleared her throat. "You took pictures of me. I mean, really me. Your father makes me look like all of his models. They look like me, but I have no connection to that girl he sees." She picked up the picture of her at the makeup table. "But, I don't know, there's something here that feels like...like me."

"You're vulnerable in that one. You seem so, anyway."

"I'm not, you know."

"All of us are vulnerable. You were brave enough to show it to me."

"I don't know that I meant to. I was just sort of lost in the moment."

"You're a very good model."

"No, no. It's not me. It's not me at all." She took a deep breath and scissored her fingers. Delores handed over the cigarette. Sammi took a drag and, sticking out her lower lip, blew the smoke upward. "Give it a bit for the aspirin to kick in. We'll go to the beach."

The waves were languid that day, sanguine in their curl and crash. They sizzled up on the wet pack, sucking back into the ocean proper as tides pushed and pulled, leaving behind the brine and decay of the wetted sand.

Santa Monica Beach was never empty. On hot days there would be the big show: tanners, muscle beach men and their admirers, or surfers and their admirers. But any day of the year would bring some locals walking their dogs, holding their shoes to feel the soft cold grit between their toes. People moved to Santa Monica to be near the beach, and no weather could keep them away.

Sammi and Delores walked north of the pier, up the beach to where there were clubs and houses, because that's where fewer people were. Delores set up a camp with a blanket on the cool sand, and then she assembled a privacy screen from some bamboo poles they found lying in the sand. A blanket across the poles flapped in the light breeze, sounding when the wind whipped its edges.

"It's too cold for a bikini," Sammi said. She was made up, a stop in the studio to do her hair and face before they walked the half mile down the hill to the shore, but her lethargy and a whine in her tone gave a nod to her overall state of mind and body. She bundled her throw tighter around her shoulders as proof of her chill.

Delores handed her the flask. "I don't care," she said. "I want to shoot you in one."

"At least your dad has heat. And heart."

Despite her protestations, Sammi stood with her back to the curtain so as not to be exposed to the houses or highway, and Delores held a towel for modesty from people along the shore. Sammi offered one final dramatic shiver and dropped her clothes.

Delores looked up. It was still overcast, but the clouds were thin in places, throwing a diffused glow evenly on the beach.

When Sammi had the bikini bottoms on, Delores picked up her camera, holding a corner of the towel, poorly, in her mouth.

"Hey! Keep that up."

"Nobody's looking," Delores said, voice muffled by the towel, and she turned to make sure that was true. A few figures down by the water break, but so far away she could tell only the color of their jackets. They certainly couldn't discern any detail of Sammi's body.

She dropped the other corner of the towel and just let it drape in her mouth, ineffectual for its supposed purpose, and removed the lens cap. Sammi's complaint melted into a smile as soon as that glass was exposed to the salt air.

A few shots of her in just those bikini bottoms, black with white polka dots. Sammi there, hands on hips, toes in the sand. Delores came around to get the water far behind (but with the narrow depth of field, disappearing into blur, like the sand behind them).

Then a few of Sammi tying the bikini top around her midsection, face twisted into concentration, albeit comically, as if this were a pose for Dad in one of his whimsical paintings.

They left their little encampment and made their way down to the water. Delores made Sammi pause a few times, lie down in the sand. When they got closer she had Sammi fetch wet sand with a little red children's pail they happened upon, and Sammi built sand castles on command.

Delores threw down a towel and got some faux sunbathing shots, including one of Sammi face down, cheek against her folded arms, while the bikini bows on her back lay open, as if to avoid tan lines, a pose that carried a hint of vulnerability, a bit of accident that could end in exposure. The unbroken line of her spinal indent sloped and disappeared between the dimples on the back of her hips.

Delores called three teenage boys over and had them stand next to Sammi so she could get the bathing beauty surrounded by adoring men. She persuaded them to ditch their shoes and socks, to roll up their cuffs and show their feet and ankles standing around the model. She cut them off at the knees with framing, but she saw how Sammi arched her back with these boys around.

She beckoned one to retie the bikini, and then Sammi flirted with the boys after she stood. She touched them and laughed in a showy way. Delores took a photo of them standing in a line shoulder-to-shoulder, holding Sammi in their arms, as if she were lying in a bed, on her side, head in hand, a smile on her face. They were young and earnest and wanted to stay with Delores and Sammi, but Delores sent them away with five dollars for their trouble.

The two of them would pause whenever Delores would swap film, each time meticulously using her bag as a clean room, brushing away sand with a stiff brush she kept in her kit, and using a small squeeze bulb to poof air across her lens. And, as if on ceremony, Sammi huddled around Delores at these times — ostensibly a windbreak — and they nipped at that flask until it went dry.

The weather proved no real deterrent. Sammi either became warm or faked it so well that Delores felt no compunction over making her stand in the lapping waves, letting water wash her feet. Any hangover was gone by then, whether through will, or aspirin, or whiskey. Or, if not the hangover, at least the malaise that attends the early stages of one.

As Delores shot Sammi against the water she again found in her work that purified moment. That satisfaction and drive, that feeling that perhaps she was very present and doing important work. It was an alien sort of thing, a feeling like this. She became conscious of it, and that awareness very nearly toppled it. But just like recognition of a nascent dream could either wake her when she was on the cusp of sleep, or she could sometimes calm her mind enough to go back toward the dream instead of away from it, she was able to draw her attention back to the craft at hand and away from grandiose conjecture.

She ran three rolls of film at the shore, and they decided to walk back to their encampment. About halfway there Delores turned and saw the pier looming to the side of them, shafts of light from very thin clouds bringing it bright into the day.

"Stop," she told Sammi. Sammi struck a pose, a smile, an arched brow, a hand on the hip. "I want to do a nude."

"No way," Sammi said. There was nobody close, but down toward the water people walked. People on the pier could make them out, if not in detail certainly enough to see what would be happening. A dog barked at its owner to throw a stick, and the two women watched to see which way they would go, but the owner threw the stick into the water and dog tore off to fetch it.

"One shot," Delores said. "Fully nude. Standing tall, arms at your sides, back arched like a dancer."

"No! I'm not going to get arrested for public indecency."

"I'll bail you out and pay your fine."

"This is not negotiable. I will not strip naked in public in front of all these strangers."

"Come on. Don't be chicken. I'll give you a reward."

"What reward?"

"A kiss."

"What makes you think a kiss from you is incentive to begin with?"

"You're not running away."

Sammi bit her lip. She looked around her again, then back to Delores.

"Fine. But you're going to give me your sweater after so I don't have to fiddle with my top again."

"Fine. Deal."

Sammi ducked her bottoms first, tossing them over to Delores, where they would be out of the frame, and then ripped away her top and, taking a breath, took a pose that reminded Delores of photos of early film starlets, who were probably echoing paintings of the goddesses of mythology. She had mussed her hair a bit doffing her clothes, but it was perfectly mussed. Wrong in just the right way. Lovely.

Delores smiled, got on one knee, and framed Sammi against the pier in the distance, a blurry backdrop to offer a level of distance and perspective. She shot, wound the film, shot.

"Hurry up, would ya?" Sammi said.

But Delores just lowered her camera. She had the shots she wanted, but the view was so marvelous. Sammi, back arched, the line from her neck undulating down her shoulder blades and waist, over her behind and smoothing down her curved legs until it swooped under her foot into arches as pronounced as her waist. Her stomach curving past the hip bone, down to her pubic line, dusted with sandy hair. It was heaven here, Delores decided, and she didn't want it to end until it absolutely had to.

"Really!" Sammi said, looking around. "Hurry it up."

"Yeah, I'm going to back up a bit. Don't move."

"Just hurry!"

She turned and walked away from Sammi, then took a few more pictures with Sammi in the middle distance, full framed, so vulnerably naked amidst all that sand. Small figures out of focus in the background told the story that they were not alone.

Then, as quickly as she could muster, suppressing a laugh, she turned and ran in the opposite direction, the sand working hard to steal any momentum from her footfalls.

"Hey!" Sammi yelled, but Delores was running, laughing. "Hey, wait!" She looked back to see Sammi coming up the beach at her. She was able to pop off a couple of quick shots and set her camera aside before Sammi hit and tackled her. Grasping hands pulled at her sweater, working one arm out of it, then the other, then finally yanking it away from her.

Sammi stood and pulled the damn thing on, covering herself while

Delores laughed. Sammi kicked sand onto Delores, then she walked toward their little encampment.

"Hey!" called Delores. "Your bottoms!"

But Sammi just turned, and jutting her hips forward lifted the minidress-length sweater, exposing herself. She held it long enough for Delores to pull out the camera again and get the shot, framed over a small dune in the sand. Then Sammi stuck her tongue out while holding the same pose, and Delores got that shot too.

They walked up the hill, which kept the chill at bay, but a breeze buffeted their backs as they climbed and nipped at exposed skin.

"God, I need a shower," Sammi said. "I'm gritty." Delores could feel it too. That dusty, worn skin the beach left as the residue of a visit.

At the house Delores unlocked the door and motioned for Sammi to go first.

Then, inside, Delores pinned Sammi to the wall, not with violence or aggression, but using steady firm pressure that told the model what Delores was doing, and that it was a desire that had weight behind its momentum.

Delores pushed her hand under the thick strands of sweater to feel Sammi's warm skin. Her hand went to Sammi's waist, feeling the slope of her hip. Sammi breathed in. Delores moved her hand up Sammi's side, enough pressure not to tickle, not enough to be aggressive. She moved her hand up until it was beside Sammi's breast. With a thumb under, and fingers around, she pushed the flesh up, lightly, and then let it descend beneath her hand, letting her fingers and palm just gently graze the nipple.

A groan came from Sammi's lips, a gasp, and that broke a resolve. Delores kissed Sammi firmly. A kiss came back to her, Sammi reaching behind Delores's neck to pull her in.

Delores glossed Sammi's lips with a wet gliding mouth, then moved down the cheek, the neck, and left a small light bite on her clavicle. She pressed Sammi into the wall with pressure from her body, then she stepped back abruptly and strode off to the bathroom at the end of the hall. Sammi followed.

Delores ran the shower hot, the water steaming the tile where she had washed away her hangover not so many hours ago. She undressed Sammi, who just stood there, letting her. Who just stood there as if Delores's stealing that kiss was enough to trigger a passive response to everything to come. As if she were a lizard that Delores had flipped on its back to stroke its belly. She watched Delores, open, certainly, but maybe confused and out of her depth. Delores had never seen Sammi not appear in charge of herself, which for Delores was a kind of rush, making her lover apparently respond to the puppetry of her touch.

She took Sammi by the hand and led her into the stream. Delores positioned her so that the stinging spray soaked the model's hair, and then took some shampoo and lathered it luxuriantly in her tresses. She massaged Sammi's scalp, moving soapy hands down her neck and shoulders before coming back, folding the hair up and around, pulling it gently into shapes, and wringing out the excess foam while Sammi stood with her eyes closed, mouth parted just so.

Delores rinsed her, soaped her from a white, unperfumed bar. Delores turned her, then tipped her chin upward and washed her face with easy massaging fingers, working away the rouges, powders, and pigments of her makeup. Sammi's breath came deep and hard, and she pressed her mouth together and swallowed as Delores massaged and worked her.

At one point, Delores moved up against Sammi, and whispered to her, water dropping from her nose and lips, from Sammi's ear: "I've never wanted anything as much as I want you."

She moved Sammi to the corner of the stall, where she stood at the edge of the spray. Sammi pulled her arms in, as if cold, so Delores pulled her back, close. Delores washed her own hair. Scrubbed herself while Sammi's arms encircled her waist, and her head lay against Delores's chest, despite the water cascading down her cheek.

"Do my back," she told Sammi. The model lathered her hands, then with a great lethargy moved them up and down Delores, soap gliding on skin. Delores turned and rinsed, took Sammi's hands and rinsed them too.

Then she cut the water, and the drain whirlpooled the puddle at their feet. Delores pushed the glass door open with a click and retrieved a towel as a rush of cool air invaded the sauna of the shower stall. She stepped out and then reached back to pull Sammi to her. She wrapped Sammi's hair and then dried her. Sammi's face flushed, little pinpricks on her skin as the water, or the ardor, or both, brought blood close to the surface.

She combed Sammi's hair once it was dry enough, and then she left Sammi standing there and walked into her bedroom. She drew the shades, something she rarely did thanks to the room offering a measure of privacy despite its windows. When she was done, Sammi was leaning in the doorway. Hair in moist strands. Towel around her.

"I've never done this," she said.

"You've never taken a shower?" Delores said. Sammi didn't laugh, she bit her lip. Delores dispensed with joking and said, "But you've always wanted to?"

"Yes."

Delores sat on the edge of the bed. "And when you've thought about this, what exactly did you think about?"

Sammi pursed her lips. Shrugged a bit. "I don't know. I like it when you kind of take the whole thing over. I'm not sure I know what to do."

"Okay," Delores said. "Then come here and I'll show you what I've been thinking about doing with you since the moment I first saw you, and let's see how you like it."

Sammi came to her. Delores reached up, and with studied deliberation she unhurriedly moved the towel away from Sammi's body. Sammi made to cover herself but stopped her arm after thinking it through.

"No, be modest, if you'd like," Delores said. "It's fetching."

Sammi covered her breasts with one arm, and with her hand, she covered her pubic area. When she was a "model" she stood naked without a thought. Something else was being revealed to her, and Sammi seemed unsure about it.

"Poor girl," Delores said. "Poor girl." She reached up to take the lower hand and placed it at Sammi's side. She took the hand from Sammi's breasts and drew her down so that Sammi was sitting on Delores's lap. She moved her hands up Sammi's leg, over her hip, waist, rib cage, and back down again.

"I want you to be mine."

"Why?" Sammi said.

"Because I want to be yours."

Sammi bit her lip, and Delores kept up that steady movement of her hands. She nuzzled her face against Sammi's neck and littered it with tiny kisses, moving up to Sammi's ear, down her cheek. Her hands still moved over skin, as Sammi shifted. She lay her head back, and Delores grasped her, laid her down on the bed, kissed her neck like it was the only thing she had ever wished to do.

"I'm yours," Sammi said, half whispering.

Delores kissed her, and stroked her hair, and held her. She moved so slow, using each touch to clarify desire, proof of just how much they belonged to each other.

Sammi lay on the bed after, under the white sheet. Delores stood, as naked as the model, holding her camera. She leaned back against the chest of drawers to get a shot. Delores began comparing Sammi's body to her own. The width of her hips next to Sammi's, the overall proportion of breast to rib and waist, the shape of their faces even, how Delores was wide and curvy while Sammi was slender and curvy. Standing to take pictures gave her a task to occupy her wandering mind.

"Who is that woman without a face?" Sammi said, pointing to the picture of Tanaquil Le Clercq on the wall. At Tanny's feet, three men sat, looking at the viewer. They were the creative team behind the ballet. But Tanny rose above them. Before it was torn, her face engaged the viewer with a conspiring glance. The men might clothe, choreograph, and direct her, but when the house lights dimmed, it was she who stood and delivered.

"A dancer. Ballerina. Her name is Tanny. She dances with the New York Ballet."

"She must have been your lover."

"Tanny?"

"Yeah. Tanny."

"What makes you think that?"

"It seems a certain kind of statement to put a nail through somebody's face. I figure she did you wrong."

"Pull the sheet down some," Delores said, and she moved in closer when Sammi did, exposing her breasts, the white fabric making a line between them, exposing one hipbone but covering her sex. "You look so good after you've been ravished. You're flush. Your cheeks are red and glowing."

"That's just because you know how to make a girl feel something. I mean, my god."

Delores moved around, getting different angles, pulling the shades to let in some of the late afternoon sun.

"So was she or wasn't she?" Sammi said.

"Take your foot out of the cover," Delores said. "And I'll tell you." Sammi brought out both feet, leaving the sheet draped up to just under belly button, pulled between her legs but exposing them both up to the curve of her waist.

"I tried. With Tanny, I wanted her and I tried," Delores said as she walked around, pushing Sammi to pose her instead of telling her, onto her side, onto her stomach, onto her knees as if in prostration, moving the sheet to drape her in ways both revealing and teasing. "Cora and I had been together four years or so. We didn't live together yet, and our relationship was boring, predictable. I always wanted sex more than her. I told her she was treating me like a domestic worker, which is how I felt. Especially at that time.

"I went to a performance that Tanny did with Merce Cunningham, in his new troupe, and because Cora gave a lot of money to support Merce, I was given entrée into their world. I went backstage and said hello to Merce, and he introduced me to Tanny, and I asked her to get dinner with me, and she said yes."

Delores sat on the bed, put down her camera. "I've never told this story," she said. "Maybe it doesn't make me out to be a very good person."

Sammi sat up. Wrapped an arm around Delores's chest, and kissed her between her shoulder blades. "You're a good person," she said.

"Well, for some reason Tanny said yes. Probably because Merce had told her how much money we give them, even though it wasn't my money, it was Cora's money, and I was ostensibly just her private secretary at the time. But she said yes, for whatever reason.

"We went to dinner later that week. She was very kind, and funny, and the type of person whose presence fills a room. She told me the most fascinating thing. She said the one thing that marks a prima ballerina is not always talent of movement, although of course that is indeed true, but the ability to mask pain while performing. They are extremely athletic and strong, ballerinas are. They suffer greatly and turn that pain into something beautiful and worthwhile."

"If you like ballet," Sammi said.

"You don't?"

"Never mind me," Sammi said. "What happened at dinner?"

"There's a little French place I like near the Village. It's small and stuffy in an old world way, but it's always quiet. So I took her there — on Cora's tab, mind you — and after a few glasses of wine I got up my nerve and I placed my hand on hers and said, 'I want to get to know you better.'

"It was a very subtle thing, what she did. She didn't even move her hand. She just held it there, although she didn't grasp mine, or give any sense of affection back to me. And then, she said, 'I would like that. We really appreciate your support. Come backstage and visit me after any performance.'

"So there it was. I was a patron, not a lover. I withdrew my hand and made small talk, but I was withering with embarrassment. I had no information that she liked women in that way, so my move was bold and stupid. But I figured she was bohemian, as most performers are, and so wouldn't be all that shocked. It was stupid. It could have ruined me if she hadn't been kind and graceful about it.

"We kissed cheeks and I walked towards my apartment, but feeling rejected, and now also guilty for having turned away from Cora in this way after trading on her name. I decided I needed to end our romance."

Delores took a deep breath. Sammi moved her hand lightly up and down her arm, running from neck to shoulder to elbow to fingertip and back, in a sweep of affection. Delores wriggled.

"Could you please do that harder? It's too light and it tickles."

"Sorry," Sammi said, and she continued with a firmer hand.

"I steeled myself, brave with wine and feeling sorry over my pathetic attempts at seducing one of the most desired women in the city, I entered Cora's building just off the park. The doorman sent me up, used to seeing me all hours. Cora was surprised. I said, 'We need to talk. I'm unhappy and this isn't working for me.'

"She took my hands and said, 'I know. And it's because of me.' She said that! Then she said she had something that might prove her devotion to me, and that this was what would repair our union. It was a surprise, and not quite ready, she said, but since I was there she would show me anyway.

"We exited her apartment and crossed the hall, and she opened the door opposite hers. Mind you, her apartment took up the whole floor. This door was just a servant's entrance. But she had separated it into its own apartment. It was a modest place, two bedrooms, but had the same view as hers, overlooking the park. It was a pleasant, beautiful apartment in a prestigious building. Not ostentatious like hers, maybe, but roomy and cozy at the same time.

"She crossed to a table in the main room, and on it took up an envelope that she handed me. The deed to that place, in my name. 'It will be yours,' she says. 'Even if something happens to me, even if my family tries to take it from you, they can't. It is yours, in your name, if you sign this paper. What I'm saying Delores, is I want you to be my wife. To live next door to me and be my wife. Will you marry me?'"

"That's very romantic," Sammi said.

"Can you believe it? I try to cheat on her, and she does this. She does this and has people working on it while I'm scheming. And she hid the whole thing from me, since I was keeping her books! I found out how later and never let her hide anything again, but that's another story.

"And there's more. There were two bathrooms. One she had converted into a dark room. There were materials in boxes there, chemicals, an enlarger, trays, and sitting atop it all like a capstone was this very camera here, this Hasselblad. A camera I had attempted to save for, with no results."

A sliver of sunlight, a reflection off a window or car, hit the shades and flickered, and Delores parted the shades to look outside, then closed them again.

"What did you do?" Sammi said. Delores sat again. Put her camera on the bedside table, the light going too dark for shooting. She fell back onto the bed, then scooted up to be next to Sammi, who threw a leg across her.

"What could I do? I was overwhelmed. I buried my guilt and bad feelings about Tanny as deep as I could and said yes. I signed the paper and became her wife, in theory if not in name, of course. We were together every day. Inseparable until I came to California."

"Do you miss her?" Sammi said. "Cora, I mean. Do you miss her?"

"Not right now," Delores said, nearly in a whisper. "Not at this moment. I came here to find you, you know. I left her to find you."

Sammi crooked her finger around Delores's chin, and drew it back until she could reach her lips, and kissed her in that deep passionate way that only lovers unworried by being exposed to the other can. Delores fell back into Sammi's arms. Sammi, for her part, kissed deep and let the range of her traveling fingers expand until it was finding all of the places on Delores that Delores had found on Sammi.

It was the thing that said this affair was not about one person expressing certain affections or desire toward the other, but in fact, about something mutual. An energy given mass and force and direction by the four hands that guided it.

For it is one thing when you are allowed to touch someone you desire. It is quite another when they in turn touch you back.

IX

"PLEASE TELL ME you are hiring some man to do your work for you," Diego said. "I cannot stand a woman being this talented." He was bent over the table, one eye squeezed shut, the other at the loupe. He stood and circled one image with the grease pencil, then leaned back down to inspect the others.

"Don't be an ass."

"I'm not an ass. I'm a traditionalist."

Delores spit out a laugh.

"Don't be bitchy, now."

"I'm picturing it. You. A traditionalist."

"Well," he shrugged. "About some things, for certain. I certainly don't like my ideas to be challenged."

"By women, you mean. You don't want women challenging the idea that you hate women."

"Oh, darling," he said. "I don't hate women. I just don't want to fuck them, which makes them think I hate them."

"You have that wrong. Women don't like you because you're an ass. Sometimes a woman finds it refreshing when a man doesn't want to bed her."

Diego waved his hand to dismiss the thought. "Point is, you're as a good as a man. There. I've said it. You're as good as a man. I mean, look at those rosy cheeks. You got a flush from her, for sure."

"Did I tell you she's engaged?"

"What's the score?"

"I can't get a bead on it. He's older. She could have any guy her own age, better looking. There's something fishy about him."

"I'll bet I could take the shine off."

"What do you mean?"

"I have a few dicks that owe me. Put a tail on him for a few days, something'll come up."

Delores laughed. "No, thank you. That's a bit much. I told her I'd give him another chance. In fact, I'm meeting them for lunch after I leave here."

"Okay, then. Let's talk about this instead: I've got a buyer interested in your work."

"For the love of Pete, Diego, I told you none of that."

"Better to beg forgiveness than ask permission."

"You and your back-alley bullshit."

"No, no, no. It's not like that. I did some asking around. I sent some of these to Chicago. You remember, you asked me?"

"Chicago?"

"Chicago, doll. *Playboy.*"

"You're pulling my leg."

"That Hefner fellow called me himself. Wants you to do more work for him, too. I may have to step out of the middle and let the two of you deal straight. Just so long as you remember me when it's check-cashing time."

"Not sure I'd be very popular at home if my name got published under a picture in *Playboy.*"

"Use a nom de plume."

"With Dad's model?"

"You were the one who wanted *Playboy.*"

Delores sighed. "I don't know what I was thinking. He would be so upset with me."

"Look, I like your pop plenty, doll, but you're the one that said you need to start getting some money rolling in, and that's what I'm proposing. Your daddy is a big boy and has had a successful career. Time for some new blood."

He walked over to the table, picked up a manila envelope tied with a red string, and gave it to her. "Here you go. Model releases and contracts, the whole deal inside. You take a look and tell me what you think."

"You never fail to surprise, Diego."

"I'm a man of the ages. Don't you ever forget it."

"How many lesbians does it take to screw in a light bulb?" Pal said, eyes bright with the pre-humor that comes when people project the joke. Delores sat in a booth, Sammi and Pal across from her. The tavern was a dank place, just across the avenue from his dealership. The remains of a few sandwiches sat on plates, next to a nearly empty pitcher of beer. In front of Pal were a couple of empty shot glasses, an inch apart, with a matchbook bridging them.

The table was rough thick-lacquered wood, between straight-backed wooden benches. Neon glowed in the high simple window that, though tinted, showed some light from outside. Several regulars sat at the bar, nursing drinks.

"None," Pal said. "Can't do it. Lesbo light bulbs only got a socket."

Sammi and Pal were already there when Delores made it from Diego's. Pal in a crumpled gray suit with a bright yellow tie, a silkscreened blue bird at its apex, a big open avian eye peeking over the table edge. Sammi jumped up to give Delores a hug, bouncing in her arms and planting a kiss on her cheek, then wiping the cheek clear of the lipstick she left. Sammi was in a fitted tan shirt with pearl buttons, tight black Capri pants, and a black bow in her hair.

Pal had started complimentary, telling Delores how much he liked her Dad. "I don't know from artists, I mean, like they say, I can't tell if it's good or not, but even to me there's something about the way he paints that is just wonderful. You know, I bought a painting of Sammi from him."

"He doesn't sell his originals," Delores said.

"He does if you give him a good chunk off a new car," Pal said with a wink. "And even better, it's of my little Sammi here laying across the hood of a big new Chevy. It's a beaut. Hung it in the office, and when those fellows come in to buy a new car they can't but help wish they were me." He put his arm around Sammi and pulled her tight. "I got it all."

"You're a lucky guy all right," Delores said. The words came out nearly fine, but she projected a bit of sarcasm, and the glint in Pal's eye changed when he recognized it. Here was a man, Delores realized, who was very astute about people. She tried to recover with an over-the-top joking tone and said, "I just can't imagine what she sees in you."

"If I knew," he said, "maybe I'd put that into a book and sell it so that everyone could be so lucky as me. The Pal Birkness story. Riches beyond belief. Learn from the master." He laughed.

Delores picked up her pint glass, swished the last bit of beer in it, and drank.

"I hear you worked for that Cora Fournier in New York," Pal said.

"Delores was her private secretary," Sammi said. "She ran all of her affairs. Very important position."

"Must be something to get a glimpse at the lap of luxury like that," Pal said.

Delores shrugged. "She's just people. Puts her pants on one leg at a time."

"That's what I heard about her," Pal said. "That she wears pants. What you say, Dollie — oh, you mind if I call you Dollie? Maybe you don't like that. Some people don't like it when you take liberties with their names, and I'm gonna respect that if you are one of those people."

"My name is Delores, not Dollie."

"Okay, okay. No insult meant. Well, anyhow, I'm not one for any celebrity gossip, but I am curious about this little tidbit. Is it true what they say about that Fournier woman? Is she a big old dyke?"

Delores put down her pint glass. Wiped her hands to remove the condensation. Tried to sound disinterested.

"What makes you say that? Who told you that she was any which way or another?"

"Little birdie whispered it. I mean, she is a public figure. On the society pages and such."

Delores shot a look at Sammi while Pal took a deep drink from his beer. Sammi shrugged and then shook her head. Wasn't her.

And that was when he started with the jokes.

"Say, I got a few good ones about lesbos. You ever hear the one about that little boy who stuck his finger in the dyke? Boy, was she sore." Pal laughed, slapped the table. Delores startled.

"Aw, Pal," Sammi said. "Those jokes aren't funny."

"When I find the right one, you're gonna bust up. Say, you know, two dykes can't get a marriage license. But that's okay, see, because in order to stand two women in the room all the time you need a liquor license."

"I don't like these jokes," Delores said. "Miss Fournier was a good employer, and my friend."

"Aw, Dollie. Maybe she ain't even a dyke, hell if I know. Don't you go thinking these jokes are about her, now." Again, Pal sent himself into fits of laughter. "Liquor license!"

He followed up that joke with the one about the light bulb. Delores felt them on the back of her neck, in a heat creeping from her collar to her hairline, dipping her ears in a red dye. She lifted her beer and downed the last few drops.

She tried to let the whole thing slide off, mostly due to Sammi throwing her panicked looks that this whole lunch was going terribly wrong. She tried to counter in as lighthearted a tone as she knew how, which was not very. "Now Pal, you know there's a ton of car salesmen jokes out there."

"Know it? I wrote half of them myself. I'm telling you, a person has to be able to laugh at themselves. You ask any of the fellows at the dealership. I can laugh at myself. Why, they pull little pranks on me all the time. Put milk of magnesia in my coffee and such. They love to see me blow my stack, but I come out of it laughing along with them. Of course, then I get them back. I always get them back."

He stopped, nodding at his own wisdom. "Hell," he said. "You best ignore me. I'm just a bit drunk, being so excited having lunch with two such lovely companions. I'm probably showing off a bit, just like the goddamned peacock that I am. Bet you I sell three cars this evening. I'm always best after I have a few. Nice and loose. But anyway, I'll stop now, I promise."

"All right, then," Delores said.

"You are the worst," Sammi said, giving him a slap, which to Delores seemed a little too playful.

"Oh, I forgot, I have one more. Just one more. What did the dairy farmer call his wife after the dyke screwed her?" He looked at Delores, like she was the only person in the world. He leaned toward the table, arms crossed.

Delores leaned forward, too, both arms on the table, coming just a face's width from being nose to nose with him.

And Delores said: "Satisfied?"

Pal's eyebrows went up in surprise. He slapped the table again and leaned back in the booth, laughing. He pulled Sammi to him. "Did you hear that? That's good, that's really good. Better than what I was gonna say. Satisfied. Okay then, let's just call it that. Let's just call that the punch line. You got it, you really do. You got and you took it."

Pal pulled out his wallet and dropped some bills on the table, all smiles and chuckles. They walked out, the sunlight searing after the bar interior, bleaching their eyes. Pal donned his fedora, shading his brow. Sammi pulled oversized sunglasses from her purse, but Delores in her cat-eye glasses had to wait for her eyes to adjust.

Sammi gave Pal a hug and a kiss on the cheek, which he immediately wiped away like a boy might a mother's kiss, perhaps worried about lipstick. Sammi climbed into the 210 on the passenger side, since Delores was giving her a ride to the house. But before Pal ran across the avenue, he held out his hand for Delores to shake.

"I tell you, that was a good one. Thanks for coming out and having lunch way the heck out here. That's mighty nice of you."

"What was it?" Delores said. "What was the punch line?"

"What punch line."

"The dairy farmer."

"The dyke joke?"

"Yes. Tell me. What was it?"

"Well, let's see if I can remember. What did the dairy farmer call his wife after the dyke screwed her?"

"Right. That one."

"Well, the real answer is salt lick. But, to be true, my answer? If that was my wife? Then the punch line would be that he'd call her an undertaker, because I don't abide any woman who plays me like a fool."

He shrugged. Patted Delores on the shoulder and jogged across the street, back to his dealership, full of shiny hoods in many tints, reflecting the bright light of the sun.

"What did you tell him?" Delores said as soon as she climbed into the car.

"Well, nothing, of course. I mean, he knows you worked for that Fournier woman, but I didn't tell him nothing."

"How does he know, then? He wasn't talking about her, he was talking about me."

"Aw, don't take him to heart. He's full of bluster that one. Like you said, lots of jokes about used car salesmen."

"He's a horrible man."

Sammi's face tightened.

"Pal? He's rough around the edges all right, but I wouldn't go that far."

"He threatened you. He said he'd kill you if he caught you cheating."

"He did not."

"He did. When you got into the car, he did. That prick."

"Are you sure he said that? Doesn't sound like the Pal I know, even when he gets a little herky-jerky around the edges when he drinks."

Driving in her agitated state didn't seem wise to Delores, but neither did sitting and arguing across the street from a huge sign that said Birkness Chevrolet, like a beacon of success for a man she was coming to realize was her rival in more than one way, so Delores put the car in gear and pulled into traffic.

"I don't know, Sammi. I don't know what you see in him. What is it that he's got?"

Sammi reached into Delores's handbag. Pulled out her cigarettes and put two in her mouth. Lit them handed one to Delores.

"Can't say I can put it into words, really. I mean, he was good to me at a time when I was on my own and needed someone. He encouraged me to start modeling to reach my dreams. Supported me when I found work. But, I guess, anybody could do that."

"Parents could do that."

"Yeah, they could do that if they aren't the ones I had."

"Doesn't mean you have to marry the guy, though. Even if you owe him."

"Well, there's the thing I can't say I can put into words. I guess I love the old guy. It's like he took his heart out and showed it to me all red and bloody, and ever since then when I look at him I see that heart and only that heart, even if he says funny things or gets a little rough."

"Rough."

"Well, not like he means it, only when he drinks a little."

"Rough, like he hits you?"

"Well, no, I mean, he's not done that," Sammi said. "That's one way he isn't like my pop."

They drove for a block or two along 3RD, just looking at the big houses, not saying anything to each other.

"Someone wants to buy my photos of you."

"You don't say!" Sammi brought a leg up under her and turned to Delores. "Is that so? For real?"

"Of course. *Playboy*, even."

"Wow. Imagine that." But then Sammi's face fell. "I can't do it."

"Do what?"

"Let you sell those pictures. I mean, those were for us. For fun."

Sammi put a finger to her mouth and bit the nail.

"Thing is, Pal said I couldn't. I mean, I told him about the pictures we took and he said I couldn't ever sell them, that it wouldn't be fair to Gael, and that that sort of thing could hurt a movie career."

"Marilyn Monroe was in the first *Playboy*."

"Well, sure, she can get away with it. She was already famous. Look at her."

"Look at you."

Sammi stubbed out her cigarette, half smoked.

"Do you really think people would buy a magazine to see me naked?"

"I would."

"Look, it's flattering and all, but I have to listen to what Pal says."

"Maybe you don't."

"What's that mean?"

"Maybe Pal isn't the one for you after all."

Sammi laughed. "You got a better man all lined up for me?"

Delores looked over, and understanding broke across Sammi's expression.

"Oh, Delores," Sammi said. She scooted over the bench seat until she was right next to Delores and laid her head on the driver's shoulder. "That's so sweet."

"I sell these photos, they want more. I can make a career out of this. I can support us."

"Dollie, it's sweet because it's a dream. Can you imagine, living in this world as two women? Nobody does that."

"I do it."

"Okay, maybe women like you. But not me. Not in Hollywood."

"Not in Hollywood? You ever heard of Barbara Stanwyck?"

"No! No way!"

"Sure. Joan Crawford?"

"You're making that up."

"All you have to do is just say that you're mine. Let me take care of the rest."

Sammi moved back over to her side of the car. Looked out of the window. They were coming into Santa Monica, the canopy of trees overhead as they turned onto the wide street that led to the house.

"I can't. I'm sorry, Dollie, but I can't. You have to share me with Pal, and you have to keep those photos private. That was for me and you. To get us ready to...you know, get ready."

"I hate it when people call me Dollie."

"Okay, fine, just don't be mad at me, okay? Please don't be mad."

"So, you are not coming home, that is what you are saying?" Cora said, her voice a thin reedy crackle. Delores sat at the table in the kitchen, a rare moment of privacy while Mother was out gardening and Dad was up in his studio with Sammi. The scene with Pal, the uneasiness of the talk in the car, meant that delicious ache in her abdomen was now floating on a bed of worry.

"Can we just let it be for a little bit?" Delores said. "Do we need such huge declarations?"

"Declaration? You *have* declared something, darling. You have declared that you are inconsiderate of my emotions and time and attention. That our six years together —"

"Seven."

"— yes, yes, fine — seven years together are not enough for you to trust me. I guess I just don't know where this is coming from."

"I know about the show," Delores said.

"What show?"

"My show."

"Your photography show?"

"Yes, my show. I know what you did."

"What do you mean, what I did?"

"You bought out the whole show. And you did it by subterfuge. By giving money to other people to buy prints. You subsidized the whole goddamn thing."

"Ah. That." A deep sigh over the line. "How did you find out?"

"I do your books. You don't spend money that I don't know about."

"Well, I tried to be sneaky about it."

"Yes, you did, and it looked funny, so I did some digging."

"Just hold on a minute here. Are you saying that you left me because I bought out your show because I was so proud of you? Because I wanted you to have a stellar opening and kick off your new career?"

Delores could see Mother planting some new starts in a bed to the side of the kitchen, a bed that got lots of light as the sun traveled overhead.

"That is mischaracterizing it. You bought it out because you didn't think I could sell it."

"That is just not true."

"Of course it is!" Delores said, lighting a cigarette. "If you thought I was going to sell, there would have been no need to buy."

"Are you smoking? I can't believe you started that up again."

"Don't be a nanny. I'm just having one. In case you hadn't realized, talking to you causes me great stress."

"It's a horrible habit," Cora said. "Just horrible."

"Your disapproval is noted and filed with all of your other disapprovals. The disapproval department is well staffed, between you and Mother. Working overtime, in fact."

Delores exhaled right into the microphone, causing a windy rumble.

"Did you ever think maybe I wanted to collect your work? As an investment?" Cora said.

"Of course not. You're attempting to argue it backward and cover yourself. The truth is, if my show wasn't going to sell then I needed that to happen for my artistic process. That informs what I shoot. Unless you think the work was poor and had no chance of selling."

"Oh, Delores." Another sigh. A cough and a deep breath. "Okay, you got me. I just didn't want this to be another thing you gave up. Like writing. Like dancing. Like painting. Like every creative endeavor before. I wanted you to have the flush of success that would carry you into your career. I wanted some wind beneath your wings, and to be completely blunt, I felt it was my place as your partner to be that wind."

A flush of irritation worked its way down from Delores's itchy scalp. "Something I gave up? Photography has always been my desire. You were the one who pushed me into writing, dancing — which I was terrible at, I might say, and you might have realized that before the fact if you looked at my body — into painting, for which I gamely took classes with you to do as time together even though I had no desire to paint, knowing full well the temperament it takes to be an accomplished painter, having, you know, grown up with one."

"Now listen, don't be sharp."

"So, you never listen when I tell you that this skill I'm working at is the one that I care about. You never listen when I tell you those other things are things I do for you because you have this concept of your lover being a magnificent artist, so you could be my patron and the history books will write lovingly about the wealthy Cora Fournier and her lover, the famous and scandalous Delores Sarjeant. This is what you want. Notoriety."

"I wanted success for you! How horrible am I that I wanted you to succeed? Oh, that Cora, she is a cruel woman who only wants the best for the woman she loves. You are such a selfish child. You can't even see when someone is working to support you. And yes, maybe you didn't see exactly the method of that support because I kept it hidden, but only because you're so damn sensitive that I was afraid a spotlight would spook you, and you'd run away into some corner like you do. Like, if I may point this out to you, you did to me when I was in Europe. Like a coward."

Outside, Mother patted the beds around her new plants, little buds closed tight on nascent shoots. She used her arm to wipe her forehead, her trowel streaked with dirt, a white pail of soil on one side of her, a tin watering can on the other.

Delores took a drag off her cigarette. Stubbed it out. Exhaled, then took a clear breath. Delores knew that the line between them was sticky, and whatever she said next would be fixed between them for some time to come.

"My mother is outside right now, on her knees, planting some flowers. Maybe that's what you thought you were doing? Planting flowers? Tending to your garden? Aligning your interests in such a way that they would flower like returns on your investments? Like the value of a painting or sculpture?

"I say I'm coming into my own, no thanks to you. You say you wanted me to succeed, but what I see is that you have no faith in me. In fact, I think that I rather disappoint you, don't I? Just because I don't bloom in the morning sun, that I'm not worth tending?

"This is it, Cora, why I left. You have no faith in me. I don't care to belabor this metaphor, but if you were the gardener to my plants you would rip me up and cast me in resin rather than give me soil and light and water. That's it, Cora. That's why I left you. Maybe you had faith in me at one time, but you lost it. And I can't trust you anymore."

Delores lit another cigarette, and made sure to do it in the noisiest way she could.

Cora said, "Okay. Okay, I'm sorry, I spoke too —"

"And no, I'm not coming home. I'm going to make a life for myself in Los Angeles, and do it on my own terms, in my own time. I see now that this is something you would never allow of me in New York." Before Cora could respond, Delores ended the call.

She toggled her finger on the cradle button until she got a dial tone. She dialed Diego. Once he answered she said only, "Call your guy. Put him on Pal, see what he can dig up. Get ready, I'll give you the address of his lot."

Then, when that was done, she pulled from her satchel the envelope holding the contract and model release, and where it said *Model's name* she wrote "Sammi Brill," and where it said *Model's signature* she forged Sammi's signature. She put the whole thing into the envelope Diego had prepared for her — complete with a stamp — and grabbed the keys to the 210 to head out to the post office.

Just as she was pulling into the driveway, returning from the post office, Mother waved her down. "Darling, I need to shop. Take me to the shops." When Delores agreed, Mother said, "I'll be just two minutes. Wait here."

That turned into a half hour while Mother changed out of her gardening gear, and Delores sat in the 210 until she couldn't stand it anymore. She was almost at the front door when Mother came out, looking fresh in black fitted pants and a gray fitted blouse, a little pillbox hat capping her head.

Mother held out her hand and motioned with her fingers, wanting something. The keys.

"I'm driving," Delores said.

"Not in my car, darling."

"You made me wait so long that I'm going to drive so I can keep my hands from wringing your neck."

"Oh, somebody's cranky!" Mother said.

"Yes." Delores said. "Fear me."

Mother sighed, but she walked around to the passenger side.

"I have a favor to ask of you," Mother said when they were en route, applying lipstick in the rearview mirror, which she turned so that Delores couldn't use it. "I need you to go to San Francisco and look after your grandmother for a bit."

They drove the wide streets, each block punctuated by a dip into a rain gutter, like a boring roller coaster; the 210 bounced on its floating shocks every time. Mother would pause until they were over the dip before going back to her lips.

"What do you mean, for a bit?"

"She's not well. I think she's less well than she is letting on. Your dad has agreed to drive you up this weekend. You can spend some time looking after her and giving your dad some peace of mind. She called last night and seemed very confused. I'm surprised she even knew to call us."

"I'm surprised you didn't hang up on her right when you heard her voice."

"Oh, come now. It's not that bad between us."

"Were you even going to ask me?"

"Darling, that's what I'm doing. You love your grandmother. And you love San Francisco."

"I'll go up with Dad this weekend. I'd love her to see her. But I'm not just going to stay up there."

"I think it's best if you do."

"I thought you wanted to take me to dinner for my birthday."

"We'll do it when you get back. You won't be up there forever."

At the market, Delores saw a close spot, but picked one farther away just to annoy Mother.

Once the car was off, Delores put her face in her hands. "You'd think I'd know better than to go on car rides with you. You always pick fights with me in the car."

"Don't be dramatic," Mother said as she opened the door. "And just sit tight. I'll only be two minutes."

A few days later, on Friday afternoon, Delores rode the bus to Sammi's apartment. They headed towards Central Los Angeles, away from the beach. A few seats behind Delores was a group of grousing teenage girls. It seemed to Delores that each of them had a sunburn. She tried to imagine them on their way to the beach in the morning, all bubbly sunshine and expectation. Then a day of sunburns and too much fun, too much candy, too many boys perhaps. She knew that gritty sunbaked feeling of the trip home. They were probably heading toward Pasadena or Eagle Rock, or some other farther-away location.

The last time Delores was in Santa Monica, streetcars were still running. The Red Car and the LARY streetcars used to make it to the beach, but both were torn out because of declining ridership.

Sammi's place was on the second floor of a pink stucco apartment house on Mascot Street in Mid-City. The first time Delores had visited she was giving Sammi a ride home, so taking the bus was a new adventure. Sammi had laid out all the lines and times, since she rode the bus whenever Pal was too drunk or too busy to come get her.

The bus ride out took almost an hour. Delores read the advertisements overhead. A cartoon tooth invited her to try a new dentist. A placard for an upcoming auto show. A car wash with dancing bubbles said to mention the ad for a free detailing on her first visit.

Behind her she heard the low murmur of the girls, their voices not loud enough for Delores to make out their words, but at just the right frequency to cut through the rumble of the bus with a shush-sha-shush-sha sound. Trying to make out their talk was distracting, but when the bus would stop and open its doors, they would clam up, as if their topic was so important it shouldn't be overheard.

Delores pulled the cable for her stop, near where La Brea and Washington crossed. One of the girls, a freckled redhead sat up straight, and said loud and clear, her voice tremulous and declarative, as if standing up to great impropriety, "Girls, what's between us is between us forever." As Delores exited she looked at them, bathing suits tied around necks under loose shirts, flimsy tennis shoes, skinny lobster-red legs sticking out of shorts.

Delores found Sammi in a folding chair across the street from her building, in a little triangle of a park. A halter top that, like the girls' bathing suits, was tied behind her neck. Shorts. An empty Coke bottle sat beside her hand, and a magazine lay open and folded back on itself. Sammi smiled when she saw Delores approaching. She stood.

"Don't say a word," she said. Leaving the chair, she grabbed Delores's hand, and they turned toward her building. Her apartment had a Juliet balcony on the second floor, above the main door. There were slim glass-brick windows to the right and left of the first floor windows. A small canopy of curved Spanish ceiling tile clung to the lip of the building.

Sammi led her in and up the stairs — the banister had recently been oiled with something that smelled of Murphy Oil Soap — and along the hall to Sammi's apartment door. "Don't say a word," she whispered in Delores's ear, all breath and steam.

Delores smiled. She reached into her bag and pulled out her flask. Sammi bit her lip and smiled. Delores opened it and held it to Sammi's lips, tipping it too generously. Filling her mouth, which made Sammi laugh and nearly gag and spill some, and she pressed her hand against Delores to get her to stop. Delores took a swig herself, and after swallowing went to kiss Sammi, who surprised her by passing the mouthful of whiskey back into her own mouth. Delores laughed. The liquid spilled over her lip, down her chin, and dripped onto her shirt. She slurped, and holding back a laugh, swallowed. Sammi licked her chin and kissed her, smooth and warm and wet.

"Naughty," Delores said.

"Shhhhh!" Sammi said, and she opened the door and pulled Delores inside.

X

DELORES CAUGHT the last bus out to the ocean that night. After packing her bag she got just a few hours in bed. Then Dad was shaking her shoulder, beckoning her. It was dawn, and he was ready to drive.

He had a thermos on the seat of the 210. He was drinking from a mug when Delores emerged, hugging her pillow to her chest, sleep still pulling at her, and her efforts to fight it gave her a headache.

Dad sparked a cigar as she opened the door.

"Oh, no, that's gonna make me sick."

"I'm driving. My rules."

"It's like when I was a kid. Stuck in the backseat on the way to Yosemite, and you making me throw up into a paper bag."

"Don't throw up, then. Seems that would be the simplest thing."

She cracked the vent window and angled it to blow fresh air on her face, and she lay her head against the door with the pillow for support. She slipped in and out as they went north. She'd come to and open her eyes, watching the road pass, blurred by speed, then the scrubby hills around her slower, but moving all the same. She saw the break of dawn bringing high brown grasses into focus. Then they snaked between two hills and the glistening Pacific Ocean materialized, a morning haze hanging off shore.

They stopped at a little Greek diner dad liked up by Santa Barbara, a place called Cain's where a pretty waitress served them eggs and hash browns without enthusiasm.

Delores came around after breakfast, no longer sleepy so much as completely weary but unable to rest. She screwed up her courage to address a topic she knew she could avoid no longer.

"I sold some photos," Delores said.

"Well, hey. Good for you," Dad said. The meaty paw at the end of his right arm was at the twelve o'clock position on the wheel. The other elbow was resting on the window frame ledge, a lit cigar dangling from two fingers, "Some of those photos from New York?"

"No, Dad. They're nudes. Nudes of Sammi that I took."

He didn't react, really. He looked at the cherry on the cigar. Put it back in his mouth and puffed a few times to get it glowing.

"Where exactly," he asked after a moment. A gulf was opened by his nonreaction, by his confusing serenity. "Where exactly did you sell them?"

"You're not going to like the answer," Delores said.

"If I'm not going to like the answer, I'm sure as hell not going to play a guessing game with it. Rip that bandage off."

"You won't have to guess."

"*Playboy*?" he said. "Is that what you're saying? You sold pictures to *Playboy*?"

"Yes."

Dad pursed his lips. Sucked in spit in a rush of breath. Knitted his brow. "You sold pictures of Sammi — my model — to *Playboy*? That same *Playboy* that runs naked pictures of celebrities?"

"I told you I was taking pictures of her," Delores said. "You said you didn't mind."

Dad nodded. "Can't say that's not true," he said, with self-reproach.

"I have to find a way to support myself. I thought I could sell some photos, maybe find a few other models. You know, make a go of it. Follow in your footsteps, as it were."

"And you think that taking snapshots of girls showing everything they've got and selling them to some glossy magazine is following in my footsteps?"

"Yes. I think it is."

"So, you must think that learning how to push a button is a skill as complex as learning how to render a face properly in paint, then. That it's the same amount of effort as learning color and proportion. You must think that painting is a night course you take from some fellow and then you start earning, because that's how I learned photography, you know. From a fellow doing a night course. Then I taught you, so that's how you learned. Do you think that?"

"It's not a thing I want to compare, the different skills we have."

"But you are, selling photos. You are comparing them, seeing as you used my model. Seems to me you're just thumbing your nose at me and what I've had to do to get to where I am in my career."

"Come now. If I never did anything unless I was as good at it as you, I'd never do anything. You got a good contract, and I sold a photo or two. Isn't there room for the both of us?"

Gael let out a long breath. They curved around a steep cliff, on one side the geology of the ages stretching upward to grassy bluffs, on the other the white stripe of guard rail, and then the Pacific, flat and blue, as it stretched towards the blur of the horizon.

"I made dinner plans with Norton Shale tomorrow night. He asked specifically that you come when I told him you were around. I'm sure he'd love to hear how little you value our profession."

"Dad, be reasonable."

He laughed, with a spit of surprise. "If you knew what I was thinking in my head and not saying, you would not be asking me to be reasonable. If you knew what violence I was imagining right now, you would not be asking me to be reasonable. If you could measure the extent to which I am not acting on my emotions right now, you would not be asking me to be reasonable. I am being reasonable. A judge would free me from murder for how reasonable I am being right now."

"I'm sorry," Delores said. "I didn't do it to hurt you."

Gael didn't answer. Just tightened his lips together. He smoked his cigar to a nub before shoving it into the ashtray with its fallen brethren.

"You haven't seen your grandmother in quite some time," Dad said. "She's getting older, you know. She's not as spry as she used to be. You might just be surprised how you find her. Prepare yourself."

Etta Sarjeant owned a Victorian in the Haight. It was one of four houses designed to represent the seasons. Grandma owned winter. After the streetcar line that connected the Haight to downtown went in and the property boom began, Delores's grandfather built all four seasons and sold the other three for a tidy profit.

But the neighborhood was changing. A freeway was going in right across the Haight, and neighbors were selling left and right. Grandma refused to move. She was fighting the city alongside a small band of neighbors, convinced they could halt the progress of that monstrosity and, as they saw it, save the city.

Delores helped her grandmother fix tea in in the kitchen while Dad sat outside in the back garden, smoking yet another cigar. He barely talked in the car, after Delores's confession. He smoked nonstop.

"Don't help me," Grandmother said. She was slow compared to the last time Delores had seen her, more slumped, but she still had a spark that gave Delores hope her mother had exaggerated the need here. She was still able to climb the stairs to her front door, a story above the street, over the garage.

"I'm happy to," Delores said, reaching for delicate red-patterned china. When Delores was a child, it always lent an air of formality to their tea together, and Delores would feel so sophisticated. Now she could see that the set was tatty, chipped, and old. Didn't matter, though, for the depth of the call that simple pattern made into her childhood memories. She pulled down the pot, and the matching cups and saucers.

"I have biscuits," Grandmother said, reaching into a cupboard and pulling down some shortbread. Her white hair was wispy and gathered into a loose bun. She wore a simple sweater and pants, no doubt things of comfort. She arranged the cookies, her fingers showing a slight vibration.

Delores watched her while scooping loose tea into the pot.

"How is Cora?" Grandmother said.

"She's fine," Delores said.

"And why did you leave her?"

Delores, about to put the kettle back on the stove, stopped and looked through the window to assure herself that Dad was still in the backyard, then turned to look at her Grandmother, who had a small satisfied smile on her face.

"What makes you say that?"

"You haven't visited your parents in years. This time you come and stay long enough to come visit me as well."

"I wanted to come see you. Mother really wanted me to come see you." Delores set the kettle down. "But why do you think I left Cora?"

She tapped her forehead with an index finger. "Nothing gets by me." She crossed to the creaky round oak table that once served as a family dining area, and now held letters, papers, bills. She picked up a blue envelope with cursive on the outside. "But this helped me figure it out," she said. The return address was Delores's own in New York. The letter was from Cora.

"She wrote you?"

"We have a regular correspondence. Well, she writes me, anyhow. I've not been very good about returning them lately. Can't seem to find the time."

"You correspond about me?"

"That's where it started. She couldn't exactly write your parents, and knew that I was aware of your relationship and didn't judge you like others might, so I became the source of all Delores knowledge. But then, we would add an aside about a book or a movie we enjoyed, and soon those topics took over the writing. You know, barely a week goes by that we don't write. I'm quite grateful for it. Most of my other pen pals have died, I'm afraid."

Delores didn't know quite how to react. She took the letter.

"You can have it, if you'd like."

They served tea and sat in the backyard until dusk stole the light. Until the cherry on Dad's cigar was the only signal that he was in the yard with them, because the more that Grandma and Delores chatted, the less he said.

———————

Delores read the letter in bed. Dad offered to sleep on the couch so Delores could take the guest room. Delores heard the front door open and close as she was climbing under the thin wool blanket, so she suspected he was headed out on the town.

The room was large but so dominated by a burl vanity and bed that there was no room for maneuvering. The bed groaned and squeaked with every shift Delores made.

She held the letter, almost out of sight, against the back cover of her book as she read by the light of a small Tiffany lamp. The blue edge of the envelope peeked over the top, until finally she couldn't stand it anymore and put aside the book.

> *Dearest Etta,*
>
> *Hope this finds you well. I also hope you forgive me for jumping right to the point here and dispensing with usual formalities.*
>
> *Delores has left me, it seems. She only took a few things along, her flat is just as she left it. She left a cryptic note, saying that I will understand, and that I will know the reasons for her actions. I suppose in some ways I do know, but this is very sudden and upsetting to me.*
>
> *She went to Los Angeles to be with her parents while I was abroad. Apparently returning to the strange, possibly unhealthy environment she was raised in. No doubt she will find some solace in what is known to her, and maybe find comfort there, but this worries me.*
>
> *Delores has never talked fondly of California, with the exception of visiting you in San Francisco. She has, in fact, derailed many trips we planned to take together to visit her family, even when it included time with you.*
>
> *There are certainly things I can point to — a lack of romance, a certain settling in that might more strongly reveal the gap in our ages (I think she prefers going out whereas I prefer staying in), some disagreements over money, or at least the fact that I support us both and she has a generous allowance, but I wonder how much not earning her own way affects her.*

Despite those things, though, I found our "Boston Marriage" (as my Mother kept referring to it, despite my protests that this term was outdated and inaccurate) to be quite wonderful. We were good companions, and good friends. We enjoyed similar things at a similar pace of life. Of course, I love her.

So why would a woman like Delores who has everything just cast it aside? I am most interested in your perspective on this, whether or not you get to talk to her about it directly. Of course, I am hoping you will act as some sort of intermediary, passing information back and forth.

My goal is nothing less than convincing her to come back to me. To undo whatever damage I may have inadvertently caused. I need to win her heart, again. Please, Etta, can you help with this project?

Yours affectionately,

Cora

"Sarah!" a voice cried in the dark. Delores sat up in bed. A woman's voice. From outside?

"Sarah? *Sarah!*" But it wasn't coming from outside. Delores could make out a light in the living room, through her open door. Then, a figure in her doorway, lit from behind. Wearing a once-white nightgown. A ghostly figure haloed by unpinned hair that glowed with lamplight. Her grandmother. Delores pulled the brass chain to bring her own lamp to life.

"Sarah, Harry is drunk and won't come to bed. He's snoring."

And it was true, there was snoring. From the living room. Dad, on the couch.

"It's Delores, Grandma. It's Delores, and that's not Grandpa on the couch. It's not Harry, it's Gael."

Grandmother blinked in the light, her brow taught, lips pursed. Her face softened at Delores's words, as she tried to understand. A log-sawing snore cut the wait, and might have been comical in another context.

"Delores...?"

"Yes, dear, it's me. Sarah and Harry are both gone."

"Oh, Delores."

"Let me help you back to bed."

"What a dream I had. It was so real."

Delores pulled back the sheets and put her feet on the cool wood floors.

"No, no, no," Grandma said. "I'll get myself back to bed. Don't you worry. It's all right. I'm just fine."

Delores sat on the edge of the bed and waited as she heard her Grandmother shut the door. Then, the creak of boards, a cough. Still she waited, listening to her father's stertorous breaths, the resonant cavity of his head amplifying the ridiculous noise. She rose and shut the door, which did almost nothing to block the sound. She crawled back into bed, shut off the light, and lay in the dark, listening to him ebb and flow.

The snores were like waves on a beach, with a rhythm and cadence all their own. Unpredictable, but subtly signaled if you listened close. Which is what Delores found herself doing: listening close. Listening for an hour or so until she grew so weary herself that she slipped under during a short respite in his night animal noises.

Delores watched her grandmother closely for signs of confusion in the morning, or for that puckered face that she wore in the night. But there was none to find. She seemed herself, if slightly feeble. Was it unreasonable to have confusion in the night at her age?

Then again, was it reasonable to leave someone you love alone to have those horrifying dreams at night? Did they haunt her often, or did they come last night only because her routine was disrupted by her houseguests?

During tea at the round table, with English muffins and some cheese and jam, Delores told her grandmother that she had read Cora's letter.

"Oh, yes?" Grandmother said.

"She accuses me of being frivolous. As if my reasons for running were not good."

"Of course she does. If she's in the wrong, the pain she's feeling is her fault. It's easier to blame someone else."

"Do you know what she did? I had a show in New York. She bought every piece. Bought out the whole gallery."

"Ah. And this upset you?" Grandmother put down her cup. Her hands shook, just enough that the cup clattered against the saucer a few times. Delores noticed too that her grandmother was in the same outfit as the day before. How often did she bathe? Wash her clothes? Did she do her own laundry? Where?

"You know Mother wants me to move up here to care for you."

Grandmother rolled her eyes. "Of course she does. She wants you to be her mouthpiece because she knows I'll listen to you. She's wants me to sell and get out. That freeway thing. And your father wants me to move to Los Angeles and stay under your mother's roof."

"I can't see that being a very friendly arrangement," Delores said.

"Can you imagine? And he doesn't seem to appreciate that if my main reason for staying here is fighting a freeway, Los Angeles is the last place I'd like to be. They're mad about them there, the way they're talking. No. I want to die in this house. This is my home."

"What about the stairs? What if you can't navigate them anymore?"

"I guess we can deal with that when it happens, but if you ask me, the stairs keep me fit. They give me exercise, you know. Would you mind, dear?" Grandma pointed to her nearly empty cup.

Delores filled it from the pot, the musk of the English Breakfast tea sweetening the air. "I have to confess something to you," Grandma said. "Buying out the show. It was my idea."

"I don't understand."

"Well, I've never told anybody this, so you can't either. But I did the same thing with your dad's first show."

"You did?"

"It was the twenties, and we were doing well. Had some extra money. He had a piece in an exhibition where he won a ribbon for a still life. He put up a show at a local business. I arranged to buy all the work. Give him a little ego boost and money, keep him moving along in his career."

Delores was surprised. She spread some jam on a muffin half, but then put it down and didn't eat it.

"He never found out, unlike you, of course. Maybe he didn't want to know, after all. But in his case it worked! He found his legs and sold a few girlie paintings, and that was the start of a career. He met your mother in Los Angeles and started a life down there.

"So, when Cora wrote me and worried that you would be discouraged if you didn't sell your work, I suggested the ruse to her. If I had known the ripple that action would have I would not have said anything. But please don't blame her, blame me."

The action that Cora had taken felt manipulative and underhanded, but the same action attributed to Grandmother seemed somehow loving and caring.

Delores sighed. "Well, maybe that takes some of the sting of intention away, but even if you suggested it, she should have known better."

"Could be. But then, maybe she loved you enough to take the risk."

"You can slice it up and tie it back down, but whatever your argument, Gael, there's no doubt in my mind that all you are doing is wasting paint."

Norton Shale was the type who leaned down when he entered doorways. A gaunt man, loose-fleshed and giant at more than six and a half feet, a thin man whose clothing always seemed made for men larger even than him, and yet, oddly, they always seemed too tight as well.

They met at the Tadich Grill on Clay Street, where white-coated waiters served with impeccable grace. Delores was about half as slow as the men, but since they were on their second bottle of wine after a few rounds of cocktails, even being last in the race meant having a decent blur about her head.

Shale had an underwater lethargy as he talked, the drink robbing him of steadiness. "You are just wasting paint. Twenty-one-color palette, like me — see, I make my paintings for reproduction with modern printing techniques, and see, you only got a few colors on the press, right? They come together to make up all the colors like so." He wove his fingers together, like a small carpet, to demonstrate. "They might give it a nice varnish or something, but there's a limit to offset printing. And see, anything outside of the gamut of those colors? That's just wasted paint. Wasted paint is wasted money. Wasted money is wasted time.

Wasted time is…well, that can't be good, right? We only get so much."

Shale was the only illustrator Dad held as his equal, or better still, his rival. There were plenty of working artists Gael Sarjeant admired, or whose style he appreciated, but there was none whom he was jealous of the way he was jealous of Shale. Whereas Dad worked blue onto the exposed thighs of fleshy, sumptuous young women, Shale traded on the idea of family life in America. A pure sweetness imbued his work — playful Midwestern football games, or Thanksgiving scenes with families praying around the table, or a little girl in crinoline and hair ribbons who is accepting a lollipop from a white-coated country doctor hiding a needle and syringe behind his back — which graced every cover of *The Saturday Evening Post*. A gig any illustrator would kill for. A gig very few could deliver on.

Dad shook his head the whole time Shale was talking. "The problem with you, Norton, is your lack of imagination. I don't paint for the reproduction process. Sure, that's what pays my bills, but I paint for me. I use twenty-eight colors because I want to see that figure pop off the canvas and make me want her." He stopped, turned to Delores and patted her hand. "That was crude. I'm sorry."

"Don't mind me," she said, arms crossed, a cigarette held loosely between two fingers of a dangling hand. "But maybe one of you can answer why I was asked to this summit of monumental artistry?"

"Oh, god," Shale said. "Look here, that's my fault. My son — you met him before, right? He's got that little stationery store. Well, his wife up and left him for a sailor, and he's about your age and likes some of the same things you do, I understand, so I talked your dad into being a matchmaker of sorts."

"You did?"

"I did."

"He did," Dad said, nodding.

"And?" Delores said.

"Well, the poor guy got cold feet at the last minute."

"He did."

"He always has been a bit of a wallflower. A bit effeminate. His wife really pushed him around."

"I can't imagine," Delores said.

"Well, she did. She was one of those demanding types. Never happy. He's had some success, he has, with his shop. It supports them and bought them a little house in the Sunset, but she was still unhappy. Nag nag nag, she did. Waited until after the wedding, and then started in."

"She sounds like a cartoon from the funny pages," Delores said.

"You see, that's not so far from the truth," Shale said. "It really isn't. Anyway, she called him a pansy then ran off with somebody she deemed more manly, and the poor fellow really needs to meet some people." Shale reached over and patted Delores on the shoulder. "Now, I'm not saying you were going to be some kind of love interest for him, but I thought surely an evening at a nice dinner with a girl his own age couldn't hurt, could it?"

"Probably not," Delores said. "Send him my regards." He seemed, she remembered from meeting him as a teenager, like a painfully shy boy looking at a life of manipulation by stronger-willed people: wives, fathers.

"Delores has got news of her own," Dad said. "Why don't you tell Mr. Shale here what you told me on the drive up."

"You want to talk about that?"

"Sure I do. Tell him about selling your photos." And then to Shale: "Delores here sold some of her photos."

"Yes," Delores said, a bit shy on this new tack. "I was able to sell some photos."

"Well, congratulations," Shale said. "What style are they? What's your topic?"

"Tell him!" Dad bellowed, probably with more exuberance than intended, loud enough that a few patrons at nearby tables turned to look.

"They're nudes."

"Tell him who they're nudes of!"

"I used Dad's model, Sammi."

"That's right, she used my model."

"You used his model?" Shale said.

Delores rolled her eyes. "Yes. I mean, we became friends and it just sort of happened."

"But that's not the best part," Dad said. "Tell him what the market is. Where you sold them."

"Well, they're nudes," Delores said. "There aren't many places to sell." She stubbed out her cigarette and immediately lit another.

"She didn't," Shale said. Then to Delores: "You didn't."

"She did," Dad said.

"*Playboy*?" Shale said. Delores nodded. Picked some tobacco off her tongue and took a deep breath. Dad crossed his arms and leaned back in his chair, nodding with a self-satisfied smile.

"See, I'll tell you what I say about that," Shale said. "I say, to hell with *Playboy*. To hell with them. The idea of a mainstream magazine with that smut, with such content, next to *The Post* or *Life*. That's not the America I know."

Dad put his hands on his knees and leaned in, pulled at the sleeves of his checked dinner jacket. "That's the truth. I'll tell it right here and now. Women aren't perfect. If you want a woman to be perfect, you need to paint her. How can you rid yourself of that ugly mole or the hair on her legs or the lazy eye?"

"Right, right," Shale said, tapping the table with his index finger.

"So, they put these girls up, and sure, they're young and pretty, but they're flawed. We don't reflect reality, you and me, we reflect a fantasy. Like a movie. To show what is real like that? That's making the American male appetite into a clinical joke. We might as well be lady doctors."

"You do know that movies are made of photographs, Dad?" Delores said, but she was ignored.

"Have you seen the pay scale for these photographers?" Shale said. "It's nothing. Can't support a family on that. Can't support a career. Taking money right out of the pockets of good, hard-working painters who have wives and children. It's a total shame. A damn shame." And then he turned and apologized to Delores for his language.

"Well," Delores said, taking the opening. "These magazines have been around forever."

Dad responded to that one. "Cheap printing. Black and white. Bad photography. Shit writing. Targeted to college boys. No, *Playboy* is different. High-quality color photography and good editorial writing, great fiction and essays, good printing and impressive distribution. Mark my words, Delores, Norton and I here will be completely replaced by photographers. You won't see illustration anymore. You won't see painters working to make rent. Remember that painting put you through school and paid for the roof over your head."

"Second of all," Delores continued. "*Playboy* hires illustrators. Cartoonists, painters. There's more illustration in *Playboy* than in many commercial magazines. And talk about hypocrisy. Mr. Shale, you yourself mentioned *Life* magazine in the same breath as *The Post*. Tell me how many illustrators versus photographers they hire?"

"The girly stuff is different," Shale said. "That's editorial photography in *Life*. Capturing views of the world that you couldn't see otherwise."

"And a look into a woman's boudoir is something you see all the time?"

"That," Dad said, much too loudly, backing his volume with anger, "is *my* boudoir that you took photos of. The costuming that *my* painting bought. The model that is on *my* salary."

Delores pulled back, recoiling from the venom in his voice.

"It's a lost cause for us anyway," Shale said, maybe reacting to Dad by talking more quietly, or maybe just changing the topic to make sure he could still get a table at Tadich after that night. "Every young painter today wants to be Jackson Pollock. Nobody does figurative anymore."

Dad took a few breaths. Finished his wine and took the last half pour from the bottle into his empty glass. "I hate that man," he said. "Diarrhea on canvas. The only good Pollock I've ever seen is the floor of my studio."

Shale swirled the last few swigs of wine in his glass, more precious now that the bottle was dead. "No, no, no. You're missing it, Gael. He's a great talent, and would that I could be taken seriously as an artist like that and hung in museums. I'd be honored." He leaned in, and pointed at Dad, then Delores as he made his point. "The problem is, every young painter wants to be him. Nobody wants to do figurative work, like I said, see? They don't want to learn how the masters did it. They just want to throw paint on a canvas in some random fashion and think that makes them artists."

Shale leaned back and then continued. "No, see, where you're wrong about Pollock: the man knows composition. He knows dynamism. He knows what he's doing."

"To hell with him," Dad said. "I don't need some flipping museum curator telling me what good art is or not. I can look at a painting and know what the artist knows. I know whether he's bull or something with talent. Let me tell you, I know painters, and even if he could paint like Jan van Eyck, the bastard doesn't, and that tells me everything I need to know.

"And you, Shale, you should know better than to want to sell your canvases one at a time in some gallery who takes half of your money. You got it better. You sell reproduction rights. The painting itself? Worthless. The reproduction rights, that's where the gold is. That's why I don't sell my canvases. Worthless on their own."

He turned to Delores. "And thanks to *Playboy*, my reproduction rates are dropping faster than ever before."

"You just signed the biggest contract of your life, so I am questioning the heart of your premise," Delores said. She motioned for the waiter. "Can you call me a cab, please?"

"But I couldn't start out now and make it. It's different now."

"So it's different now," Delores said. "So what? It's all change. What, you want to go back to the thirties with the depression or the forties with the war? Maybe we'll get into it with the Russians, and then we won't have to worry about life here or anywhere anymore. Until then, I'm going to try to make my own way as an artist, and that means selling my work."

"You just keep away from my studio. No more shooting there."

"Fine."

"And no more shooting my models."

"That's not your choice."

"The hell it isn't. You stop or I'll fire her and find another. Just like that." Dad snapped his fingers.

Shale was looking around the restaurant. The maître d' approached, holding Delores's hat and coat. "Ma'am?"

He held the coat for her as she put it on. She offered a pressed smile and a nod of thanks as he motioned toward the door.

"We'll find out when we get home, won't we? Until then, drink yourself into a stupor for all I care."

"I'm not drunk."

Delores scoffed at her father, then turned to his companion. "Mr. Shale, always a pleasure."

Shale blew her a kiss with a smile broad enough to suggest he was oblivious to the argument that had just happened, or that he at least had willfully ignored it, but then he shrugged, as if to suggest that he couldn't have helped it anyway.

Delores walked into the night. San Francisco was lit by neon, making dark outlines of the buildings, and she was in a Dashiell Hammett story right there for a moment or two. She got into the Yellow Cab, which smelled of coffee and cigarettes, and directed the driver to the Haight, but she changed her mind after he pulled away.

She leaned forward. "Do you know any good women's clubs?" she said.

"Women's clubs, miss?"

Delores offered him a few dollars. "Yes. The sorts of places that women — and only women — go."

The cabby, at a red light, turned, an arm over the back of the seat

"Lady, this is San Francisco. You gotta get more specific than that. Couple places in North Beach are pretty lively, big shows, women dressed as men, that sort of thing. Tourists love 'em — well, until a few got busted last year."

"I want someplace smaller. Quieter. Less traffic."

"Gotcha. I know just the joint for you." He took the money from her hand.

The bar, Maddie's, wasn't far from North Beach. A door led to an entry hall with a heavy black curtain a few feet in. Just beyond that a woman on a stool put down her book long enough to give Delores a knowing nod. "Welcome, sister. Be watchful."

It wasn't full, maybe ten women sitting at tables with groups. The room was dark save for strings of outdoor Christmas lights that gave a nice warm glow. Delores took a seat at the bar on a stool padded in shiny vinyl. A young woman in heavy horn-rimmed glasses tended bar. She jerked her head at Delores in greeting and set down a glass of water and bowl of peanuts.

A radio played jazz, but it wasn't loud. The conversation seemed deliberately tuned to be quieter than the music, save an occasional laugh or punch line that broke through.

The bar was scratched, in need of refinishing. Looked like it could splinter you if you ran your hand against the grain of it, but Delores leaned in anyway. She ordered whiskey and a beer, then turned on her stool, putting her elbows against the bar. Two couples were dancing in butch-femme combos. The femmes wore pretty dresses, the butches, men's sports jackets and collared shirts.

"Breaking the law," said a woman on the stool next to hers. "Just for dancing: breaking the law. Can you believe that? What a farce."

Delores turned to face her. Early forties. Short hair, a bit long over the ears, largely gray. She wore a sports coat, too.

"Ridiculous."

"You know, those gals out there, they do that on purpose. They been in busts before. They know what the score is, so they dance. They dance to tell the cops that nobody can't tell them not to. Of course, the cops got different ideas about that."

"You a dancer?" Delores said.

"Sister, where I come from butch don't dance with butch."

"I wasn't asking. Just curious if you're like them. A radical, as you say."

The woman leaned on the bar, laying her head in the crook of her arm. Her eyes bleary. "I'm no dancer. I'm a drunk."

"Drunks can't dance?"

"Listen." She sat up again. "I used to be a factory worker, managed a whole line during the war, but then all that skill I gathered and scraped and fought for was for nothing when the men came home. I was a manager, goddamnit. But had to give the asshole his job back — *my* job — just because he had to go fight. Got fired by the pricks. Came out west 'cause I heard it was better here for people like us. It was pretty good for a while, and then McCarthy, you know, that pig fucker. Bet dollars to doughnuts he's some kind of pervert. You know what? I've been in three busts in this goddamned town, but I don't know any other way to meet girls. So, yeah, I don't dance. I drink and try to find some femme to spend a little time with. And run for the back door soon as the yelling starts."

Delores nodded. Downed her whiskey and took a small handful of peanuts.

"I've never seen you around," the drunk said. "You looking tonight?"

"I'm from out of town. And trust me, I've got my hands full. I'm not going to stand in your way if you want to go pull a skirt."

"That's good, then. But you know, I'm long tonight. Too much. Too... uh, crap, 'scuse me." The woman slid from the stool and weaved her way to the bathroom.

Delores lit a cigarette and turned back to the dancers, both couples holding each other as close as they could, despite the music having a jump to it.

The femme of one couple looked a little like Sammi, if Sammi had ten years of hard living on her. She had on a simple print dress, empire waist with flowers, made herself, no doubt. She was slender, as was her butch. Both of them had their eyes closed; they swayed every four beats or so. The look on their faces showed no joy in their task. Maybe instead resignation, as if they were entrants in a dance marathon that never ended. Delores imagined them all lined up out front. Black and white, the flash goes pop, they all end up in a folder in a locked drawer in Diego's archive with a clipping of the newspaper notice.

What if Sammi were here? Would she hold Delores's hand? What if Delores kissed her lips in front of all these witnesses. Or, more laughably, what if Cora were here? She'd never walk in the front door, that's for sure.

"Mind if I sit here?" Delores turned to see a pretty femme, a curvy woman with a wide nose, Asian features. Her dark hair done in a stylish wave. She wore red — a red dress, red heels, a red flower in the turn of her hair.

"I'd be a fool to mind," Delores said.

"Now you can buy me a drink," said Red Dress.

"I can, you say?"

"Unless you got something against Orientals."

"Well," Delores said. "I'm trying to not think about somebody. Can you help me with that?"

"Oh, my goodness," said Red Dress, hopping onto the stool. "I believe that is my specialty."

"Can you do it dancing?" Delores said.

"You want to dance?"

"Yeah, I want to dance."

Red Dress hopped off the stool. She took Delores's hand, and they walked to the small area cleared of tables. Red Dress turned to Delores and put her arm around Delores's shoulder, and Delores's right hand found her partner's left hand as Delores wrapped her arm around the waist of Red Dress, feeling her body as it folded above her hips. Loving the feel of it. The sensuous unambiguity of her form.

Red Dress wore a perfume, a subtle musk. Delores pulled her tight, their fronts warm against each other, bellies together. Delores had only an inch or two on her, but Red Dress laid her head on Delores's shoulder anyway. Delores caught the eyes of the other butches, who each gave her a nod of approval, or respect, or resignation perhaps. Maybe, even, of warning. A kind of "Hey, watch out for that one."

But who cared if this didn't last? It was all about that very moment, in that bar, in those arms. Delores looked at the door, at the girl on the stool, reading the book.

It could happen tonight. They could decide to bust Maddie's. They could come through the door any moment. Flashlights, billy clubs, photographers. So be it. Arrest her for dancing. She stood a little straighter and closed her eyes, and just felt Red Dress against her as they swayed more or less to the quiet music and social chatter of those women who just wanted to keep the company of other women.

What was it about California that drove her to drink? Delores awoke hung over here more often than she had in the last ten years in New York. She felt the malaise before she opened her eyes, and then after doing the mental checklist and finding at least a modicum of equilibrium, looked at the ceiling of a strange room. It was high, painted white, with a round floral medallion surrounding a naked light bulb.

Where did she end up? What neighborhood? To her left, warm skin. Warm skin? Sammi? Delores looked over and saw the back of a head of thick, now tangled, black hair. Red Dress. That's right, Red Dress. Hardly able to be called that now, since she was naked, asleep on her stomach. They were on a mattress on the floor. A round-mirrored vanity against one wall that was nearly identical to one Sammi had in her apartment, which gave Delores a slight sense of worry, as if it were an omen. Posters with bright primary shapes that resembled trumpets, saxophones, and drums hung more or less square with thumbtacks on the white walls.

Delores lifted herself from the bed, stepping on that pretty red dress so carelessly thrown on the floor. She picked it up and brought it to her face, inhaling, entertaining a fancy that it might have been perfume more than anything else that seduced her. She held it up against her body in the mirror, the silky fabric smooth and cool, but too small for her. And the color was wrong on her skin, brought out her ruddiness. She folded the dress, quick and neat, and put it down on the chair next to the vanity, wishing for a moment she had one of those ribbons from Mother's lingerie to tie it up as a token of affection for a night she was almost sure that she enjoyed.

She remembered listening to jazz, some recital of a poem having to do with a politician and a dog, but it was blurry. There was a cab ride to some apartment in a house, some roommates Delores could not picture now, a joint being passed around. A performance of some kind that was funny, very funny, then huddled drunk fumbling in the dark of this room. Unfastening and stripping. Fingers and warm breath. Sighs, moans, sleep. She was sore, but it was hard to tell if it was due to pleasure or just efforts.

She dressed, going slow as an icepick hacked behind her eyes. She walked into the living room, now empty, a dinner-plate sized ashtray overflowing on a kidney-shaped coffee table. Wine bottles and glasses crowding it. Some with splashes of red still in the bottom. One or two with swimming cigarette butts. Then, eureka, a pack of her cigarettes. She grabbed it, and shook it to see if it held anything, but it was empty. She crushed it and threw it down. She remembered giving them freely when asked, and also remembered that smoking her last was one reason she and Red Dress had retreated to the bedroom.

In the small kitchen she took a glass from a drying rack and filled it over the dishes that topped the sink. She drank slow, looking out a back window at an overgrown garden. She put the empty glass back in the drying rack. She did a mental check of her person, a physical check of her purse, and then left the place by a long staircase that led to a very steep hill, which she was halfway up. The morning was misty, cool, and close. Absurdly quiet. She decided to walk down, instead of up, and went in search of either a diner or a cab, whichever appeared first.

When she arrived at Grandmother's an hour or so later, they were in the kitchen. Dad sat at the table, hands over the back of his head while

Grandmother stood over him.

"You're a bad example, Harry. You can't run the store drunk. What are your workers to think, if the boss comes in this way?"

"I'm Gael, Mom," Dad said, with the resigned cadence of someone who had repeated those words more than a few times already. "Harry died in the Great War."

"Don't you argue with me. You brought shame to us with your liquor and your whoring."

"Grandma," Delores said. Grandmother spun, surprised by the new voice in the mix. "Grandma, listen to me. That's not Harry." Grandmother looked at Delores, again with that face Delores had seen a few nights previous. How it turned from anger to confusion, an open softness, and a desperate need, a yearning for meaning unfound.

"Delores," she said. She stuttered a time or two, then said, "Your grandfather is being quite bad," but her voice held less conviction than it had a moment earlier.

"That's Gael, Grandma. Your son."

She looked down. Dad uncovered himself, and looked right up at her, spreading his arms wide as if to say, "Here I am."

"It's me, Mom. Me. Gael. Your favorite."

"I don't have a favorite."

"Of course you don't," he said.

Delores approached the old woman. Put her hands on her shoulders. "Do you want to sit? I think you should sit." She led her grandmother toward her chair in the living room, where her radio was, where her magazines were, where she kept some knitting and busy work, some books that Delores noticed were dusty. She wondered if her Grandmother was able to read them anymore, able to follow the stories.

"Your father — your father acts just like his father," she said in a mumble. "His voice is just like his father's."

Then Grandma shuffled back to the kitchen, out of Delores hands, to a tissue box. She took one and blew her nose. Then another, and she wiped her eyes. Delores went for one as well, but then saw the box was empty. She picked it up and was about to throw it in the garbage.

"Don't!" Grandmother said. "Don't, give it to me. I'll take care of it." But when she noticed her reaction drew quizzical attention from Delores and Dad, she explained. "I'm particular about my trash. Thank you."

She took the box and walked from the room.

"It's been a hell of a morning," Gael said. "Where have you been?"

"I better follow her."

"Somebody should have been here with her. Where the hell were you?"

"She lives alone, Dad. I'm sure she was fine last night. I want to see what she's doing."

Delores acted the spy, following Grandma as she stole into her bedroom. She walked into her closet, closed the door behind her, and emerged only a moment later.

After Grandma had gone to sit in her chair and Delores had fetched her a new cup of tea, and the radio was playing some crooners, Delores went into her room. There was a minty smell there, medicinal. Some jars of rubs and ointments on the vanity. A jewelry box Delores remembered looking through, as a girl, whenever she could. A nubby white cotton throw over the bed, unmade. A pile of used tissues on the bedside table. Delores opened the closet. Against the back wall, and the sides under the clothes, were stacks of boxes. Tissue boxes, like bricks, against the wall nearly to the level of the high shelf. A hundred or so. Delores took one, and then another. Completely empty. She picked up a third and felt something rattling inside. A piece of costume jewelry.

She began to dismantle the wall, looking into each box. She found old cloth, a handkerchief, a torn stocking, two short knitting needles still attached to a small ball of blue yarn and the beginning of a baby sweater. Soiled underwear. She found a long box from a jeweler and opened it to find a beautiful set of white pearls nestled in black velvet. A card in the box with them: "Merry Christmas, Love, Gael and Lily, 1950."

She took the box and went to find Dad. Grandma was sitting in the old rocking easy chair, with news on the radio. Eyes closed, a blanket on her lap.

She handed him the box. "You have to come see this."

He did as she had, going through boxes, pulling them down at random, looking inside. One had a small collection of desiccated moths. At that, he went and roused his Mother.

"What are these, Mom?" Gael held up a tissue box. "Why do you keep these?"

"I just don't want to waste them," she said, with obvious embarrassment, and pride enough to attempt to cover it. "They may be useful."

"How? How will they be useful? They're garbage, Mom. Garbage."

"They are useful. Sometimes they stop...well, the noises in the closet. You know."

"I don't. I don't know, Mom. You have to explain. Why keep these?"

"They come through the closet at night unless I give them something," she said, blurting it out as if trying to crest the hurdle that had kept her from saying those words for some time now.

"What happens if they come through?" Delores said with measured calm, reaching out to stroke Grandmother's arm. She pulled away with a quick jerk at the touch, and looked at Delores with vivid panic.

But then her eyes went sad and Grandmother leaned into Delores, and whispered it in her ear. "They touch me, Sarah. The wicked, wicked beasts. They do horrible things."

XI

MOTHER'S HAIR blew across her face in de-
fiance of whatever product was supposed to hold it at bay. They walked
down onto the pier, she and Delores, the morning after Delores and
Dad were back from San Francisco. They walked out for a spell, then
leaned on the rails to look at the sand, to smell the waves, the coconut
oil perfume of tanned bodies walking by, cigarettes, and alcohol.

Delores tried to find the spot where Sammi had stood naked, and
she wondered what the view would have been like from up here.

At his request, she had shown Dad that photograph, and a few others, after the drive home from San Francisco.

"Aren't you tired from the drive?"

"Show me."

As she had done with Sammi, she made the reveal slow. One picture,
then a pause, then another, in a deliberate row.

"Hmm," he said as she lay down each print. Tapped his finger on
the table. Then, when the last was placed, he drew a breath and ex-

haled. "Well, these are good." He picked them up, stacked them, leafed through them again, then tapped their edges on the table to stack them evenly. "I wish they weren't."

"Well, thanks."

Maybe they had become partners facing Grandma's mental quirks, the evidence of her senility when it finally came. In comparison, maybe their squabble seemed petty. Or maybe he was truly impressed with the work. Whatever the reason, Dad's view softened.

"Here's the deal," he said. "My schedule comes first. If you shoot her, it must be on her days off."

"Fair enough. That's what I do now."

"My clothing and costuming are off the table. You want her in lingerie? You foot the bill."

"Okay."

"No shooting in the studio or at the house."

"Fine."

"And you have to pay her. At least what I do."

"I can't afford that."

"Then you can't afford to have a model. If you're doing commercial work, you have to respect the other professionals who allow you to make the bulk of the profits. Speaking of which, where did you get these developed?"

That was a question Delores was dreading.

"Just a place in Hollywood I found."

"Just don't use Diego."

"Why not?"

"He's a blackmailer. I don't mean that figuratively. He's bad news. You don't want to be near him."

"Okay."

"I want you to promise me. I stopped all dealing with him because of how unethical he is."

"Okay, okay, I get it. Does this mean that we're okay, you and me?"

"What are my options here, kiddo? I'm angry with you. This situation goes against the grain of me. But I'm trying to give you an olive branch and see the thing from your eyes. Certainly would be a lot easier if the work was no good."

"Thanks."

"You're about to turn thirty, Delores. This is your shot at making a career. But I'm only going to be patient so long. Go behind my back again, and I'll pack you up and send you back to New York myself. Let Miss Cora Fournier be your protector instead of me."

And so it was that a weight of worry and dread that felt sure to topple her at any moment had been lifted. Dad's approval, however reticent, was a balm on the open sore which festered under the worry that she wasn't pleasing him. That she was failing to be a good daughter. Then some defiance kicked in and she was irritated with herself, because wasn't he the one who caused the wound in the first place by demanding such devotion from her?

On the pier, Delores looked over at Mother. She had seemed gaunt before Delores saw the pall of Grandma's skin. But Mother was very nearly radiant in comparison, besides being trim and fit. Her skin was clear and tight, just some smile lines around her face to give it age. Especially when she frowned. Delores watched her move hair from her mouth and tuck it behind her ear.

"Maybe I should have stayed," Delores said. "I can't help thinking she must feel so alone. She was so desperate and confused when the spells would hit."

"Maybe you should have," Mother said. "But maybe it's right that you didn't. If she doesn't even know who you are, then it wouldn't matter if you were there."

"She knew who I was when we said goodbye."

"Your father is sparing no expense in this facility."

"There goes your boat."

"Yes, he was almost gleeful when he told me. Very irritating. He said 'The two happiest days of a boat owner's life are the day they buy it and the day they sell it. We're avoiding both.' And then he convinced me we could rent. Go out with Pal again sometime. Anyway, it's a worthy sacrifice if it means your grandmother is comfortable in the days she has left. That facility is highly recommended, top-notch. And, close to her home, so she knows the neighborhood."

"She still thought Dad was Gramps. I wonder how much our being there made her worse."

"I wouldn't want to be haunted by that man."

"He couldn't have been that bad." Her grandfather had died before

Delores was born, fighting in World War I. They had brought home a picture of him, full uniform, flying-saucer style helmet and round glasses, saluting. A serious, dour man, by the look of it. They had found the picture in a folding silver frame, tucked into the bottom row of tissue boxes.

"He was that bad," Mother said, tucking hair behind her ear again. "He was a drunk. But he's also long dead, so I should just forgive him and be done with it. That would be the Christian thing, wouldn't it?"

"If you're capable."

"Of forgiveness?"

"You are not the most gracious creature, Mother."

"I know you think I'm too hard, darling, but it's not that I don't care. To be honest, I think I care too much." Again, she tucked her hair back. "Your grandmother was horrible to me, you know. Just wicked. Treated me like a servant when I met your father."

"So you've said. Many times."

"Did you know that she cut your father out of the will for marrying me?"

Delores looked at Mother. She did seem stoic today. More thoughtful for some reason. Less judgmental. More resigned.

"No, you never told me that," Delores said.

Mother snorted. Used both hands to move hair from her face, pushing with her palms.

"And she said since my father was a labor leader that I was a traitor to America. And then there's Sarah. She called you Sarah, right?"

"Yes."

"You know who Sarah was?"

"No. I asked Dad but he didn't know."

"He does know, he just probably didn't want to explain it. Your grandmother did have a good friend named Sarah, whom she met in the Women's Temperance Union. Supposedly they were very, very, very close."

"Really?"

Mother shrugged. A large gust mussed her hair again, and it fell across her forehead and cheek. She slapped at her face, pushing it back with an unmeasured flail, an overanimated reaction, a frown on her lips. "We have to get the out of this wind tunnel. It's driving me mad."

They walked back toward the avenues and the shopping.

"Look, your father told me about you selling photos of Sammi," Mother said as they walked. "Just be careful, okay? Be careful not to hurt him. And just be careful."

It took nearly a week for Sammi and Delores to get a day together. They met again in Sammi's apartment, Pal off playing cards, Mother and Dad having a quiet night in.

She had seen Sammi a number of times since they got back, but only around other company. They had to maintain the illusion they were simple girlfriends, not lovers. It was torture to Delores, whose furnace of desire was stoked by pretending that it didn't exist.

Free in her apartment they were more expressive with their attentions. They lay in Sammi's bed as a breeze from the open window smoothed across them, drying the sweat on their skin.

"Did you miss me?" Delores said.

"What do you think?"

"I don't know what I think. That's why I asked."

"Did you miss me?"

"I missed you. More than I thought I would."

"How much?"

"So much it hurt."

"Liar. You found some little birdie to sing for you in San Francisco."

Delores reached for a cigarette, and knocked over a half-full tumbler of wine, set on the floor next to the bed.

"Shit!" She sprang up.

Sammi sauntered to the kitchenette, while Delores picked up her camera so it would be out of the way of the rivulet snaking its way along. She put it on the bed.

Sammi came back with paper towels and Delores pressed a wad into the red, soaking it up.

"I found something in San Francisco," Delores said. Sammi didn't reply right away, so Delores kept on. "But it wasn't a new lover. I found that I don't want to hide anymore. I'm tired of pretending to be something I'm not. I want to be public. About who I am. About who I love."

"What does that mean, be public?" Sammi said.

"I don't want to lie anymore. I mean, I'm not going to publish a newspaper article or anything. I'm not going to make a lesbian float for the Rose Bowl Parade, but I want my family to know. I want my friends to know. I want them to know who I am and who it is that I'm in love with. I want to socialize with other women who are like us, who have loves of their own."

She watched Sammi walk back to the kitchenette, watched the shifting of her backside as she went tip-toe across the floorboards, hitting a squeaky area twice, to throw away the wine-soaked paper towels. As she turned and came back, Delores took in the shape of her. The hourglass, the downy patches, the smooth lines.

"Well, bully for you," Sammi said. "I hope you make her very happy."

"Her? Who?"

"Whoever it is you want to take with you to your new fancy public spectacle."

"Not who, you."

"What makes you think this is what I want?"

"Well, you love me, don't you?"

"I don't see the point of talking about that."

"Sure, but...say, are you just annoyed because I spilled that wine?"

Sammi flopped back on the mattress, sat with her back against the wall, threw her legs over Delores's midsection.

"Give me a cigarette." Delores lit one and handed it over. Stayed on her back to look Sammi in the eye.

"Look," Sammi said. "I mean, I told you I love what you do to me. You tie me all up in knots and then pick at them for hours until they come loose and just fall at your feet. But that's different, right? What we're doing is different than what you're talking about. About this getting married stuff, or the being serious stuff. Why can't this just be the fun that it is?"

"Don't you think it could be more?"

"Oh hell, I don't know. Don't confuse my comfort with being with you with wanting to be with you forever. I mean, I *am* engaged to be married."

"And you'll never leave Pal, is that it?"

"Aw, sweetheart, I don't know what I want, but I've already told him

I'm going to marry him. What do you want me to do?"

"Leave him. Dump him and come live with me. Can't say it more plainly than that."

Sammi laughed. "Live with you. You can't afford me. I make more money than you do."

"I'll sell photos."

"Of who, exactly? Our sessions get me riled up, I admit it. They're the best kind of teasing. But how long do you think this could last? Someday in the future we'll have a fight, and it will take the gloss off things, and I won't feel it when you look at me, because you'll be seeing me through the fight and not as I am now to you."

"I can't see that happening."

"Everybody loses their desire for another person. Everybody."

Delores took Sammi's hand in her own. She guided Sammi's fingers, down over her stomach, past her patch of pubic hair, parted her thighs, made Sammi's fingers go down there and kept them in place by holding her wrist, and clamping her thighs together again.

Sammi squirmed her hand, at first trying to pull it away, testing Delores's will in keeping it there, but then it settled into its role, and Sammi started exploring, wiggling the fingers, and Delores bit her lip when that went on. Sammi drew on her cigarette, looking down.

"I want you all the time," Delores said, and she opened her legs again. Sammi kept her hand there. She gave Delores the cigarette. Delores took a drag and stubbed it out in the ashtray next to the fallen wine tumbler. Sammi placed her free hand on Delores's belly and felt it rising and clenching with her breath.

"You're my muse," Delores said. "My sweetheart."

Sammi's warm hand went north to Delores's breast, alternating a light and feathery touch with pressure, in just the right cadence. Delores released Sammi's wrist and gave herself to the mercy of the mood. She threw her arms above her head and moved under Sammi's touch.

"I want you forever," Delores panted. Her hips took their own direction and rotated, moved, undulated.

Sammi readjusted, leaned down and kissed Delores, and then pulled her mouth so that it was just right there and Delores couldn't reach her for another kiss. Sammi's mouth was open, a bit of a smile, her eyes wide with what she was invoking in Delores. Delores bit her lip, tried one more time to reach Sammi's mouth, but Sammi moved back each time, then her hair fell from behind her ear, and it framed a warm little space for their faces to be close to each other.

"I want you forever," Delores said again.

Still Sammi teased Delores, refusing to kiss her. Delores turned instead to Sammi's arm and kissed it, up and down its length, strained to reach a breast with her mouth.

An orgasm for Delores was like being tied to a wall by a giant elastic band and trying to reach the wall opposite, each push of effort getting her a bit closer, each push of effort demanding more of her, putting her more into the moment. Just as Delores was about to touch the other wall, Sammi kissed her hard on the mouth — a lip-bruising, hard kiss, passionate and bracing, and Delores grabbed a handle on the far wall and pulled herself flush to it, cool brick against her body, and as Delores was right there in the rush of the storm she let go, and the band dragged her submissive body back across the space, the herky-jerky approach now in reverse, coming as a beautiful gloss of release.

Delores gasped air with squeaks and vocalizations she didn't recognize. And then her body slumped. Small electrical impulses ran her, causing her to twitch every few moments as she whispered to her lover.

"I love you. I love you, oh god, I do. Oh fuck, oh fuck, I love you so much." She looked up to Sammi's eyes to meet a deep smile, a moment of connection and presence.

After, Sammi stroked Delores from her knees to her shoulders with a nearly pressureless hand, and then when Delores was almost asleep from the affection, she heard the telling sound of a shutter being released, and film being wound. Alarm almost caused her to sit up in bed, to take the camera from Sammi. Delores was never the subject, Delores was the observer. But then a warm flush of embarrassment, and maybe even arousal, held her still with her eyes closed and she let Sammi take pictures of her naked, as she pretended to sleep.

The dim red bulb of the darkroom was the only illumination. Diego, in a black apron, held the end of a plastic tray slightly aloft, washing chemicals over exposed photo paper, the image — Sammi sitting on a simple wooden chair in her apartment, leaning over, her hands on the floor, her face down, her hair draped — coming up from ghostly white.

"Well, ain't this arty. Nobody's gonna buy this."

"That's personal."

When the image was fully present he moved the paper to a water bath, holding it gently with tongs, and then he hung it on a clothesline, now full of Sammi, and a few of the nudes of Delores that Sammi had taken. They were framed poorly, the exposure was wrong, and Delores did not like the way her body looked, but they still gave her a visceral thrill. They stood in for a near-secret vulnerability Delores was not sure she possessed previously. Each was a kiss from her lover.

Diego looked at his watch. "Ah. I believe my friend will be here by now."

"Who?"

Diego hung his apron on a hook and motioned for Delores to follow.

In his office sat a man in a cheap suit. His belly rolled over his belt, a hat sat on the couch next to him, his hair was stringy and greased over his balding scalp. He had a cigar in one hand, a drink sitting on the side table, and a newspaper folded back to expose the racing pages.

"Delores, this here is Mr. Cohen. He's a private dick." Cohen nodded his head. "You two can talk. I know nothing." Diego left the office, closing the door on his way. Delores watched him through the glass panels as he walked toward the dark room.

"Miss Sarjeant," Cohen said, his voice a baritone gravel road. "Our mutual friend here asked me to look into a certain matter for you, and I have something to report on said matter." He stood and crossed to Diego's round table desk, where a manila folder sat. He opened it and removed a photo. "First off, let's establish that I was on the tail of the right tomcat. This is the fella you had questions about, correct?"

He held out a picture of Pal, standing in his car lot, resting one hand on the roof of a new Chevy, and looking off into the distance.

"That's him."

Cohen picked up his cigar and puffed, drawing the cherry back to life and giving Delores a moment to study the photo of Pal. When she turned back to him he continued.

"Then okay. Now that we have that established, I did find that this man was carrying on with a lady. I was able to get some candid shots to establish that they were not just, let's say, bridge partners." He pulled a leather satchel from a chair next to the table and handed over a manila envelope, weighted by a number of photographic prints.

"Please tell our mutual friend Mr. Peck that I consider our debt square, and that unless he wants to hire me for good cold cash in the future and retain the high quality that I bring to all my endeavors, well, unless he wants that, he can keep his faggot ass out of my affairs. Would you be so kind as to let him know?"

"Yes."

"Fine," Cohen said, handing over the envelope. He walked to his drink and downed it in one gulp. He touched the brim of his hat in a modest gesture to Delores. "Good day, then, ma'am. It's been a tremendous pleasure."

When he was gone, all but the sour smell of him, Delores opened the envelope and pulled out a thin stack of 8 x 10 photos. The top one showed Pal behind the wheel of a dark Chevy. Shot from the driver's side through the window and showing the legs of a woman. Could be Sammi for all Delores knew, nothing to identify her.

But the next photo was far less ambiguous: Pal walking around the parked car, which was stopped outside a motel, and the passenger also on her feet, closing her door, in profile view of the camera, her lips pursed. Delores's hand went to her mouth.

The next photo was even clearer: The two of them entering a motel room, the woman turned back and looking around as if to make sure the coast was clear. Then, shots through a gap in drapes, faded to blurred white on the edges where the curtain blocked the lens, the woman ready to step from the puddle of her dress. She was dressed in elaborate lingerie, black garters and panties, black bra, her hair done up on top of her head, her hands fixing it as Pal undressed in the background.

Then, a few more direct, explicit photos.

They were blurry, but as the woman's obvious pleasure turned her mouth upward, Delores could clearly see her. Those French-Persian features. Unequivocally, definitely, unmistakably: Mother.

"I don't know who else to talk to," Delores said into the phone, looking out the kitchen window to make sure the car hadn't returned yet, that Mother and Dad were still out on their errands.

"I'm glad you called me," Cora said.

"I found something out. I don't know what to do about it."

"All right, then," Cora said. "Tell me everything,"

Delores looked outside again. "Mother is having an affair."

A laugh. "Really? An affair?"

"It's not funny."

"No, of course not. I'm just surprised, that's all. I'm sure it's especially not funny for your father. Have you told him?"

"No! Nobody knows."

"How did you find out?"

"I'd rather not discuss it."

"You collect secrets like some ladies collect hats."

"I will tell you someday, but it's irrelevant right now. Let's just say there is no confusion about the matter. She's having an affair with this fellow named Pal. Quite a piece of work, he is."

"You know him?"

"Yes. He's the fiancé of Dad's model."

"Your mother is having an affair with the fiancé of your father's model?"

"Yes."

"That sounds very complicated."

"Yes! That's why I called."

"All right. And you are trying to decide who, if anyone, to tell. Correct?"

"Yes, and it's unnerving, Cora. I cannot tell my dad. That would break his heart. I can't tell Sammi —"

"The model, right?"

"Yes — she's the one in Dad's paintings, the one on that polar bear rug in the print I have in my apartment."

"Ah. The one you have the crush on."

Delores leaned back, resting her head against the glass. "Am I that obvious?"

"Well, yes." There was a pause, maybe Cora calculating how honest she would need to be at this point. "I do pay attention, you know. Even when you don't think I do."

Delores made a sound, a kind of "mmm" of reluctant agreement.

"Can I just say I'm really touched that you called me to ask my opinion on this? It makes me think I'm still a part of your life."

"I never said you weren't part of my life, you know."

"Thank you for that, Delores."

"I hate Pal."

"Is he a violent man?"

"He's a man."

"Could you confront him? Use the information to get what you want?"

"Blackmail, Cora?"

"Social pressure, Delores. I'm not suggesting you do anything illegal, but since he's misbehaving maybe if you inform him that you are aware of it he will modify his behavior."

The lot had twenty or thirty cars. Big numbers on cards in the windshields listed the prices, bubble letters with highlighting, as if the sun glinted off the curve of them, as if they were made from inflated balloons. But it was dusk on the lot, with big lights above, like ones at a sports stadium, pools of white light on the playing field.

Delores walked along, looking in windows, the stitched vinyl seats, the whitewalls, the fins and fans that defined modernism on wheels.

"Waiting for your husband?" The voice came from somewhere behind her. A man, bucktoothed and large nosed, with a wide smile. A bow tie on a wrinkled short-sleeved shirt, poorly fitting slacks.

"I'm here to see Pal."

"Sure, sure. Mr. Birkness is with a client in his office — he's just putting a nice young girl like you into a good family car that can hold a dozen kiddos. So let me help you. Maybe give you some good points you can use to convince your husband that you want to go Chevy?"

"I'll look around on my own, and please have him find me when he is done with his business. It's most urgent."

"I got your number," said the salesman. He put two fingers to his temples like a psychic. "I'll bet I can read your mind. You're a frugal sort. Don't like spending more than you have to. But you recognize quality. I'll bet you're the sort that brings good facts to the table when your husband is making decisions. Say, I get it. I get that you want to scope things out before he gets involved and —" he made air quotes " — 'makes the choice.' That's okay with me, I'm a modern guy. My wife always tells me, 'Jake,' she says, 'Jake, the hardest part of being a woman is making you think what I want you to think without you knowing that it's me making you think it.'" Jake laughed. "I do say, she is mighty good at it. Probably like you, am I right?"

"Tell Pal to find me when he is free. Until then I will look by myself."

"Okay, okay, I can take a hint. When you're ready to talk, here's my card. You tell Mr. Birkness that I showed you around and helped you out now, won't you?"

"Oh, I'll be sure to," Delores said.

Jake winked and walked off toward another couple. He raised his hands as he greeted them.

She wandered for another twenty minutes or so, found herself next to a Corvette. A two-seater car, so intimate. Fast-looking. She opened the door and sat in the driver's seat, running her hand over the wheel, the gear shift, turning the radio on and off again with snapping clicks.

This was the kind of car she should get. The kind of car that would let her just leave, go anywhere. Drive up the coast to see Grandma. Find herself in Portland or Seattle or anywhere.

"These things sell like you wouldn't believe." It was Pal, suddenly next to her, leaning in, not so much as a footstep giving away his approach. He smelled of cinnamon gum and freshly-applied Lilac Vegetal.

"This is a nice car."

"I'd be happy to sell it to you."

"I'm not in the market."

"Everybody's in the market," he said. Then, with a smile, he added, "For something."

"You have somewhere private we can talk?" Delores said, exiting the Corvette. She pushed into Pal's personal space enough that he backed up as she stood. She walked toward the showroom, assuming he would follow.

Pal's office had a large desk atop a carpet with glittering gold specks, some photos of Sammi — one that Delores had taken that was cropped to her face, she was surprised to see — but mostly her as represented in paint. Behind him an original: Sammi in a bikini holding a foamy over-sized sponge and lying across the hood of a Chevy, one graceful hand draped over the shaft of the airplane ornament, a rivulet of soap and suds dripping off the bumper into a pool at her feet, the sponge drip-ping white onto her leg. It was signed: "To Pal, with warm regards and thanks, Gael Sarjeant."

"Can't tell you how many deals that has closed," Pal said, noticing her gaze. "Husbands come in here and can't stop gawking, so they love it. Wives want to get out of here as soon as possible. Make sure their men don't get any ideas that they can get a pin-up model for a fiancée like this old schlub. I should probably pay your old dad a commission."

"You probably should."

"So, what's the story here? Why do I get a nice visit?"

"I know about you and Mother."

Pal laughed. Leaned in his chair and opened a lacquered wooden box of cigarettes. Offered one to Delores. She accepted, and he stood and stretched across the desk to light it, then did one for himself, and settled back in his chair.

"I do like your Mother. She's a firecracker. Hell of a sailor, too. I'd like to say I can call her a friend. Her and your pop, of course."

Delores pulled the manila envelope from her bag and slid them across the desk. Pal opened it and pulled out the pictures. He looked through them, and then carefully replaced them. Opened a desk draw-er with a key, placed them inside, then closed and locked it again. Leaned back in his chair.

"Something about you just loves getting in my business."

"Really, I want nothing to do with you."

"I find that hard to believe. What are you going to do? Put some pressure on me? Try to get me to end it with your Mother? Tell me you have the negatives and other prints?"

"I want you to end it with Sammi."

Pal laughed.

"And Mother."

Pal leaned toward the desk, stubbed out his practically unsmoked cigarette in a clean ashtray, a Corvette logo silk-screened on the bottom. When it was out to his satisfaction he dumped it into a metal trash can next to his desk. He took a tissue, spit into the ashtray, and wiped it clean. Then he placed it back on the desk, just so.

"You got balls, I'll give you that. But I'm not changing anything. Sammi's gonna give me a family, and I want a family. I want a son and a daughter to share my hard work with. I want a wife to make me dinner every night and keep my house and make the neighbor's jealous. As for your Mother, well. Your Dad left her out to ripen on the branch. Is it a wonder somebody came along and plucked her?"

"You disgust me." Delores said, one arm across her belly, the other up at the elbow, cigarette dangling, ash growing.

"I have to confess, Lily is a bit older than I usually go for, but she's got something. Maybe it's all of those pin-ups I saw when she was modeling for your dad, all the Sarjeant's Sergeants stuff during the war. Man, I thought she was gorgeous. Still is. It's a little bit of a dream, to me. Really is, I tell you."

"Why would you think I want to hear this?"

"You're too emotional about this. Because there's a choice here. You could try to blackmail me, put those photos out there. Sure, you could. Maybe I would even bend a little this way or the other. But you're the one who hides things, Delores. You're the one who has something to lose if people find out about you. About you and Cora Fournier. What a scandal. She is a pillar of society. Too bad she's a pervert. What would the boards of all those charities she sits on say about a queer amongst them?" Pal's brow wrinkled. "Wait, is queer just a term for faggots, or can you use it for ladies who love ladies, too?"

Delores reached out to her side without even looking and ashed her cigarette, the spent gray flakes falling onto his golden carpet.

He leaned back in his chair, put his hands behind his head. "Well, whatever. It's rich, if you think about it, a lesbo trying to blackmail someone, anyone, in this day and age. You got nothing."

"You don't know what my dad is capable of if he found out."

"I'm not scared of your dad, sweetheart. He looks he can handle himself, but he's not the only one."

Pal leaned in again, palms on the desk, an open stature. He was not only unflappable, he actually seemed interested in this conversation.

"But hey, this has taken a dark turn. How about we shake hands to just leave each other be. In fact, as a show of good faith, I'm willing to slash the ticket on that Corvette.

"Imagine," he said. "Driving up the Coast, the top down, the wind blowing about your face, nice music on the radio. In fact, let's work something out right now. You take the car tonight, just drive it off my lot, and we'll figure out the rest later. I know where you live. I know you're good for it. Come on, Delores. Let's be friends. Let's make a deal."

Delores stood. Dropped her cigarette in the clean ashtray, let it lie there, its little steel-blue ribbon of smoke rising into the still air. "Sammi is so much better than you."

Pal sat again. "Oh, sweetheart, you really don't know anything, do you?"

It was full night by the time that Delores returned to Hollywood Film. The door was locked, but she went around to the alley, sidestepping garbage and sludge, and buzzed the doorbell by the back door. A moment later it was opened by a handsome young man.

"Yes?" he said, with a thick Mexican accent.

"I need Diego."

"He know you coming?"

"Get him."

The door opened. Delores followed the man inside. He was trim, in high-waisted pants and a crisp white shirt. All of eighteen, if that.

"You wait here," he said, and jogged to the office.

Through the windows Delores could see them. Could hear them. Men's laughter. Five or six of them, cheap suits all around. One with his jacket off and a revolver in a shoulder holster. They were around the round table. Diego, his cuffs rolled up and red suspenders keeping his pants aloft, laid out photos.

He placed one, they'd pass it around. Each jowly middle-aged fellow made some comment before passing it to the next. Everyone was smoking.

The young man put a hand on Diego's shoulder. Whispered in his ear. And Diego looked over and saw Delores. She waved. Other faces turned to look at her. Faces fell, got serious. Pictures were gathered into a single pile.

Diego held out his hands as if to say that all was fine. He made some joke and everybody around the table laughed. He came out of the office, took her arm, and pushed her to the very back of the space.

"Are you crazy? What the hell are you doing here? I'm doing business."

"I need something from you."

"You got some kind of addiction for favors?"

"That fellow in the photos your dick took. I need you to...put some pressure on him."

"I don't know what you're talking about. I saw no photos."

"Don't bullshit me, Diego."

"Even if I did see photos, I don't know what you mean, 'pressure.'"

"I want him to break up with his fiancée."

"Look sister, I don't know what you're implying, but just to be straight: did you come and interrupt my little moment with the police detectives in there to try to convince me to blackmail someone on your behalf?"

"I tried myself. He won't listen to me. If a man did it, he'd take you seriously. He'd listen to you."

"Jesus, doll. What the hell are you thinking?"

"Look me in the eye and tell me you don't do that."

"Even if I did, what makes you think I'd do it for you?"

"Don't. Do it for you. Get a little cash out of it. The mark is loaded."

Diego turned from her. Took a few steps to look back in the office, then came back.

"You need to leave now. You need to leave and never talk to me about this again."

"So you'll do it?"

Diego growled, flashed anger in his eyes. "You wait right here. Right here. Don't move. Don't come close enough to see in the office. You don't want those men to recognize you. You don't want to recognize them, if you saw them on the street."

He walked, stiff, leaning as if into a wind, into his office. He cracked some joke, and she heard laughter. A minute later the young man came out, holding a small package.

"Diego said to give you these. Your prints and negatives. He said you're done here. Don't come back. Some things are happening, understand? Don't come back."

"I want to talk to him."

The boy gave her a look of consternation. He was ridiculously handsome, even featured, dark complexion, black hair in a luxuriant wave. His skin had the kind of healthy suppleness that made one self-conscious, even under the horrible lights in the back of the shop.

"Who are you?" she said.

"I'm Carlos. I'm Diego's friend —" emphasis on the word *friend.* "I'm your friend. Please, you must leave now, is important. Stay away."

"I just want to make sure we're —"

"Go," Carlos said, his eyes pleading. Another round of laughter from the office.

"Okay, okay." Delores turned to leave. She reached for the door, and was stopped by a hand on her shoulder. Carlos whispered into her ear.

"He wishes he could say more. You *must* stay away. You must."

She nodded. Left the way she came. In the alley, a stumble drunk had just finished urinating but hadn't put away his business when Delores exited the building and startled him. He turned to her, a flash of white floppy finger against his dark pants. To walk away from him would take her down a long alley and away from where she left the car. She walked around him instead. As she passed he tried to whistle at her but was too drunk to accomplish the task. He just ended up blowing spittle on the side of her face before losing his balance and falling against the wall he had just peed on.

Delores headed toward the beach, wrapped in that bulky cardigan she wore when she shot Sammi on the beach.

In the package the boy had given her were indeed all of her Sammi negatives, as well as negatives of the pictures of Mother and Pal. She took the illicit shots, bundled them together, and put them inside her sweater.

She went down the hill to the beach, not knowing what she was doing, but needing to do something. The night was cool, but not chilling. It was a weeknight, but the beach was bustling, as always. The pier lights' colored halo blotted out the stars. People smiled, walked with stuffed animals, too late now for children. It was the realm of young lovers.

She went out onto the pier, intending to throw the photos in the trash or possibly tying them to a rock and tossing them off the pier into the water. But what if they washed up? What if a garbage man found them?

She wandered past the rides and the hawkers, the ratty cheapness sold by bright gloss and sugar. The uneven boards massaged her feet through her ballet flats.

She went to the rail, very close to where she had stopped with Mother not so long ago, where she could see that spot Sammi posed, the goddess of the beach. Wasn't it funny how that whole thing played out in a matter of minutes, but now it was the defining part of the beach to her?

A few minutes on a beach full of decades of such memories. The couple who met here, or had their first kiss there, or the woman who was attacked here, who might never feel safe to return. All of those memories that overlapped hers but were invisible. As if the place were storing them all, like a bottomless sponge containing all the water that ever crossed it.

Down on the beach some kids had a bonfire. They stood around, surfboards upright in the sand like sentinels that defined the room of their party. She left the pier and made her way along the beach and across to them, took off her shoes and let the velvet shore run between her toes.

They were college age. About fifteen of them, all standing around a fire that licked up to her height at times, maybe ten boys and five girls. One fellow had a guitar, but Delores could barely hear him across the fire, his voice and the strings getting lost amid the wind and fluttering of the flames.

She came up beside a young man with dark hair, made shaggy by the wind, who wore a white windbreaker and jeans.

"Mind if I join you?" Delores said.

He turned to her, amusedly gave her a once-over. "I'd say I don't mind at all, just so long as you'll drink a beer with us and give worship to the goddess of the flame." Then he cupped his hand and bellowed, "Sergeant at Arms! A beverage, if you please!"

Across the fire from them a skinny fellow with a beard stood to attention and saluted, then he took from a cooler a bottle and haphazardly tossed it toward them, tumbling in its trajectory.

White Windbreaker snatched the bottle out of the air deftly, then produced an opener from a pocket and uncapped it. He handed the frothing, overflowing beer to Delores.

She nodded her thanks and took a drink, then she said, "How do I give worship to the goddess?"

The man nodded, face open to her. "Yes, yes, a good question. There are many ways one can worship the goddess. You can do so in a carnal fashion." He waved a hand toward a couple just outside the firelight, lying together, making out on the beach. "Or, perhaps, you could be like the bard and offer song." He motioned toward the guitar player. "Franklin over there —" a man lying face down in the sand, laughing at girl who was poking him in the ribs "— well, Franklin pulled down his pants and broke wind at the goddess, who repaid him by ridding his hindquarters of bodily hair via sacred flame. I give honor by sharing our repast with beautiful strangers who may be convinced to become new indoctrinates into this religion we ourselves have discovered this very evening."

Delores smiled and took a swig from the bottle. "In that case," she said, "as a goddess worshiper of the old order, I offer my approval, and I do have a sacrifice." She reached inside her sweater and withdrew the envelope. She stepped closer to the fire and held out the package, gripping the envelope with the tips of her fingers to get it as near as possible. The paper caught fire, and Delores held it upright as it burned, a small torch throwing orange light on her face.

"And if I may be so bold as to inquire, m'lady, what exactly are the contents of this envelope you so sacrifice?"

Delores looked at him, his drunken swagger, his humorous air. She threw the envelope into the fire, and watched the whole thing catch. The front of her body fevered with the warmth of the flames, her back chilled by the cool, humid beach air.

"Those are the negatives and prints of pictures of my mother screwing my lover's fiancé," she said, hugging her arms.

The man's face fell into a serious countenance. He held the look for a few beats as her words penetrated his hazed thoughts. Then he laughed, a sudden guffaw.

And then he started jumping into the air, again and again, arms stretched above him, as he called out, "God-DESS! God-DESS!" with every leap. Others joined him: Sergeant at Arms, then Franklin, who got to his feet, and the girl with him. Even the couple making out stopped to join in.

Delores felt a lightening at burning those negatives. She was not the sort of person to join in this stupid revelry. But she was not, she hoped, the sort of person who didn't take advantage of a moment presented to her. Arranged, perhaps, by the goddess. How could she not pay homage? She held her beer aloft, sloshing it down her arm. The group of them jumped in tandem and shouted, "God-DESS! God-DESS! God-DESS!" as the remnants of the negatives and prints curled, turned to char, and were safely removed from existence by the goddess of the fire.

XII

A WEEK LATER, on a bright and beautiful af-
ternoon, Delores came to Sammi's apartment. She laid out a series of
photos on the kitchenette table while Sammi was in the bathroom, ar-
ranging them, then considering and rearranging again, until they sat
just so. A diorama, of Delores asleep in Sammi's bed. There were only
two photos, but Delores had Diego pull multiple exposures and crops,
trying to draw some interest out of the fairly mundane pictures.

"What the hell are these?" Sammi said when she returned.

"They're me. They're the pictures you took of me."

"Why did you bring them? Why even print them?" Sammi was in a
bikini, black with white polka dots. Sunglasses held her hair back atop
her head. Barefoot on the cool wood of the floors, toes recently painted
red. A scar across her right knee caught the light in such a way that Delores noticed it for the first time, and wondered if it appeared on any of
the photos she had taken. She had kissed that knee without seeing it.

"You took them. I thought you might like to see your handiwork."

"I just wanted to see what the big thrill was on the other side of the camera. And they're not very good, anyway."

"You don't want them?"

"What if somebody finds them?"

"As long as you don't inscribe 'My lesbian lover, Delores,' on the back, I suspect anybody who found them would simply think they were amateurish nudes."

Sammi snorted. "Amateurish. Thanks for that."

"Oh, come now. You were the one who said they weren't very good."

"Fine, I'll keep them."

"You're welcome."

"Fine. Thank you, I guess."

"You are completely out of sorts. Do you want me to leave? We can shoot another day, you know."

Sammi shrugged. She sauntered to the bed. "Nothing else to do." She flopped, lying on her side, one arm stretched out as if she were doing a sidestroke, her head resting on her bicep. Her other hand held a cigarette close to her mouth.

Delores reached into her satchel and picked out an envelope. Dad had given her an advance on the money she'd earn from *Playboy*, once they paid.

"This is for all of the modeling you've done for me."

Sammi sat up. Put her cigarette into the ashtray. Took the envelope and looked inside. "I thought we were doing it just for fun."

"It is fun. But I made a bargain with my dad. I have to pay you to take photos of you."

"Well, isn't that just grand."

"You're upset?"

"Well, you've gone and turned me from a slut into a whore in one fell swoop."

"Whoa, wait a minute. I just want to respect your time."

"My time isn't yours to do anything with. I'm the one who chooses where to spend it."

"My god, you are driving me mad. What the hell is on with you?"

"Can't a girl just have a day? Why do you have to jump down my throat if I'm not perfectly peachy for you. Maybe other people's lives aren't perfect sometimes. Have you ever thought about that?"

"I think I missed something," Delores said.

"Oh, yes, you missed something, all right. Maybe spend a little less time gawking at my boobs and legs next time and spend a little more time really looking at me." Sammi held up her left hand and waved it around.

"I don't understand. Can you just tell me?"

Sammi gave Delores the bird with her left hand. No, she wasn't — it was her ring finger that stuck out. And it was empty.

"Oh god, did you lose your ring?"

Sammi snorted. "Yeah. And the fella who put it there for safekeeping."

"Pal broke it off?"

Sammi lit another cigarette, even though the one in the ashtray was still burning.

"He might as well have, that coward," she said.

"Tell me what happened."

"Hell if I know!" Sammi said. "One day everything was normal, and the next he says that maybe things are moving too fast and maybe we should slow down and maybe he thinks I can do better than him."

Delores sat next to Sammi on the bed. Put her arm around her, and Sammi lay her head on Delores's shoulder. "That fool."

Sammi was leaden. Delores held her, supported her weight. Sammi's cigarette, resting lightly in her hand, threatened to drop ashes on her bare lap. Delores took it and ashed it, then put it back between Sammi's fingers. Its smoke curled in the sunlight of the room.

"You know what the worst part is?" Sammi said.

"Tell me."

"I don't love him. But he broke my heart anyway."

Then she pushed Delores away and stood. "Let's go take some photos."

"We can do it another time."

"I need to do something. I hate this feeling sorry for myself."

They started on the roof of the building. Sammi walked the stairs slow, shoulders slumped, hips swaying with each step. She held her arm against the light when she pushed open the door. A hot day, but gauzy with brown smog.

Sammi muttered, "What a beautiful goddamned day," flopped into an Adirondack chair, and lit a cigarette.

Delores loaded film, and when she turned the lens toward her model, Sammi responded as if injected with some serum. She sat up, her body responding to a silent call for action. A wry smile replaced her frown as Delores pressed the trigger, moved, pressed the trigger.

Sammi spread her legs, thighs apart, the polka dots of the bikini distorting as they went under her. A smile just on the tip of one side of her thin lips, a drag of the cigarette, a peek over the tops of her sunglasses.

Delores knew it was false, that inside Sammi was turmoil and disappointment, but maybe the constraint of being present and aware of the camera pushed that down to a more manageable place.

A couple of rolls later they decided to go down to the apartment. Delores had Sammi stay at the top of the stairs, the light of the transom door enveloping her, leaking around her silhouette. She shot Sammi on the stairs with the aluminum nosing. Sammi descended, glasses atop her head and holding back her hair, a windbreaker over her shoulder, heels making her leg muscles defined as she took the steps down one by one.

Then she sat on the bottom stair and moved her body around, leaning back, leaning over, leaning forward and planting her palms on the floor. Delores moved, framed, and shot, disappearing into the moment of her work.

Sammi lit another cigarette. "I'm bored." Her face fell, the smile only for the camera, and a whiff of annoyance lifted one side of her mouth. She motioned to her apartment door. She blew a bit of hair from her face, and it flopped back. "Let's go in."

Back inside, Delores went to the closet and pulled out Sammi's most feminine dress. She threw it onto the bed. Picked out some heels, stockings, and a teddy to go underneath.

"Get dressed," she said. "I'm taking you dancing tonight."

The bar was called Jack's Waves, a quiet-seeming tile-fronted joint in Hollywood. The feeling there was very different than in San Francisco, where recent busts had turned the women into activists. Here it was casual. It followed the conventions of most lesbian bars Delores had been to: butches in menswear and femmes in dresses. Here, some men were mixed in — obviously gay men out with their lesbian friends. There was a jukebox, and occasional half-hearted dancers or ladies who liked to show off would get up and move around a bit. Delores was sure she could get Sammi on the floor after a drink or two, and the idea of swaying with her as she had with Red Dress gave a heartbeat to the night.

Delores sent Sammi to get a booth while she got drinks, a beer and a whiskey for her, a white wine for Sammi. The bartender, dressed like Delores in a suit coat and men's shirt, hair parted in the middle and falling down the sides of her face, delivered the drinks to the bar. As Delores was laying out her payment, the bartender nodded her head to where Sammi was sitting.

"Best watch out for that one," she said. Delores turned to find a young greaser leaning over the table. Jeans, motorcycle jacket, dark hair combed back.

"You got a problem if your place has men hitting on folks here."

"You got it all wrong," said the bartender, turning her back to Delores. "But be careful all the same."

Delores carried the drinks to the table.

"She's with me," Delores said. The greaser turned around, and Delores saw a young woman's thin face with a sharp nose and a sneer. A very fine-featured feminine look, big animal eyes with long lashes. The leather sent a different message than the delicateness of her features. She looked Delores up and down.

"Aw, look at the little butchy. Wants to play dress up and be like a businessman." She turned to Sammi. "C'mon. Come dance with me, sweetheart. I know how to have fun."

Delores couldn't get a bead on Sammi. She didn't seem to be discouraging this pick-up. Surely she saw through this cry-for-attention in leather. This two-bit idiot dressed up like a cheap Hollywood tabloid version of tough.

Delores felt invincible. Whatever happened, she needed to hold her ground and defend her turf. It was the code of the butch: a butch did not hit on another butches' femme. This bitch was breaking the code. A good butch defended her femme. Kept the predators away, be they men or other women.

"You're not hearing me," Delores said. She put the drinks on the table. She scooped up the whiskey and took it in one gulp, then slammed the empty shot glass face down on the table. "She is with me, sister." She stood tall, facing the little leather punk.

The greaser was shorter than Delores. Skinny, but that was hard to tell in those square cut dungarees cinched overly tight with a black belt that extended a good four inches past the buckle, as if she had tried on Daddy's work clothes. To go with her long face she had a long torso, in a crisp white tee. The shirt rode beneath her black leather jacket and was tucked into the jeans. She smelled like Brylcreem and gasoline. The greaser threw back her shoulders.

"Fuck you," she said. "I ain't no sister of yours. I'm just talking here. It's a free country, ain't it? I wanna talk to her, seems like it's her choice whether she wants to talk back, and she ain't told me to leave yet."

"I'm the one telling you to leave," Delores said, teeth clamped together.

"Who the fuck are you? This is my bar. My bar, my town. I've never seen you before, and I know every dyke in Hollywood. You come in here, thinking you got it all figured out. Dressed in that stupid uniform, following some stupid rules some stupid hags all made up before any of us was born. Fuck that."

Delores pushed her. A solid hit on the shoulder. The greaser fell backwards into some chairs, but managed to hold herself upright. The whole bar turned, twenty pairs of eyes now riveted on what was unfolding.

The action surprised even Delores, who had never been in a fight. It was as if she was pushed to a precipice by the greaser, a line she couldn't help crossing, like the moon's gravity pulling water until it hits the upswell of land before the beach.

"Push me again," she said. "I dare ya." Click. A knife in her hand.

"No!" came a voice from behind the bar, and then the unmistakable sound of a shotgun getting pumped. The bartender held the weapon to her shoulder and pointed it at the greaser. "Not in my place, Sally. You're banned. Out. Now."

The greaser held up a hand as if to say *okay*. She slowly folded the switchblade closed and held it aloft. "Okay. Okay, Jack. Didn't mean to start anything."

"Out!"

She jammed her shoulder into Delores as she passed. Sprung the door open with all of her might and tried to slam it, but its mechanism caught and pulled it closed with a whisper.

The bartender pointed the barrels of her gun to the floor. "I told you she was trouble," she said to Delores. "Why the hell'd you have to start something?"

"She was hitting on my lady. I couldn't peel her off."

"Look, you best drink up and get out too. I don't need this kind of grief in my place."

Delores sat down, her hands shaking from the adrenaline of it all. Sammi took two big gulps of her wine, eyes wide.

"Why didn't you tell me it was like this!" she said. "This is the most exciting thing I've ever seen. You shoulda took me out ages ago."

After Jack's they went to another place Delores had heard of. Smaller, less crowded, more men in the mix. The Midnight Lounge.

But this place had no dancing, so Delores wasn't able to take Sammi in her arms and show her off, wasn't able to feel her warm body against her while other people paid attention or didn't.

"I wanted to show you what it could be like. That it could be normal, us being together. Just like any other people. Guess I failed."

"It's true, no fellow ever hit on me while I was out with Pal."

"Why do you think he broke it off?"

"I told you. He said it was better for me. Sounds like bullshit."

"Sounds like bullshit," Delores agreed. "He ever make you feel something? I mean, like I do?"

Sammi laughed; looked around; leaned in.

"No way. Nobody ever made me feel like that. I used to think Pal was an okay lover, but he can't hold a stick to you."

"That's because you're a lesbian."

"Stop saying that."

"Why?"

"Because I'm not."

"Could have fooled me. Have you ever had a man make you feel as good as I do when I touch you?"

"No, but that's not the point."

"What is the point, then?"

"Do we have to go into it? Why work so hard to tie a neat little bow on it?"

"Because I love you. I want to be with you."

"For the love of Mary, you don't listen, do you? We're not going to be like that. I'm not going to be with you except like we have, and if you keep talking you're gonna ruin that too."

"Look, it's just that I really got it when I was up in San Francisco. I learned it, and I want to teach you. It's so much better if you're honest with yourself. If you admit to yourself what you really want. Stop lying to yourself."

Sammi rolled her eyes. "You lie to yourself about me. You don't know who I am."

"I know enough."

Sammi laughed. "Really? Did you know about this?" She reached into the dress, over her breast, and pulled out something she had tucked there — a little scrap of paper. "Here's the phone number of that hot number in the leather from the last bar. I was gonna ditch you later and give her a call. Bet she wouldn't get all sappy on me, would she?"

Delores took another drink of beer. Put down the glass.

"You're bluffing."

"Do you really think so?"

"You would do that to me? Break my heart like that?"

"You don't own my heart, Delores. Nobody gets to own my heart but me. I mean, I'll be clear, you taught me a lot. You gave me a boost and confidence to jump off the cliff. But now that I jumped, I'm not going to settle down. I want to see what the rest of the world is like. I'm not going to be your steady girl. I'm not going to be *anybody's* steady girl anymore. I'm going to do what I want, and nobody is gonna get in my way anymore. I'm gonna go steady with myself and treat myself real good for a change."

One part of Delores — the part that was filled with helium and wanted to just be herself in the world — was rising, but the other part of Delores — the part that wanted Sammi on her arm, to show the world that this was part of who she was — was all lead weights. The push pull of the rising and falling made her a bit crazed. All this after she had fought that greaser for Sammi? This was how she was repaid?

Delores took another swig of her beer and put it down extra gently. She leaned in and told Sammi: "You're going to be in *Playboy*. I sold a photo. Everybody in the country is going to see you naked."

"I didn't sign your damn contract. You can't do that."

"You're going to love it. You love being watched, being seen so much."

"You didn't, Delores. So help me. I'll get a lawyer and sue you blind. I'll make you wish you'd never met me."

She stood. "Call her, then. Call her for a ride home." Delores tossed a five dollar bill on the table. "Or call a cab for all I care."

She stopped as she was leaving. Turned back to Sammi, who had her arms folded, her lips pressed into a pout.

"Why is it, Sammi? Why is that I'm surrounded by only the cruelest of women?"

Sammi scoffed. Made her hands into fists and pretended to rub her eyes. "Poor wittle Dewores. All the girls are mean to me. Boo hoo hoo."

XIII

THE TORTURE of staying with her parents was that Delores could not escape. Lying in bed she heard Sammi's voice that next morning. She opened her eyes, looked at the nail wall, Tanny Le Clercq's impalement. Sammi's laugh, without a care, from outside. How could she be happy this morning? How could anybody?

Delores snuck from her bed, onto her knees, over to the drapes and parted them. She peered out to see Sammi ascend the stairs with Dad, a mug of steaming coffee in his hand, the other on the small of Sammi's back, guiding her, smiles on their faces. Did nothing happen last night? Sammi should've been sullen and cross.

Delores sat and looked out again. Just at the top of the stairs, before they entered the studio door, Sammi turned and looked right at Delores. Delores gasped and let the drapes fall shut. When she peeked again a few seconds later, the door of the studio was closed.

She tried to sleep again, but even after pulling the covers over her head, the tick-tick-tick of her bedside clock was amplified into a telltale rhythm, disturbing and relentless.

In the kitchen she found Mother, still in her own robe, working the percolator. They sat, both wordless, both sporting the signs of weariness on their faces, waiting for the brewing to stop. Circles under their eyes. When the light went out, Mother poured two mugs and placed them on the table. They both reached for a cigarette at the same time and bumped hands, paused to let the other go first, and then bumped hands again. Mother snatched the pack, took one, and skittered it across the table at Delores. They smoked and drank in absolute silence together.

Finally, Mother gave a sigh after getting in a few sips. "I think Perino's for your birthday."

"I've never been," Delores said.

"How many? I'll take care of reservations."

"What about just the three of us? If Dad will stop working long enough."

"Really? I thought you and Sammi were as thick as thieves."

"What's wrong with the three of us? How much time do we spend together alone?"

"Nothing wrong with it, of course. I'll make the reservation."

Each of them lit another cigarette.

"Look, I don't know about you," Mother said, "but I could have slept all day. Maybe it looks like you could have too. Why don't we play hooky and go watch a matinee of *The Blackboard Jungle*? It's showing downtown. Maybe get some lunch while we're at it?"

"That's a marvelous idea," Delores said, "sitting in a dark room."

Mother turned her head quick, like an animal watching for a predator's shadow amongst moving leaves. Delores looked too and saw Sammi coming down the stairs. But she saw them, stopped, took one step forward, then gave a quick huff and turned again, climbed the stairs and closed the door to the studio.

Then Delores had hope again. Because Sammi had looked annoyed at seeing her, so, Delores knew, she was suffering because of last night as well.

———

This was the first stretch of time Delores had spent with Mother since learning of her affair. While Delores again pulled on the clunky cardigan sweater and blue jeans she wore to the beach, her mother made an effort. She wore green Capri pants, white tennis shoes without socks, and a white blouse with embroidered flowers on the shoulders. A scarf contained her hair.

Delores watched her during the movie. Mother brought the popcorn to her mouth a kernel at a time and chewed it slowly during the dramatic scenes in the film. A film full of bombast and explosive moments. Mostly, it held Delores's attention, but at times she just closed her eyes and replayed the night before, wondering what she could have done differently. Wondering whether Sammi called that greaser girl or just left on her own. What a fool Delores had made of herself.

After the movie Delores waited in the lobby while Mother used the restroom. A girl with a messy head of dirty blonde hair, eleven or so, right on the awkward transitional cusp of adolescence, was standing before a poster for an upcoming movie titled *Rebel Without a Cause*. She wore a simple cotton dress, saddle shoes, and white ankle socks. She was chewing gum slowly, mouth fully opening with each jaw descent, enraptured.

Perhaps sensing Delores's attention, she turned. She smiled. "I'm waiting for my mom," she said.

"As it happens, so am I."

"You're not waiting for my mom."

"No, I meant mine. We just came out of the movie."

"We're just going in. Did you like it?"

"Yes, I did. Why aren't you in school?"

"Oh, you know how moms are. She took me out for a couple days to go bum around and have a good time. Says it's good for the soul. Plus, I get good grades, so the teachers need some time to catch the rest of the class up. My mother is very bohemian, you see." She rolled her eyes.

"Yes. I do see. What do you think about that?" Delores pointed at the James Dean poster. "Do you think you'll see that?"

"Oh, sure! Didn't you see *East of Eden*? He was quite spectacular. A real presence on screen." The girl flapped her lips as she chewed her gum, smacking and making cracking sounds every few chews.

"I just met someone who reminds me of him, in that picture." The poster was split in two. The right half showed Dean leaning against a brick wall, one foot up, rolled jeans, a black motorcycle leather, a white shirt, one hand on his hip, the other holding a cigarette.

"Was he dreamy?" said the girl.

"She, and no. I thought she was horrible."

"Huh. A girl? A real tomboy type, I'd say."

"You could say that."

"Well, I'm not judgmental. If that's how a friend of mine wanted to dress, I'd just judge her on other criteria, I think."

"Such as?"

"Well...." The girl bit her bottom lip, which Delores was grateful for since it stopped the chewing and smacking. "Well, I think I would judge her mostly on how she treated me."

Then Mother was there. "Are we ready?" she said.

"Ready," Delores said, then to the girl, "That's wise advice. Nice to talk to you."

"Likewise," said the girl.

"Darling," Mother said, leaning across Delores. "Chew with your mouth closed. I'm sure your mother tells you, too, but it's very unladylike."

The girl clamped her mouth and gave a sheepish grin. Delores turned back when they were going through the doors. She was staring at the poster again, mouth flapping just like before. Spittle spittle snap.

Clifton's was right across the street, so that's where they had their lunch. They each picked a salad, and Mother got a BLT for them to split. Delores drank a fountain 7-Up.

Sitting at the table closest to the wildlife scenery, Delores watched as Mother picked at her food. She opened her sandwich and pulled out a slice of bacon, nibbled the end of it for a few moments, then put it down. She took a bite of salad, chewed slowly, then put down her fork.

"I guess I'm not really hungry," she said, with a sigh, and lit a cigarette. Delores was already done eating.

"Something has you down. You seem out of sorts." Delores said, aware that the same could be said of her.

Mother rolled her eyes, waved her hand. "I'm just off today. Nothing more to say about it than that."

"Did you like the movie?"

"It was fine. I could stand to see a double feature, to be honest."

"You really are blue about something, aren't you?"

Mother waved her off again, but Delores could see her eyes fill. She blinked, frowned, looked away, snorted, then put a hand over her mouth to subsume a sob. She put down her cigarette and reached for a napkin to dab at her eyes.

Delores reached out and took her Mother's hand. Mother took a few deep wavery breaths, steadying herself, but a trickle of tears came down each cheek no matter how hard she tried to keep it back.

"I hate crying," she said, bleary. "God."

"Tell me what it is," Delores said.

"Oh, it's nothing. It's just silly emotions."

"If it's about Pal, if that's what has you down, I know about him and you."

Mother made a surprised jerk of the head, which struck Delores as almost chicken-like.

"When you moved back and I said a little warning would be nice because we have lives, well, this is what I was referring to. Some of us like to keep private things private."

"Did he dump you, too?"

"What do you mean, 'too'"?

"Well, he broke it off with Sammi."

"Ugh," Mother said. "He told me that. He's such a fool." She took another cigarette, looked at Delores as if deciding whether to broach the topic fully or attempt to let it remain private. She dabbed at her eyes again and then took a deep breath.

"Okay, fine," she said after a moment. "For your information, I dumped him, as you put it. He got it into his head that I could be all his. So he dumped Sammi to convince me that he was serious and I should sail away with him into the sunset. Literally. On his boat. Into the sunset. What a fool.

"Why the hell would I want that? I have a husband who provides for me. Who knows who I am, and I know him. He is predictable, a fact I give no small amount of allegiance too. Why throw it away for some momentary excitement? Excitement fades. He would find some girl to bed inside of a month of having me to himself. He is not a loyal type, he's a hunter."

She looked at the ceiling and blew smoke upward. "You know, Delores, I'm the opposite of what my mother warned me against. I give away the milk, and the village idiot wants to buy the cow anyway, just so he can brand it."

"So, then, you dumped him?"

"Good riddance."

"What does Dad think about all of this?"

Mother sighed and brushed some ash from the table.

"He doesn't know?"

"Would you take the habit of informing your husband you were seeing somebody behind his back?"

"I thought maybe you were some of those progressive people you read about."

"Delores, don't think badly of me. Your father does nothing but work. I was bored silly. I needed some attention, and that oaf couldn't keep his eyes or hands off of me. I was flattered and gave in and had a little fun with the whole thing. You can always count on a good time with him. It's always a party with Pal. But all of us knew it was a lark."

Delores stacked the dishes on their table, then used a napkin to clean the crumbs. Then she lit a cigarette.

"It seems cheap," she said.

"So, you've learned I'm not above cheapness." Mother sighed, obviously more comfortable with defensiveness than vulnerability. Then she stood and gathered their things, signaling that lunch was done.

In the car, driving home, Mother was struck by a thought and blurted, "Oh, god, you didn't tell Sammi, did you?"

"No. And I won't. I won't be seeing her anymore."

"Oh? Did you two have a falling out?"

"You could say. We had a big fight."

"About what?"

"You are just not going to want to hear this," Delores said, "but I'm going to say it anyway. I want to be more open about who I love. I want to be open with my family that I love women. I want to tell you this, even though you already know."

Delores paused, wondering why these words made her tongue so thick and clumsy. "Mother, I'm a lesbian."

Mother sat up straighter in her seat. Looked at her mirrors. There was one thing about Mother, if you agitated her she needed to talk it out. She could not hold back a negative emotion. She had to toss them off herself, like a dog shaking off rain.

"We don't need to talk about it, dear. And I didn't know that you and Sammi were anything more than girlfriends. I'd prefer not to know."

"I get the feeling you'd rather talk about your affair than my love life."

"Neither is a topic I'm all that comfortable with."

"Well, here's the truth of it. Sammi and I had a love affair. I was bored with Cora — I was bored with my marriage, just like you were with yours. I left because I wanted some excitement and adventure. *Quelle surprise!* The apple lays right next to the tree."

"Please do not compare your employment situation with my marriage of thirty-two years."

"My employment situation. You are so good at using plain words as knives. When are you going to accept that I am a lesbian?"

"God, I hate that word," Mother said. "I've always hated that word. It's so libidinous."

"What about Sapphic? Does that rise to your level? Or how about I say I'm a daughter of Diana? A dyke?"

"Oh, for the love of...now you're just poking me with a stick."

"If there is no language you will accept from me, then you aren't even seeing me as the person I am. You're like a company denying that a worker has rights."

"Oh, Jesus," Mother said.

"Cora is my wife. We are married."

Mother laughed. She gestured, perhaps to cars around them, or people on the street. "Who here would recognize that marriage? What a farce you are presenting. A marriage. There is absolutely no truth to it. What church would recognize it? What state would offer a license?"

"We're married in each other's eyes. In our friends' eyes. We're married by our choice of being together."

Mother thinned her lips. She pulled the car to the curb. Put it into park and turned it off. She turned to Delores and spoke sharp and sure, a finger wagging in stern reproach, like a little hammer to pound the nails of her point.

"You make a mockery of that word. Married. Indeed. First, by assuming that it applies to whatever sickness you have involved yourself in. Second, in that even if I were to accept that the word applied to you, how good is your marriage now that you have left her? You don't have a marriage. You are playing house at the behest of a powerful woman who seduced you with a luxurious lifestyle beyond your means. She took you away from yourself. You've been lost to us for years."

"You don't know her. You don't know what she is like." Delores surprised even herself with the vibrancy she brought to defending Cora, and defending a relationship that, until the last day or so, she considered dead.

"You don't think I know money? I've seen what money does. It corrupts and pollutes the souls of those who possess it. Every dollar she holds was taken off the backs of working men, and the families they could barely support. Your grandfather —"

"My grandfather has been dead for nearly twenty years, and I'm a little tired of hearing him preach to me from beyond the grave."

"Your grandfather fought your 'wife's' grandfather tooth and nail. Industrialists like him were the worst kind of villain. Good men died in his factories and mines, leaving children and wives without any means of support. Union men beat senseless by paid security guards. By the National Guard. By police whose salary was paid by the taxes imposed by the corrupt state on those same working men, and then the bosses didn't have to pay any taxes themselves, thanks to getting the politicians in their back pocket.

"All those people — all they wanted was to work a fair day and earn a fair wage, and the Fournier family and the Rockefeller family and the Carnegie family and the Guggenheim family all sold the very humanity out of their souls to stomp their faces in the mud because they could. Because it gained them another five percent of the already obscene profits.

"So, that park view apartment you like to crow about? That apartment is paid for in blood. So don't you tell me I don't know that woman. I know that woman. She bought my daughter. She bought any hope of a grandchild by turning you into some sort of freak. She's horrible, and I know her, as surely as I know myself. I know her kind."

Mother exhaled a bull's breath through her nostrils. She took her cigarettes and lighter, having to snatch at them a few times. She threw open the driver's side door, a truck swerving just in time to avoid taking it off, a Doppler of honks down the road as it went. She walked around the car, and Delores saw her attempting to light a cigarette with a visibly shaky hand.

Nearby were a median strip and a park, mostly shaded by gnarled old trees. Mother walked to a bus stop and sat on the wooden slat bench, smoking, fuming.

Delores exited the car into the sweet green stink of recently mowed lawn. She walked to Mother and squatted next to her. She lowered her voice so as to mask her anger. To not let Mother feel like anything she said had any effect on Delores.

"Your stories are stuck in seventy-year-old battles. Stories an old activist told his impressionistic daughter around a labor camp stove. You want to be political? Take your pick. Fight for negro integration rights in the South. Fight for women to be fully recognized partners in marriages and society. Fight for my ability to love the people I want to love. Stop being such a coward and fight a fight that's happening right now, and happening to your own daughter."

Mother's gaze remained fixed in the distance, on a gas station across the street. Delores herself wondered whether she'd meant the words rhetorically or literally, but Mother didn't look away from whatever held her attention for a full minute. So Delores sat next to her Mother on the bench. A bus came and stopped, opening its doors, but Delores waved it off and the driver shook his head, and muttered loud enough for them to hear "stupid broads" before it pulled away.

"You need to see this like I do," Mother said, softly, after another minute or two passed.

"No," Delores said. "I'm tired of seeing it your way. I need you to see me. I came here because I need you. Can't you see that?"

Mother's angry, stern energy dissipated into something softer at that idea, that her daughter needed her. "There is no authority in the world that thinks having a sexual relationship with a member of your own sex is healthy. Trust me. I read everything I could get my hands on."

Delores snorted. "You know who they always neglect to ask? People who are in those relationships. Somehow they never ask us if we're healthy or not."

"Well dear, what would you expect? Would you ask an alcoholic if they have a good relationship with vodka?"

"You need to read the Kinsey Report. It's not a sickness. It's not an addiction. It's not even that rare. It's been written about since our earliest histories. I'm the opposite of confused about who I am. I'm not going to change."

Mother sighed. Sat up straight.

"Fine. I will never approve. Never."

"I'm not looking for you to give me your approval, Mother. I'm looking for you to see me with truth and honesty."

Mother nodded but didn't reply. They sat, watching the shadow of trees fall across the road.

They sat quietly a long time, occasionally smoking. Finally Mother said, "Do you suppose there's another movie on tonight that we could go see?"

"God," Delores said. "I really hope so."

XIV

"LISTEN, WE ALL just really love the work, and we want you to do more for us. Did you get the contracts?"

"Yes, Mr. Hefner," Delores said into the phone handset.

"Fine, fine. This is a bit rare, having a girl photographer. Just so you know, I have a very clear idea of what I want. If you meet those standards, that's just grand, but you may have to suffer quite a bit of rejection. Are you prepared for that?"

"You're the boss," Delores said. "I can take direction."

"We do have themes. We'll give you a call and let you know, give you time to find a model and shoot her inside the purview of that theme. Speaking of which, your model is fantastic. She's somewhat my ideal Bunny, although her breasts are a bit modest for the tastes of my readers."

"There's no lack of busty models in Los Angeles."

Hefner laughed. "No, I suspect not. Just make sure they're not too Hollywood or too burlesque. We want the kind of girl you could see in

Anytown, America, but the one who makes the boys turn and look as she strolls by. We're looking for a kind of nostalgia. To present our readers with the normal girl in their lives that they had an unfulfilled desire for.

"I have your first shots slated for October currently, that's an issue date. Street date will be much earlier of course. Probably close production on them in July."

"I have one problem I need to discuss with you," Delores said. "I think I need to get you a model release."

"I'm quite sure you did. It's noted in your file that we have it."

"That signature...well, I need to get you another one."

"Go on."

"Look, I just need to make sure she signed it in her right mind."

"Right mind? Does she have any mental issues? Is that what you're getting at?"

"Oh, no, not like that. She's not getting taken advantage of. I just need to...look, when would you need the release by?"

"Look, I don't have time to muck around with basic things like model releases. Why don't we pull this photo. We haven't sent a check yet. You have things to straighten out, fine, but you have to do it on your own time, not mine."

"Thanks. I'm sorry, it was just that —"

"Look, Delores, this is 101 stuff here. It's totally unprofessional of you to not have this all in hand before you approached us. I'm working with Bunny Yeager down in Florida. She's doing knockout work for us, but she knows how to run her shop. If you need tips, look her up. Get your house in order, okay? Maybe try us when you've got that all figured out. Best of luck to you, Miss Sarjeant. Please do tell your pop I'd love to work with him. Sorry it didn't work out this time."

"I miss you today," Delores whispered into the phone.

"I can't tell you how happy I am to hear that," Cora said. "I miss you every day."

"I feel that I'm not in control of my own destiny here," Delores said. "I did sell some photographs for publication. To *Playboy*."

"Really? Nudes?"

"Yes. Of that girl I was telling you about, Sammi. But the whole deal fell apart."

"Oh, dear. Is the affair going poorly?"

Delores clucked. "She's a model. She only cares about whatever lens is paying attention to her."

"Well, congratulations. I suspect there are more models in the world than skilled photographers to capture them. I'm sure you can make a good living at that."

"I'm surprised to hear you say that."

"I believe in you, Delores. I'm just going to say it, and you can choose to believe it or not believe it."

"I'll choose to believe it."

"Well, there you go. Did you decide where to have dinner for your birthday?"

"Yes, at Perino's. Mother made the reservations for three of us."

"Well, that's a small party. What night?"

"The twenty-third. On my birthday."

"Wonderful. It's going to be a wonderful night."

Then Delores was flooded with sudden regret. Cora had always been true to her. Cora had always stood by her. Cora was trustworthy and stable. Cora loved Delores in a way that Sammi seemed incapable of, with an ongoing extension of trust and unequivocal forgiveness. The only way to put it was that Cora loved Delores as a wife, and Sammi — if she loved Delores at all — only loved her as a fling, a short-term lover. Wasn't this why she argued with Mother about it? Calling Cora her wife? My god, so many ways that Delores had taken wrong turns in this life.

With that regret, Delores saw Sammi in a different light. As a juvenile, someone who needed guidance and an adult hand to help her react to things the right way. How could you be angry with a toddler for hitting you in frustration?

"I want to say one thing, Delores, and then I won't mention it again. When I talk about you coming home, I'm not talking about you doing all the change. I'm willing to own up my responsibility for what happened. I want you beside me, and I will open up any part of me for inspection and discussion if that is the price of winning your hand again. I want you here again, beside me."

"As what?"

"I don't follow."

"As your secretary? As your friend? As your companion?"

"No. No, Delores. As my partner. As my lover. As my wife. Where you belong"

Delores snuck up the stairs, trying not to make a sound or telegraph that she was coming. She peered in the glass inset with one eye, hoping that however Sammi was posing, she was facing away from the door. She was — her head turned away from Delores. She was fiddling with a strap attached to a zip-up flight suit, ripped across one breast and down her front, unveiling brightly colored lace. Ropes were tied to pulleys in the ceiling. Delores could picture the painting being made — a parachutist caught in the trees, suit ripped open, showing her extra-military lingerie.

She watched Sammi having trouble with some tether. But then Dad came over and unhooked the clips on her harness while she bounced on her toes, and then once he got her free she ran off to the bathroom.

Delores tried the door, found it unlocked.

"Haven't seen you come up those stairs in a spell," Dad said.

"I didn't want to wait any longer to get your books in order."

"Well, sure, be my guest." He went back to his easel. Delores followed and looked, and was right about the scene. The model was mostly painted, save for the face, which consisted of blotches of bold simple colors and slightly darker lines charting Sammi's features. The tree she sat in was just rough brown strokes and dark green foliage.

Delores loved watching Dad's process. The painting started in rough charcoal strokes — the literal "cartoon" — then bold outline filled in by blocks of color. He looped back again over each section, adding paint and detail, refining each time he gave attention to a particular part of the body or scene. Every cycle of resolution Delores would find herself thinking the work might be done, but Dad came back again and again, getting the undertone — the mask of counterintuitive colors that made up a simple skin tone — then bringing out some rouge or detail in the flesh, mixing in colors Delores thought would surely ruin that bit, only to find them blending magnificently when he was done. Then freckles or features brought the model to life, made her appear almost real, and then finally the highlights and sparkle on the skin, the reflection of the bright overhead or window lights. It was that last bit that sold the painting as a living being, those glints in the eye or on the skin where light caught the natural oils of the body.

"I like this one," Delores said.

"I still have time to mess it up," Dad said, his stock response.

"Fat chance," Delores answered. "You're the best artist I know. You're my inspiration." She patted his back, then found herself leaning in and kissing his cheek.

"Well! Where did that come from?"

She shrugged, all the fighting of the near past catching up to her, rendering her mute for fear of her voice cracking.

"Darling, if I hug you I'm going to smear you with paint," he said. But she just came at him, put her arms around him, put her head on his shoulder.

"It's okay," she said. "I'm wearing your shirt."

He held her like that for a minute. He kissed her head. "Love you, kid," he said.

"Love you, Daddy," she said.

She pulled away to see Sammi standing at the bathroom door, watching them, a very unsure expression on her face.

"You want I should go?" Sammi said.

"Hell, no, we have work to do," Dad said. "Delores is just doing some office stuff. And she can flip the record. And she can take a look at your arm."

"My arm is fine."

"What's wrong with your arm?" Delores said.

"Nothing," Sammi said, pulling the ripped part of the flight suit over her shoulder.

Delores went to her and put a hand on Sammi's shoulder.

"Don't be stupid," she said to Sammi. "Let me see."

"You can't just get away with anything you want," Sammi said under her breath as they looked at Gael, who had walked over to flip the record himself.

"Stop being such a baby." Delores moved back the fabric to show a dark bruise circling Sammi's bicep. A hand print? Gael went off into the bathroom as the music started, and he shut the door behind him.

Delores shook her head. "You sure can pick 'em. Or they sure can pick you, more like it."

"It's not like that. It wasn't violence."

A stab of cold jealousy came at Delores, sharpened ice into the chest. An aria from *Rigoletto* swelled.

"Oh, Sammi," Delores said. "Let me sell the photos. Please. They're so good. Never work with me again, but let me sell them. Please sign a release."

"Why? You betrayed me. You're a liar and a thief."

"They're so good. We can sell them."

"Did you know I have a meeting with a producer next week? They're looking for a girlfriend sort. That Elvis fellow — they're going to put him in movies. So no, I'm not going to sign anything. You're just gonna have to keep those photos to yourself."

"I was really hoping we could part as friends."

"Part?"

"Pretty clear you don't want me the way I want you, so yes, part."

"Just like that? You're not gonna fight for me?"

"Not if it's you I have to fight against."

Sammi pulled the flight suit over her shoulder. "Fine." She rolled her eyes, every bit the petulant teenager. "You really don't know women, do you?"

Which made Delores laugh. "Is that what you are now? A woman?"

Sammi punched Delores. But not too hard.

Delores gave her an extra-hard pat on the arm, right on the bruise, and Sammi winced.

Then there was Gael to help string Sammi into her getup and get back to painting.

At the desk, Delores opened the oversized ledger and sorted through bills, mail, and returned checks, making sure they were all noted. She double-checked her math (although she rarely got that wrong, maybe because she always double-checked) and listened to the opera. It was the last scene, when Rigoletto opens the sack that he assumes holds the murdered Duke of Mantua and finds instead Gilda, his daughter, in the duke's place. The daughter who cries out, "I have deceived you, father!" before she dies in his arms. Poor Rigoletto! He's shocked, and cursed, and then devastated, at the end of his schemes.

XV

THE TELEGRAM came on Friday, the day
before Delores turned thirty.

```
I DID NOT FORGET YOU ON YOUR DAY
I WILL TOAST YOU ANY-WAY
ACROSS THE STATES AND IN THE WEST
A CAR WILL COME AT NOON BE DRESSED
FOR DINNER YOU'LL BE DELIVERED ON TIME TO
PERINOS
- CORA
```

"What is this all about?" Mother said. The three of them — Dad, Mother, and Delores — had split the morning paper, and behind their sections they dug at fruit with spoons, drank coffee with milk, and even had a bit of cold cereal. The doorbell caught them all by surprise. Even more so when it was the Western Union boy. A telegram was an unusual thing. Anachronistic, even.

"Got me," Delores said, handing the paper to Mother.

"Is she prone to rhyme, this socialite of yours?"

Delores rolled her eyes, sighed. "It is not uncommon."

Mother read it again. "Well, now I'm curious. Come to dinner with a story. But don't you dare be late."

Dad looked up at the clock. "Unlike my model, who is running behind today." He leaned back and looked down the path. "Ah. The devil has been summoned," Dad said. The front door opened without a knock, and there was Sammi, all sunlight and daisies.

Not only was she dressed in a bright yellow blouse that matched her flats, and gray tapered pants that Delores didn't remember seeing in her closet the last time she looked through it, but she also wore the broadest smile Delores had ever seen grace that face.

"Good morning!" she said. She helped herself to some coffee, then sat next to Delores and, with a great show, put her left hand on top of the stack of discarded newspaper sections. Sammi rolled her fingers.

"Well," Mother said. "You appear to have something shiny on your finger, Sammi."

Sammi giggled, too excited to contain herself. "He came crawling back. Begged me to take him."

The three Sarjeants had a round-robin moment of glances exchanged before they all put on smiles.

"Well, that old dog Pal," Dad said. "Good for him. Good for you."

"Yes, congratulations," Delores said.

"You two should come with us tomorrow," Dad said. "Let's make it a big party. Just like that night at Musso & Frank."

"I don't think that's a very good idea," Delores said.

"Yes, Gael, come now," Mother said. "It's a family thing tomorrow. Just the three of us. For Delores."

"The more the merrier," Dad said.

"It's so expensive," Mother said. "We can't just keep adding people left and right."

"I'm sure Sammi wouldn't want to come," Delores said. "Nor Pal."

"We'd love to!" Sammi said.

"For the love of Pete," Dad said. "It'd be rude to exclude them. They're family. I'm paying, and I say they come."

Delores gave him her most serious, mood-telegraphing face. "It's my birthday."

"Stop being selfish," Dad said. "Just think of it as more people to help blow out all those candles. That cake's is going to be chock full, old girl."

Mother looked at Delores, who just shrugged, resigned. "I'll call Perino's again," Mother said.

"Sounds grand!" Sammi said. "I've always wanted to eat there. Lots of stars do." She stood, walked to the end of the table, and just beamed down at them. "I'm really so, so happy right now," she said. Then she turned on her toes and, with the hum of a Disneyesque tune, took her leave.

"Guess I'm painting a smile on that picture today," Dad said, excusing himself.

"Well, what do you know about that," Mother said, once they were gone. Delores looked up to see her lips pressed tight, her eyes twinkling with amusement.

"They'll be very happy together," Delores said, and they simultaneously burst into a round of laughter that left them weak, slumped on the table, gasping for breath, and generally unable to recover for quite a few minutes.

Delores was ready at noon the next day. She showered, used a bit of her mother's hairspray just to get her misshapen bulk to behave, and in looking through her closet uncovered the black dress Mother bought her when she first arrived, the one with the squared neckline and the little divot over the breastbone. She put it on, raided Mother's closet for a light gray scarf to throw around her shoulders, ostensibly for the weather (sunny and coolish) but maybe for covering her arms, or at least hiding them enough so they didn't draw her eye when she looked in the mirror. She raided Mother's jewelry box for pearls, a strand long enough to hang double, kept in a soft purple velvet bag. She also picked out some black Mary Janes with a kitten heel.

On the bed lay Mother's outfit for the night: A crimson dress with a white sumi brushstroke floral pattern and voluminous skirt. Red heels.

Her stockings and underwear laid out neatly for when she was done with her gardening, done with her showering, ready to be ready.

Delores checked herself in the hallway mirror and decided that she needed a little color in her muted palette. She fished around until she found one of Mother's darkest lipsticks, a rouge noir, and painted her lips thick and inky, taking something subversive from the act, something that felt like little knife cuts to her butch personality. She pocketed the tube in her clutch, ready for the night when the day had barely begun.

A driver in a black Cadillac picked her up, and he relented in allowing her to sit up front with him instead of in the back. He was mum about their destination, but after twenty minutes or so of navigating and chatting, he pulled onto a Ford car lot, new models all in neat colorful rows.

They pulled up to the glass-paneled offices, and the driver came around to open Delores's door for her. Standing there in a double-breasted suit with a flower in the lapel was a large man in his late fifties, thinning hair combed back over his pate.

"Miss Sarjeant. Welcome to Franklin Ford and Cadillac. Please come with me."

She followed him into the lobby, saw a portrait of him on the wall. A brass plaque beneath the painting bore the caption "Sten Franklin, president." He led her into a glass showroom, where a light-blue two-door sports car sat, a massive red bow atop it.

Franklin gestured. "Ma'am, this is the 1955 Ford Thunderbird, in Thunderbird blue. A brand new car from the most exciting car company in the world. They are extremely hard to come by, and I have it on good authority that many strings were pulled in this regard on your behalf. I've not been able to procure one for my lot, mind you, but this one just arrived by truck a few days ago with some very specific instructions to follow. In other words, you have a very powerful fellow who wants to impress you."

"This is for me?" Delores said, still a bit unsure of what was happening.

"Yes ma'am. This is your car."

And with that, he held out a set of keys, attached to a winged metal keychain, and an envelope that was addressed to Delores.

"Happy birthday, ma'am. Enjoy the car. And please remember to come to us for regular maintenance that will keep the car running for years to come."

It was a fast car. Delores almost lost control giving it gas on Sunset. The 210 had a slushy feel, like she was sailing a ship, and it took a moment for a press of the gas to get the message down to the engine room. The Thunderbird, however, felt like a mechanical extension of herself. Responsive and immediate. She tempered her foot and used a lighter touch.

The men at the dealership had taken off that ridiculous bow, and they showed her how to lower the top. She signed a few papers, and two men rolled back the large showroom doors, then one man drove the car onto the lot. She sat in the white leather interior and opened the letter.

I'm sorry I couldn't be there to present
Your present, but don't be hesitant
I have one more surprise to coordinate
Drive to these coordinates, don't be late.

A map showed the route to Griffith Observatory from the car dealership. A point on the observatory deck was marked with a red *X*.

Unsure just what it was exactly that Cora was playing at, Delores drove up the winding hill to the observatory, for the first time flush in this new idea that she absolutely loved driving. Was it a sign that Los Angeles had truly overtaken her? Was she ever really a New Yorker?

New York felt oppositional, like a lover you had to coax before she'd open her heart to you. But Los Angeles was desperate to be loved and wanted to give you immediate satisfaction. She was surprised by how much it had inhabited her bones and become her true north. But that same eagerness also led to a feeling of dissatisfaction, like saving money for years to buy something that you found out you weren't that keen to own after the cash was gone.

The road to the observatory wound through foothills, brown and weedy, and she took each curve slow and steady, not feeling the need to push herself or the car to fully enjoy it. She recalled reading an interview with a race car driver who said that when one is driving competitively, if it feels like the wheels are stuck on the ground, and you're cornering smooth, and it is as if you are on rails, then you are going too slow and risking too little. But Delores was not racing.

She rolled into the parking lot and was able to find a spot very near the observatory. She parked, reluctant to leave the car. From the large lawn that lay before the white building she could see the smog hovering in the still air over the city, coloring the air with an acrid tang. The light was direct and bright, the sun almost directly overhead, so shadows were short. She took in the shape of the iconic building, domes on either side ready for study of the heavens.

It was funny to her to come to a place dedicated to looking up when almost everybody who drove that windy road up here did so to look down. There were many vistas in Los Angeles where one could take in the city in all of its expanse and bulk, but this one was among her favorites. It was an oasis in the hills.

She stepped onto the balcony that ran around the entire building and walked until she rounded the planetarium. The X on the map directed her to the southernmost part of that balcony, the apex of the arc around the structure, with a view of the hills below and Los Angeles beyond: the dream of a city, the impossible metropolis.

There, at that spot, on a small round tile-topped table, in the Greek style, sat an elegant glazed vase, turquoise in color, deco in fashion. In it, a small group of weedy flowers, purple buds all closed. Leaned against the vase, threatening to topple whenever a breeze came through, was an envelope with her name on the outside. Delores opened it to find a handwritten note on Cora's imprinted stationery.

> *This is your real present. This vase of* Mirabilis californica.
> *I love you, my Californian. Stay where you are happiest and live a full life with my blessing.*
> *— Cora.*

Delores looked around but saw no one. Who had put this here for her? Was she supposed to take the table? Was she supposed to just leave it? Her real present was scrubby flowers, not the car? This whole thing was very confusing.

She picked up the vase and used a finger to pull a petal back from the bud, seeing a yellow-tipped stamen inside.

"They call them four o'clocks, those flowers." That voice. Smoky and warm, low and commanding. Sounding more like home than any city ever could.

Delores turned and saw Cora, standing with her arms held behind her back, in a gray Chanel suit. Cora was taller than Delores, dark hair with a few fetching gray streaks turned in a kind of mature bob. She was radiant, trying to hide her smile, her obvious mastery of surprise.

"Why do they call them that?" Delores said, a quiver in her voice.

"Because they bloom late in the day." Cora took one step toward Delores. "Especially if you leave them the hell alone to do their work."

Delores felt the sunlight gather in the black of her dress, heating her back where it was exposed to the vista of the city. The city laid out behind them, crossed by a thousand streets that Delores had not yet driven.

"You came a long way," Delores said.

"And I'm stuck. Do you know anybody that could give me a ride down the hill? Maybe show me this ocean I keep hearing about?"

And Cora took one more step to Delores. Delores came to her, and they kissed, just briefly in greeting, lipstick to lipstick, and folded into each other's arms.

XVI

AT PERINO'S the maître d' led Delores and Cora through the creamy peach interior to the table. The rest of the party was there, a bottle of champagne already opened. But whatever cheer they intended to show when Delores arrived was tempered by the surprise appearance of this glamorous, mature woman with her. Cora was striking, more commanding in her presence than Delores, more serious in her countenance.

"Sorry we're late. Family, friends...I would like to introduce you to Cora Fournier."

Nobody said anything. In unison, they all looked at Cora, then Delores, then Cora again. Then Mother said to the maître d', "I need to increase our reservation by one."

Oysters Mornay, Half Cracked Crab, Marinated Herring, Prosciutto and Melon, Shrimp Nantua, Crab Eggs with Mustard Sauce. Rounds of Champagne.

"I'm so pleased to finally meet you," Cora said to Mother, taking one of Mother's hands between two of hers. "Delores has told me so many stories about your father and his leadership in the labor movement. She is so proud of her heritage in this. I know he would have dismissed me for my name or questioned my motives, but would you be open to working together to establish a chair in his name, maybe at UCLA? I want his legacy, his lessons, his sacrifice to reach and inform as many people as possible."

"Oh," Mother said. "That's an interesting idea. How large an endowment?"

Petite Marmite, Consommé Bellevue, Cream of Fresh Tomatoes, Vichyssoise, Cream of Peas. Two bottles of White Bordeaux.

Leaning into Dad, Cora said: "So Jackson said to me, 'Painting is self-discovery, and we must celebrate American painting in all its forms as such. In fact, look to so-called illustrators like Norton Shale, or Gael Sarjeant. They are American painters and create a landscape as grand as any modern or abstract painter I know.'"

"Well," Dad said. "That kind of breaks my heart to hear you say that, it does. Because it means that my friend Norton was right, and that this paint tosser has good taste after all, goddamnit."

Spaghetti Bolognese, Linguine alle Vongole, Risotto Milanese, Cottage Fried Potatoes, French Fried Potatoes (Long Branch or Julienne), Peas Paysanne, Stewed Tomatoes, Spinach en Branche. Two bottles of Burgundy.

"You have the body of a dancer," Cora said to Sammi, who was radiant in a loose floral silk blouse in lilac that fell like water from a flat ribbon collar, and a matching form-fitting skirt. Patent orange heels echoed some of the highlights in her blouse. "Doesn't she look like a dancer, Delores? You have the body of one of my favorite dancers, Tanaquil Le Clercq. Doesn't she look just like Tanny, Delores?"

Boned Royal Squab Stuffed with Wild Rice & Montmorency, Veal Cutlet Cordon Bleu & String Beans, Steak Tartare, Calf's Sweetbreads Mas-

cotte, Grilled Saddle of Baby Lamb & Potatoes Boulangère with Mush-
rooms and Sauce Béarnaise (for 2).

"Well, had I known I would have bought from you. Maybe I would have bought her a Corvette instead, although I hear they're underpowered. But I have to say, the Thunderbird has more feminine lines, a more Pacific feel to it. I don't know. Maybe you should buy out a rival Ford dealership across town so you have your hand in both pockets."

"If only!" Pal said. "But no, they don't let you do that."

"Well, don't tell them, of course. Use another name. Use Sammi's name to buy the second one. Don't tell me a little aggressive capitalism to get ahead isn't the American way. Anyway, I'm sure you don't want a woman telling you how to run your business, so let me change the subject. Delores tells me you have some marvelous jokes. Do you have any jokes you'd like to tell me, Pal?"

Cream Broule with Grand Marnier, Pear Flambé, Baked Alaska (for 2),
Crêpes Suzette (for 2). Dessert Port.

Espresso.

Delores excused herself after the first few courses, as much to get a moment to herself as for the call of nature. Cora had her charm offensive going, and Delores's smile was starting to feel taped on. To her credit, Cora had turned the table, and now everybody wanted to be the one talking to her, asking her questions. It was as if a famous historical figure had emerged, and everyone wanted to know her, as if knowing her meant knowing the legacy of her family. Everyone but Sammi, that is, who sulked and did not seem very happy that Cora was with Delores.

Delores was touching up her lipstick after washing her hands when Sammi came in the anteroom of the ladies lounge. Their eyes met in the mirror.

"You look lovely tonight," Delores said.

"I can't believe you brought her."

"It was a surprise. For me. She just showed up. What was I to do?"

"I was waiting for you. To be with you tonight. To talk to you."

"Is everything okay?"

Sammi took her hand, and led her to sit on two rococo chairs, wood frames with upright oval cushions. She kept Delores's hand in hers. She looked around, nervous. Delores could feel Sammi's pulse in her hand, her heart aflutter like a bird.

"I want you back," Sammi whispered. "I want to go back to normal." Then Sammi let her hand go, and her face soured. "And then you brought her. Why *her*?"

"You're back with Pal now. What do you care?"

"She's a phony. And it's like a knife stab to those of us who care about you. Don't you remember what she did to you? How can you just forgive her?"

"It's complicated, darling. We have a long history. Maybe I was wrong. Maybe she's changed."

"Maybe she'll say anything to get you back so she can control you again. Let her go back to New York alone, and you come with me. Come spend the afternoon at my apartment. Take pictures of me. Love me, like you do."

Sammi had a plea in her eyes. Her hands were held together, white knuckled. She was like a round bottomed wooden doll, knocked off balance and trying to find her center again.

It was Sammi who called to her from across the country, through a painting. And that was just it, wasn't it? Delores was a sucker. She had fallen for Dad's advertisement, his illustration of beauty. His falsity. There was no Sammi like Delores thought there was. There was only a confused beautiful girl who knew how to coax a lens. Like that last shoot, where she was in a terrible funk but put on a smile for the camera. Sammi didn't know what she wanted. Sammi would never be true.

"No, I'm sorry," Delores said. "It's too late, I think."

Sammi's face screwed up, almost like she was going to sneeze. She came out with a sound of muffled frustration, a wordless grunt.

"You make me so mad. You cannot leave me. Please! I'm being so nice. I'm trying so hard."

"I'm not leaving you, Sammi. You didn't want what I offered. You rejected me."

There it was again, that horrible comparison Delores hated to make, in which Cora seemed regal, mature, beautiful to Sammi's snappy popular cuteness, her high-wattage oversaturated juvenilia.

"I'll be miserable, is that what you want? I'll just cheat on Pal, you know. That girl from the bar. Remember her? She wants me. She wants me all the time. If I call her, day or night, she drives to me, just like that. Not like you. She comes to me, and I just let her do anything she wants."

"Are you trying to make me jealous?"

"I'm telling you the truth."

"Well, I guess that would be just deserts for Pal."

Sammi's eyes narrowed, processing the barb, which Delores regretted the moment she'd said it. For an instant, she had forgotten that Sammi did not know about Pal and Mother.

"What does that mean?"

Delores sighed. Rolled her eyes. "Nothing. Forget it."

"Was Pal cheating on me? Is that what you're saying?"

Delores tried a different tack in the conversation. "Do you know what Cora was saying when she called you a dancer? When she said you look like Tanny Le Clercq? She was telling me that she knew. She knew about Tanny, she knows about you, and that she has forgiven me. That it means nothing to her. That she wants me." Delores held up her right hand, where she showed a ring. A diamond engagement ring, modest and modern. "She wants me forever. We bought these today and made a commitment to each other."

"You can't just drop something like that about Pal and not tell me."

"I have to get back to the table. They're waiting for me."

"I hate speeches, so I'm going to make this one short and then we'll be done with the formal stuff," Dad said, standing at one end of the table. Everybody loose and having a nice time, except Sammi, who sat with her arms crossed, fighting back anger or tears or distrust or all of it. "It's my daughter's birthday. Today she turns thirty years old, and that's a damn thing.

"Thirty years ago this night I was waiting in that god-awful baby-blue waiting room while your mother was trying to get you into the world. I saw you behind glass, and then that first time I held you we had a little conversation. I don't know how else to tell you that, because it sounds crazy, but you were all bundled up, a little swaddle of a thing, only five pounds and some change, and you looked up at me with these black eyes and looked right at me. Right at me! And we said to each other something, I don't know if I can put it to words, but something about how we were gonna look out for one another. That we were family, and we'd always look out for one another.

"Well, here you are. A grown woman of thirty years and you can look after yourself. Maybe —" here he looked to Cora "— with a little help here and there. Your mother and I wanted to get you something that told you we were your family, but we didn't know what. You have a nice camera. We thought about buying you a car, but I'm glad now we didn't do that."

"I'm not!" Pal said, and everybody laughed, except Sammi.

"You don't like clothes all that much."

"Well, I don't *hate* them, exactly," Delores said.

"So, I was thinking back, and one memory came to me. Hiking in Yosemite when you were in high school. What, fourteen? Fifteen? You brought that old Brownie, set it up on a rock, and got a picture of the three of us. It was a great photo, because it was our family. We put it away, but that photo has always stuck with me. An image I can't forget. And so —" He reached under the table and brought out a wrapped gift, quite obviously a canvas. Delores stood and leaned across the table to take it. She put it on her lap — the table being full of glasses and the detritus of desserts — and began to rip away the paper that encased it.

It was a clear morning when they hiked up a bluff to get a view of Half Dome, the sentinel of the great parks, and the valley lying at its foot. A grand god of rock, sheared in half by impossible water magic, by a devil of a glacier on an incomprehensible scale. The picture Delores took, under protest from Mother, showed them in their camping state: Dad with a few days' beard, Mother in her nonpublic casual outfit, a scarf folded over her dark hair.

The picture, and now the painting, Delores realized as she unwrapped it, was the three of them on a bluff, Half Dome in the far background. Dad made the stone bigger in his version, and he enlarged the three of them as well. Mother, on the left, leaning forward with a laugh on her face. Delores, in the middle, about to burst into laughter herself.

Dad, on the right, his arm around Delores, his hand extending past her to rest on Mother's shoulder.

But the thing about this portrait was that it was completely unglossed. The three of them looked like the three of them, not some ideal of what they could look like or might have looked like. They looked like they hadn't showered in days. They looked like they'd been hiking all day. They looked just like themselves, apart from the world of the city, and in the world of the family. The three of them, together, and together forever. It was the most naturalistic portrait her dad had ever made.

"Oh, Dad," Delores said.

"It was my idea for him to paint it," Mother said.

"Yes, yes, of course, it's from both of us. Happy birthday, Delores. We're so glad you're our daughter."

The valet pulled up to the curb in Pal's car, a ruby-red Bel Air, fresh off the lot. Borrowed, in fact, so that he could drive everybody where they needed to go that night. With his blonde hair flopping, the uniformed valet jogged around to Pal to hand him the keys. He held the passenger side door for Mother, who stood nearby.

Pal said, "That's a good idea. You're sitting in the front with me, so we can get a little sing-along going."

Mother shrugged. She gave Delores a hug and a kiss.

"Happy birthday."

"Thank you. I love you."

"You too, darling. See you at home." Delores watched her lift the hem of her red dress just enough to get into the car without being immodest or getting stuck. She watched Pal, leaning in, looking down at Mother's legs as she did so.

"I guess it's you and me in the back," Dad said to Sammi. He also gave Delores a hug, and then gave one to Cora as well. "I'm glad you made your face known," he said. "About time." He patted her shoulder and climbed into the backseat.

Sammi, the last into the car, looked at the ground, but came in for a hug anyway. "Who was it?" she whispered. "You have to tell me."

"For the love of Pete, he didn't. I made it up to make you sore. Just go. We'll talk later, okay?"

As they pulled away, Sammi looked back through the rear passenger window, put one hand on the closed door, and raised the other to offer a small wave. A token, perhaps, a lost signal trying to find a frequency to claim.

Delores took it easy on the drive, being sober enough to know she was too drunk to push her luck. She stuck to the right lane on Wilshire westbound, letting the people slowing to park or to turn just do their business without pressure from her. She and Cora held hands, resting them on the seat between, their matching rings together as Cora wore hers on her left index finger.

"Come back to my hotel," Cora said. "It's early yet."

"It's hardly early."

"You can take Beverly Glen to Sunset."

"Look at you. Giving driving instructions like a local. I think I can get us to Bel Air. But maybe we should follow them to Santa Monica. No doubt they'll keep the party going all night. You and I can spend all day by the pool tomorrow."

"Or in the room," Cora offered.

"As the lady wishes," Delores said.

Just after driving through the country club, so dark at night that it took on the aspect of being a park, at the corner of Wilshire and Comstock they came to a stop and noticed, just up the road past the light, a strange sight. Cars stopped. People, out of them, stood in the road.

As they came through the intersection and drew closer, they saw the commotion — a car gone off the road, into a light pole. The car was wrecked, smoke coming from the crumpled hood. A buckled mess of red and chrome.

"Oh, no," Cora said.

Delores pulled as close as she could before stopping.

"Oh, Delores, oh no," Cora said.

Delores could see one body lying in the street, a pool of black oil — it had to be oil — in the streetlights. Horrifying in the electric light from other cars, the figure, half illuminated, body still, was identifiable only by her red dress, white impressionistic flowers gracing it as it fanned on the concrete around her.

Dinner rose in Delores's throat. She shut off the Thunderbird and opened the door. Stood and walked across the pavement, heels clicking with stupid loudness, the pavement made for movement, for going by, not for standing on. Not for stopping. It felt so wrong to walk in the street, as if this were the oddest part of what was happening.

The vision before her was like one of Diego's disgusting crime photos. Her mother — broken, bloodied, tossed from the car as if by some monstrous creature's wrath — lay on a square of pavement that no cheek should ever touch.

Everything happened at a glance. Delores took a few more steps toward the wreck, looking away from Mother to see the compressed bulk of a body lying on the hood, thrown through the window, head cocked sideways and motionless. Steam from the hood billowed around the still form. Pal. Another wave of nausea, of horror, of disbelief.

The back door of the destroyed Chevy opened, and a figure in lilac walked from the wreck, clutching her face like an actor doing Oedipus when he tears his eyes from their sockets, with balloons of stage blood ruptured over his cheeks. She took a few steps and was stopped by a man in a white T-shirt, who sat her down on the street, constellations of shattered glass around them. With slow care he pulled her hand away from her face, then turned and gagged. He steeled himself, pulled off his T-shirt, and held it to her face before putting both her hands on it to apply pressure. He stood, looked around.

"We need an ambulance!" he cried. "Somebody call an ambulance!"

And then another cry from the car. A cry of pain, but more than that. The cry from the backseat of the wrecked Chevy. Dad, and he cried out a single word.

"Lily!" he said. Delores couldn't see him, so she walked closer, past Sammi and the shirtless man. She gave a wide berth to where her mother lay, where she was willing a hole in her consciousness for the moment.

There Dad was, in the back, crumpled on the floorboards, his arm caught somehow in the seats. He was pulling but was unable to get free. Animal panic filled his eyes. He looked right at Delores. Looked right at her but didn't seem to see her.

"Lily!" he cried, at the top of his lungs. "Lily!"

A siren gained in volume.

"Lily!" he yelled, until the flashing lights colored the scene and the siren had drowned him out.

Delores left him there and went to her Mother. She bent over her to hear a groan, saw an eye open.

"Mother," Delores said. "Mother, can you hear me?"

"Delores," Mother said, pushing herself off the ground and then falling to it again. She raised one hand and put it into a wet mass of hair.

Then Mother cried out, a moan of pain, of animal anguish that turned Delores pale. Delores touched her arm. "Help is coming. Can you sit up?"

Mother tried, then fell again. "Hard to breathe," she said, and closed her eyes tight, tears rolling out onto the sidewalk.

"I'm going for help, I won't leave you," Delores said. She stood. Cora was there, and she put her arm around Delores.

"I'm so sorry, Delores," Cora said.

"She's not dead," Delores said, the surreal moment fading into panic and helplessness. Cora kneeled next to Mother and took one of her hands.

"Help is on the way, Lily. We'll stay with you, but help is coming."

Medics came. They moved Mother onto a gurney, causing more animal groans and yelps, and pushed her into a waiting ambulance, which drove away as soon as she was secure, all lights and sirens and speed.

Delores saw firemen with huge tin snips cutting Dad out of the car. The medics sat him down and splinted his arm. She ran to him. "She's alive, Dad. She's alive."

He nodded, not saying anything, eyes full of pain, and fear, and relief. He walked himself to an ambulance, guided by a medic.

Another wheeled gurney rolled Sammi to a second ambulance. She moaned like a hurt puppy as the devoted shirtless man held her hand and helped her keep that stained white shirt to her face.

The men who freed Dad then turned their attention to Pal. Moved his bulk from the hood onto a gurney. An ambulance driver in all white pulled a sheet up over his lacerated face.

Then the ambulances were gone, sirens wailing. A wrecker was raising the crushed Chevy into towing position.

It was after midnight. A cop with a push broom swept the glass and small shards of metal into the gutter. Delores and Cora, by that time standing on the sidewalk near where the car had crashed, watched all this activity silently, as if it were a dream.

A cop pointed at the Thunderbird. "Is that yours?"

Delores nodded.

"Well, it sure is a beauty, but you're gonna have to get it out of here. Time to get traffic moving again."

1938 – Yosemite

THE HIGH COUNTRY air in Yosemite

carries drifts of pine and fire smoke from the campsites around the west end of Tenaya Lake. Dad, whistling, cooks sausage and eggs on a blackened grill lowered over the fire pit. Delores emerges from the large family-sized tent, yawning. Mother has an oilcloth over the folding card table that is their living room centerpiece. She's set down cloth napkins and silver from the large hinged box on sawhorses that Dad built, their mobile kitchen cabinet. All but food is kept there. They store that in their car, the windows rubbed with ammonia to confuse the snouts of curious bears, who look at cars with food the way a hungry person might view a sardine can.

"Morning," Mom says. Delores mumbles something through a yawn. It's early, seven or so. Delores stretches and walks the few yards onto the rock that abuts the glassy lake face. She's in shade, but where the sun hits water the faces of rock hills that stand around the lake are perfectly reproduced in its mirror. Down a ways a thin breeze roughs the surface, and a plunk and movement somewhere draws her attention and gives a hint at the water life underneath. Rainbow trout that will, no doubt, be their dinner once Dad has his way with tackle and bait.

"Swim today?" Dad says.

"Too cold," Delores says, adding a shiver to her voice for emphasis. She hugs her arms. The day before she lasted less than a minute in the alpine water before giving up and lying down in the adjacent meadow to watch fawns prance. Their mother grazed nearby, until Delores sneezed, and they froze, then vanished amid the trees like a magic trick. But today is supposed to hit eighty. Swimming may appeal later.

"We're ready," Dad says, taking plates as Mother hands them to him and filling each with rough-cooked breakfast, something Delores likes better than almost anything else in the world. Why does food taste so good up here? Even blackened, even with the dingy color of the eggs off the grill, every bite of Dad's meal is full of salt and butter, and makes her want to keep her fork moving from plate to mouth, plate to mouth. As Dad pours coffee for Mother and himself, a punchy and woodsy note hits her nose, and for the first time it is evocative and compelling to Delores. She sniffs and almost reaches for the pot.

But then Mother lowers her head. "Dear lord, thank you for watching over us and providing for us. I hope we please you in our devotions, and you find us humble in our love for you and in our actions toward our fellow humans."

When she makes a move to eat, Delores and Dad follow suit.

"I was thinking a hike is in order today," Dad says. "I know a great trail that will give us a view of Half Dome that can barely be believed."

"I said no hiking, Gael," Mother says.

"Did I say hike? More of a walk, really."

"A walk straight up El Cap, I'm sure," Mother says.

"Oh, no. In fact, if I remember, it has a slight declination on this trail," Dad says. "Both ways. In fact."

"I hear there's a gondola," Delores says. "If you get tired along the way. In fact."

"What about the part where you must ford the mighty river?" Mother says.

"You mean ol' Trickle Down Creek?" Dad says.

"I think she means the impotent rivulet," Delores says, proudly putting together two words from the previous night's lantern-light Scrabble game.

"Of course!" Dad says. "I know the one you speak of. It's just the Nile, at one-seventy-secondth scale. Installed by model train fans, if I remember correctly. You do have to be careful. If you step in it, the poor thing is dammed for life."

"I think Mother should be more worried about the lack of wine vendors at the end of the trail," Delores says.

"They've put in a nice boutique, though. Plenty of beautiful clothes to be had."

"And the —"

"Enough," Mother says. "Don't oversell it, or I might back out and stay here with my book. And a bottle of white, chilled in the lake."

"I'll bring you a skin of wine," Dad says. "And we'll carry a nice picnic."

"I know!" Delores says. "I'll bring my new camera." A birthday present from a few months earlier.

"You don't want to haul your tripod up there and everything," Mother says.

"If the view is good, sure I do. Plus, it's barely a stroll. Right, Dad?"

"Barely a stroll, Ansel Adams."

Delores watches Mother take a sip of her coffee. She takes a deep breath of the forest, the scrubby, dirty, wonderful forest. Could somebody feel better? It's like every fiber of her is being stroked with the grain, all lying flat and soft. She pops up and reaches over to the kitchen box, removes a bent metal mug, enameled blue with white speckles, and places it on the table, with a little flourish and drama. She takes the percolator and pours herself a cup of coffee.

"Really," Mother says.

"You are about to cross a certain Rubicon, young lady. Are you sure?"

"Gael, I'm worried. The last thing this one needs is more energy."

"Might help her with keeping her room tidy."

"A fair point. And I suppose she can stay up late and study, since she'll never sleep again."

"Even better, maybe it's time I trained her to help me in the studio more. She could earn a bit of spending money."

Delores lifts the mug, taking in the vapor. The liquid moves but settles as grounds of coffee breach the surface. She blows away the steam and rests her lip on the edge of the mug. She has drawn a line in the dirt, and now she readies herself to cross.

1955 – Los Angeles

XVII

DELORES PUT IT together later. Mother had
a concussion and no memory of the accident itself. Sammi didn't want
to talk about it, and she was so drugged her memories were more akin
to dreams than truth. But Dad remembered it clearly. Dad told it all,
and the others didn't exactly refute how he laid it out.

In the car that night, Sammi was morose, leaning against the window in the back and obviously agitated. Pal and Mother sang, starting
right off with *Cheek to Cheek*. Dad tried to talk, but Sammi acted the
sullen teenager and refused.

They ended that song and then started on *Goodnight, Irene*, and
Sammi sat upright, quite suddenly. Dad said it was like she was hit by
a bolt, but he doubted it was from the song. He guessed it was from the
camaraderie that the two of them were showing. She leaned over the
furniture of the front seat and grabbed at Pal's arm.

"It's her, isn't it? You've been screwing this one, haven't you?"

They stopped singing.

"For chrissakes, Sammi," Pal said, shrugging her off.

"I can't believe I didn't see it before. You have me, and you'd rather be putting it to an old lady." Sammi said this last word with a backhand to Mother's arm, as if to make sure there was no ambiguity who she was speaking about.

"Don't be a child," Mother said to her. "And do not touch me."

It was the first Dad heard of the affair, but he was doing the math and seeing that it added up. He leaned forward, put a hand on Sammi to pull her back.

Sammi pushed Pal. "You absolute pig."

"Get off me, goddamnit!" Pal turned to shove her into her seat. She fell against Dad. The car swerved, crossed the center line into oncoming traffic.

Mother shrieked, and Pal corrected, getting the car back on the right side of the street. He pulled across traffic to the curb and put the car in park.

"Jesus!" he cried. He turned around. "Look, you keep your goddamned hands to yourself. We'll talk about it later, when we get where we're going. Don't mess around with the driver. I don't want to scratch this baby." He patted the car seat.

Sammi crossed her arms, stuck out her bottom lip. Pal watched her, as if his gaze could restrain Sammi, gave her a stern point of the finger, then turned his attention ahead again. He pulled back into traffic.

They all kept to themselves for the next few minutes. Pal, maybe in an attempt to get the drive over as soon as possible, put the gas down and kept them roaring along the avenue at a pretty good clip.

But as they were going through the country club Sammi cried out, kneeled on the backseat, leaned over the front, and started slapping Pal's ears.

Yelling at him about how horrible he was, she slapped and yanked at him, pulled at his cheek and his eyes. Mother and Dad tried to pull her off him, tried to get her to stop — and in fact, Dad did, putting his hands around her waist and pulling her into the backseat. But Pal seemed not to realize that she was gone. And somehow he hit the accelerator instead of the brake, and the car swerved off the road.

———

Sammi lay under heavy sedation in the accident ward, on a bed with a bent steel frame. Her face was half bandages. She slept. Mostly they kept her asleep. The doctor told Cora and Delores that a metal shard from the window frame on Sammi's left side had ripped a gash from forehead to chin, right across her eye socket.

"It's not going to be a pretty scar," he said. "We've got the best cosmetic man in southern California tackling it, but there's just no way around it, it's going to be very distinctive. And she's got a future of surgery ahead of her to correct it as much as possible. And, of course, she'll have to wear a glass eye for the rest of her life."

Delores sat with Sammi while Cora fetched coffee. That was their new routine. Something they did daily.

Delores took one of Sammi's hands, the skin puffy, stained with iodine and other chemicals. What Delores really wanted was to run, to leave this place and not face the suffering woman in the bed.

"Why didn't you tell me about Pal and your mother?" Sammi said in a groggy voice the first time Delores visited.

"I'm sorry," Delores said. "I'm so sorry for everything."

"It really hurts, Delores."

"I know, sweetheart. I can tell."

"No one will ever want to look at me again."

"I will look at you. I will take your picture and show you how beautiful you still are."

"It's not fair. I don't want you to ever see my face again."

Sammi's one exposed eye, the lid drooping, darted around the room. It rolled back into her head and closed, and Sammi was again asleep.

Cora kept a low profile. She would peek in the door and enter only if Delores gave her a sign. They tried to keep her out of Sammi's view.

"I don't know what to do," Delores said. "I can't just leave her like this. She doesn't have anybody."

Delores had to break it to Sammi that Pal's will had not named her, but the boys on the lot had taken up a collection to help with her medical bills. They also tried to give Sammi the painting from Pal's office, but Delores intercepted the gift. She stuck in the garage with the rest of Dad's paintings, doubting very much that Sammi would like to be confronted with what, at that time, she used to look like.

"She's had a lot of visitors," the duty nurse told Delores. "This one is popular."

"Really?" Delores said. "Who?"

"Well, I can't really say, of course, because it's her business, but some fellas came by, and a girl dressed in leather like Marlon Brando or something. You know who I'm talking about?"

"Yes," Delores said. "I know."

Mother was at home, mostly in bed. With three broken ribs, a broken clavicle, dislocated arm, and concussion, she was loopy and complained constantly of a headache.

Many people from her church came by bearing food, and to sit and chat. Delores thought Mother would hate this attention, but the pain drugs and the blow to her head made following long conversations difficult. Having simple chatter about the weather with amiable people was much easier.

Dad, Delores, and Cora would sit at the table and eat casserole dinners. Dad, arm broken and in a cast and sling, often needed assistance with the simplest of things, such as buttering his bread.

After dinner, and after taking a bottle from the liquor cabinet, Dad would go to the studio. They'd watch as he took the flight of stairs, and then the *Carmina Burana* would come on a moment later and play, and play again, ebbing and flowing with the breeze.

At first it was just muffled sounds that woke them. Delores on her side, Cora pressed against her back, arm around her, holding her tight during the night. From the other room came a raised voice. Dad's, of course. Delores looked at the clock. Not quite one, yet.

The first words to rise above the murmur stage were shouted by Dad: "You humiliated me!"

Then came more murmuring. Mother's soft voice shushed through the door, indefinable in its syllables. Father booming, Mother soothing, the argument continued.

Delores moved Cora's arm and slid out of the bed. She crept from her room and pressed her ear against the door to her parents'.

Dad said, "I had every opportunity. Do you know how many men in my shoes would have slept with every model? How many would have gone to conventions and bought some slut for the evening? But I never did. I took my vows and kept them. What about you? What did you do? You got *bored*." The derisive way Dad said the last word made the mockery clear.

"Bored with a stable, full life. Bored with everything you ever asked for. Bored because you got what you wanted."

The closet opened, and there was some kind of shuffling. Something being tossed to the floor.

"Please, Gael," Mom's voice, but it was all wrong. It had a soft edge, a pleading.

"What good is it to even be sorry? Poor Pal got worse than he had coming. I might have gone and taught him a lesson. Thrown him off of his goddamnned boat into the marina, but Sammi saved me all that trouble, didn't she? She just killed the jerk and made me feel sorry for the man who nearly stole my wife."

"I love you. I never would have left you."

"You never had the option. Pal used you, and you were cheap to trust him."

"Oh god, Gael, please. I beg you." And then an animal cry so desperate, so pleading, so horrible that Delores at first imagined violence happening inside.

A cry of pain, a sob, a mouth full of mucus and spittle. "It hurts so much."

Delores pushed open the door just enough to see. Dad stood, arms akimbo, a suitcase on the bed nearby. Mother lay on the floor before him, weeping, completely broken, her arms around his ankles.

"Lily," he said, softer. "That must be killing your ribs. For god's sake, get up."

But Mother just pulled herself to him, weeping, a woman who had lost herself to suffering and regret. Dad sighed. He bent at the knees, squatted down beside her. Raising one of his immense, meaty paws, he stroked his wife's hair and shushed her.

"Oh, Lily," he said softly. "Goddamn you. You know I'll forgive you. It will be okay. Please...I can't stand seeing you in pain like this."

The next morning Delores woke to clattering and grunts from the driveway. She looked out to see Dad, dressed before dawn, loading suitcases into the 210.

She went to him, tying her robe tight against the morning crisp, her feet in fuzzy slippers.

"Dad?"

"Sorry to wake you."

"Where are you going?"

"San Francisco."

"Oh."

"I can't just sit here and drink away my anger while some stranger cares for your grandmother in her last days. What kind of son am I?"

"A good one?"

A disbelieving laugh. "Be sure to tell her that."

He looked up at the sky, at stars showing through cracks in a high cloud cover.

"Mother doesn't want me here right now anyway," Dad said. "She's like an animal that hides when she is wounded."

"I won't be here when you get back."

He nodded. Looked up at her with tight lips. Loaded his last case into the trunk with his one good arm. He struggled a bit and used his knee to get it over the hump, and then he slammed the trunk shut.

"I'm not sorry you came."

"I am. All of this." Delores waved her hand.

Gael put his good arm around her shoulders, then pulled her close. Kissed the top of her head. "You didn't crash that car, kid. Everybody has a say in their own misery."

Delores rubbed her eyes dry. Leaned into Dad. Took a shuddering breath and then stepped away from him.

Gael Sarjeant raised a cigar, bit off the end, and hesitated as he looked at a box of kitchen matches on the driver's seat of the 210. Delores reached into the car, got out a match, struck it, and lit the cigar. He drew on it until the cherry glowed. Blew out smoke and looked at the end.

"It's a goddamned Greek tragedy is what it is. Too bad your Mother hates those old stories."

"I heard you fighting last night."

Dad nodded.

"She'd been expecting it."

"Sometimes you do things you don't want to because the other person expects it. It was like the natural order of things, like we couldn't deal with anything in our life until we had it out that way. But doing that takes it out of me. I'll be glad to have something else to think about for a while."

Delores approached her father. She wrapped her arms around his midsection the best she could with his arm and lay her head on his shoulder. He patted her head. Gave it another kiss.

He entered the car, started it. Backed out of the driveway, but paused just long enough to give her a long last look, the glowing cherry on his cigar a spot of orange in the dark expanse of the windshield.

After he was gone, Delores climbed the stairs to the studio. She turned on the lights. Gave a sigh at the mess.

She gathered the empty bottles into a garbage pail, reunited records with their sleeves, folded up the nap blanket, and put away bills. She paid the last batch so that they wouldn't be overdue when Dad returned. Sent out forwarding addresses for ones that were likely to come due while he was gone.

She cleaned the bathroom, scrubbing the tub and toilet, the sink and mirror. She went to his easel, made sure the paints were capped, and lay plastic wrap over the wet palette. She dumped out old thinner, washing it down the sink.

Then she looked into the dressing room. Stockings and a panty girdle were draped over a chair, ready to be put on another day. To her credit, Sammi had kept the dressing room clean after their first photo session.

Delores picked up the panty girdle, so tight and small in its elastic retraction, without a body to stretch it. It smelled of Sammi, of her perfume, of her body. Of that strange after-odor that inhabits worn clothes. Not the sweaty body odor, but that faint sweet echo of what the wearer was.

Delores took a lipstick from the makeup table, for future transgressions of dressing up as her own gender. She took the panty girdle, the makeup, and a small half-full bottle of Chanel, wondering whether it was Sammi's or Mother's. She turned off the lights, left the dressing room, and closed the door.

She wrapped her little sense-memory package in the brown paper Dad used around his canvases. Tied it with white string.

When she was done she allowed herself to look at the last painting dad did of Sammi. To her surprise, it wasn't the skydiving picture. That one, she saw, was off to the side, not finished. This one Dad must have started after the crash. Working from memory, or using other paintings as guides.

It was rougher than most of his work. She could see the brush strokes, and they were almost angry or energetic in their coarseness. It was, of course, Sammi. Her face turned right at the viewer, a hint of a smile on her lips. Her cheeks were lightly rouged. She wore the lilac number, the one from the night of the accident. She sat, legs together primly in a chair, hands in her lap. No slip of the dress or tease of the stocking. Just a portrait of a woman in purple.

The background was a fade of colors, pink to blue to orange, with Sammi haloed by a subtle glow. In small cursive letters, down by her feet, Dad had written a quote from *The Little Prince*: "If you love a flower that lives on a star, it is sweet to look at the sky at night."

Delores and Cora went to Canter's for breakfast, and when they returned Mother was dressed and in the living room, reading. She had managed to get herself into clothes one wouldn't be embarrassed to wear out into the world, and she wore a scarf to cover her head bandage.

"You shouldn't be out of bed," Delores said.

"I'm not going to sit around any longer."

"There's nothing wrong with staying in bed while you're in such pain," Delores said.

"If I let pain stop me, I never would have gotten you into the world. Just remember that. Anyway, I need you to take me somewhere."

Since the Thunderbird was their only car, and had only two seats, Cora offered to stay behind. It was one of those postcard Los Angeles days, clear and bright, but coming on the heels of a few days of weather.

The smog had not risen to coughing levels just yet.

"Drive toward downtown," Mother said. Delores headed south, keeping well clear of Wilshire so as not to bring forth unpleasant memories. Even so, Mother would lay her hand softly on Delores's arm every now and again, and quietly say, "Slow down, please."

Mother directed Delores to Hollywood Film Developing. Delores found parking in front, but something was wrong there. Mother stayed in the car while Delores went to investigate.

Through the windows she could see all the celebrity portraits missing from their pegs, all those little nails, each with its own short shadow, just like when Delores took down Dad's paintings in her room.

A notice was posted on the front door.

FBI NOTICE OF SEIZURE
This business, its assets, and all associated materials have been seized by the Los Angeles Branch of the Federal Bureau of Investigation. All inquiries or affected parties may contact lead agent Ronald MacNamara for further details.

"What's going on?" Mother said from the car, keeping her posture straight and forward, so it felt as if she were being clandestine in talking to Delores without facing her.

"The FBI seized the business."

"Oh," Mother said. "That is very bad news."

"Let's go around back," Delores said.

They walked slowly, since that was all that Mother could manage. The alley was deserted this time, thankfully, though it didn't seem any cleaner than during Delores's last visit. They sidestepped fallen garbage and the rivulet of diseased water running along the middle, where the ground sloped slightly to gather it.

The alley door was unlocked when Delores tried it, which made her pull back her hand as if stung, for she didn't expect it to be open. The door creaked toward her an inch or so.

Before she had a chance to make a choice of action, the door swung toward them, and there was a man in a dark suit, shoes shined to a high gloss, a fedora on his head.

"Who the hell are you?" he said, voice low, phlegmy, and coming from the barrel of his chest.

"I could ask the same of you," Delores said, standing straighter. His eyes narrowed as he sorted her response for sarcasm and maybe disrespect, which it definitely held. They were set a little too closely together, his eyes. His nose resembled a boxer's, one that had been broken at least once.

"Federal agent, ma'am," he said briskly. "This joint is closed. What business do you have here?"

Mother stepped forward, held herself straight, with lips pinched against the effort of just standing and talking. "Mr. Peck had a number of paintings that belong to me," she said. "He was photographing them, and I have come to retrieve them."

"What's your name?" The agent took out a small notebook and a pen.

"Why does that matter?"

"Lady, what's your name?"

"Sarjeant. Lily Sarjeant. The paintings were by my husband, Gael."

The agent wrote as she talked, but then he stopped, his brows went high in the middle, and his eyes popped. "Wait a second. Gael Sarjeant, as in Sarjeant's Sergeants?"

"Well, yes," Mother said.

"The painter. The painter of those pin-up girls."

"Yes, that's the one."

The man slapped his thigh.

"Well, damn, you don't say! Listen, I went through hell and back in the South Pacific, and I carried one of those pictures with me. It was a girl, cute as a button, built like tank. She was standing on a map with one foot crushing Japan, and a little Marines cap on her head. She was saluting, not wearing any pants, shirt hanging open."

Mother broke into a wide smile, and turned so that the bruised side of her face was hidden to the man. "Well, that was me. I posed for that one. The War Department commissioned it. I'm so glad it meant something to you."

The man removed his hat and smoothed his hair, regulation length and slicked back. "You have no idea, Mrs. Sarjeant. I would see things every day. Nobody should see the things I saw. Then I'd pull that picture out for a minute each night and...well." He sighed.

"Ludlow!" came a voice from somewhere behind him. He raised an index finger, as if asking the two women to wait a moment, then disappeared. Came back a moment later.

"Listen, we got stuff happening here. I can't chat. Could I bother you for an autograph? It would mean so much to me."

"Sure, whatever you'd like," Mother said, standing tall. He handed her his little pad and pen, and she turned to a blank page and began to write a message.

"Agent Ludlow, about the paintings," Delores said. Although she knew nothing about Diego having any paintings, she was putting together just why he might, and the whole thing made her feel a little impatient with this flirtation unfolding in front of her.

"Oh, yeah, look, you're out of luck." Ludlow looked behind him, then stepped outside and closed the door. "When we raided this place, that Peck fellow had been tipped. It was clean. There was nothing here but a bit of furniture and some enlarging equipment. You know, people claim he had this massive archive of photos and such, but if he did it was cleared out. Got one source tells me he took it all to the desert and set it on fire. So I guess we'll try to nail him for tampering with evidence, but frankly, we got him dead to rights on multiple cases of blackmail. So, he's going away for some time."

"Ah," Delores said, and Mother shot her a sideways glance. "Well, that's too bad. Dad would like his paintings back."

"I would have remembered them, let me tell you. I would have remembered them for sure. I did see a picture of your dad with that guy, one of those signed celebrity photos, so I sure as heck would have remembered a real painting by him."

Mother handed the pad back to the agent.

"Oh, boy, I'm glad you came by," he said. "You just made my day," Then, looking around, sheepish, he leaned toward Mother, so that his face was very near hers. "Look, I hope this isn't too forward to say, but when I got back from the war I met a girl who looked just like you. I snatched her up, stole her away from another fellow, and married her that next week. I mean, she's a good girl and she's good to me, but I never would have met her if she hadn't looked like you."

"Well, isn't that sweet," Mother said. She moved her face, and Delores realized she was going to kiss the man's cheek. A look crossed his face, like that of a child being handed a purring kitten. And then Mother took Delores's arm, and they walked away while Agent Ludlow stood and watched.

Back in the car, Delores was finally able to ask, "How long had he been blackmailing you?"

"A few weeks. He had pictures of Pal and me. In a hotel. Horrible pictures. One painting for each negative was the bargain. God, I really hoped to get those back, now that Pal is gone."

"I'm sorry, Mother," Delores said. Mother shrugged.

"The funny thing? Your dad will never know they're gone. He never looks at his archive." She sighed and then moaned. "Can we go home now? I need to take something for the pain."

Delores was quiet on the drive. Mostly because she remembered that night on the beach with the bonfire when she had burned the negatives of the same pictures Mother supposedly held. If Diego had made two sets of negatives, no doubt he had more. No doubt that the pornographic images of Mother and Pal were somewhere in the Pecker Archive, wherever it was.

Because Delores knew that Diego would never destroy his archive. It was his life's work. It was out there somewhere, and she realized the only hope she could hold was that those photos stayed out of sight for the rest of her parents' life, at the very least.

That evening Cora accompanied Delores so that she could visit Sammi in the hospital. But the bed in her recovery room was empty, cleaned, with fresh sheets on it, personal effects gone.

"Checked out this morning," the nurse told them. "We told her to stay, but of course we couldn't force her."

"Who picked her up?"

"Can't say I know what her name was, but they rode away on a motorcycle. We tried to stop them — very unsafe in her condition. But wait — what did you say your name is? I have a note here for somebody named Delores. Is that you?" She came back a moment later with an envelope. On its front, in a loopy hand, was Delores's name.

They walked to a reception area, and Delores took a seat on one of the couches.

"I'm going to go find some water," Cora said. Delores nodded. Once Cora walked away, she tore open the envelope.

Two notes lay folded inside. The first read:

> *Delores –*
> *This whole thing is my fault, and I don't know what I can do about it except take this punishment that god gave. I'm sorry for everything, and I'm mad as hell. But since I'll never be good looking again, I want you to sell those photos anywhere you want to. If I can muster up the courage I'll keep an eye on* Playboy *to see when my pictures run. Can't stop my career in pictures when there's no way I'd get hired to begin with. Hope you have a good life in New York. Doesn't matter what we felt for each other. I was bound to screw it up, no matter what*
> *Love,*
> *Sammi*

The second note was shorter. It read:

> *To whom it may concern. Photographer Delores Sarjeant has my permission to publish any likeness of me she captured in any way she sees fit.*
> *– Sammi Brill*

———————

Mother insisted on cooking for their last evening in town.

"So, I can show you I'm not an invalid. If I can cook for three, I certainly can cook for one."

She made hamburger patties, and roasted potatoes in butter and oil in a large cast-iron skillet. At one point, opening the oven, she leaned over to stir the potatoes and groaned in pain. Delores jumped up from the table, but Mother waved her off with the saying she repeated every hour or so.

"I'm not an invalid."

Cora kept her nose in her book by a new British author, Iris Murdoch, whose first novel, *Under the Net*, she'd picked up in Paris.

"Do you want a beer?" Delores said to Mother, who again waved her off. Delores opened one for herself and one for Cora, then without asking whether Mother wanted help, she got out some plates and set the table.

"Maybe we'll see some movie stars on the train," Delores said.

"You'll be disappointed if you do," Mother said, flipping the patties. "They're rarely as beautiful in person. And they're all short. With gigantic heads. It's an odd thing, but that must be what the camera likes."

"Very charismatic, though," Cora said, putting down her book. "Love to be the center of attention."

"Am I the only one here who has never met a movie star?" Delores said.

"Oh, they're just people," Mother said. "And it's messy with them here. I'm surprised we didn't see one at Musso's or at Perino's. Maybe we did and didn't recognize them."

She put the patties on plates, opened the oven, and with another groan that Delores knew well enough to avoid comment upon, placed the skillet on the stove. She dished out potatoes and carried the plates to the table. Delores took Dad's place at the head.

"Well," Mother said, a bit short of breath from her efforts and inability to fully inhale. "Since this is your last night here, should we say grace?"

"If you'd like, Lily," Cora said. "That'd be nice."

Cora took Delores's hand, and with a warm smile she reached across the table for Mother's. Delores took Mother's free hand, hot from the effort of cooking.

Mother began. "I'd like to say thanks for family and friends who have been near to us. I'd like to remember those whom we have lost. I'd like to say thanks for my daughter, and thanks for Cora. For Gael and his Mother. For Sammi, wherever she is, I hope she finds peace. I know I sound ungrateful for my life. I'm not."

She paused there. Delores and Cora, assuming she was to continue, waited for more. But after a few seconds, Mother squeezed their hands and dropped hers. She picked up her knife and fork, and began to eat.

"I'm so used to ending prayers with 'amen' that I didn't know what to do there," Cora said. "Do Quakers not say that?"

"Oh, we do," Mother said. "But I've stopped ending my prayers. I'm saying them rather constantly of late."

Cora nodded. Delores caught Cora's eye, gave a smile, and tucked into her own food.

"You are, of course, going to start paying my daughter a normal salary, right?"

Cora looked up, at Delores, then at Lily.

"Oh, Mother," Delores said.

"It's all well and good that you two are so friendly. But you were taking advantage of her by not paying her."

The phone rang. Delores reached to get it, but Mother shook her head and looked at Cora.

"Lily, if Delores doesn't leave my employ to be a full-time photographer, I will indeed start paying her a regular salary." The phone punctuated her statement with its trilling report.

Mother nodded, satisfied, and Delores picked up to find Dad on the line.

"How's Grandma?" she said.

"Is that your father?" Mother said. Delores nodded, and Mother moved out of the booth, "I'll get it in the bedroom."

"Mostly fine, but she has her moments," Dad said. "She seems to have let her guard down, now that it's all in the open. She's hiding less. It's easier to evaluate her state."

A click, a thunk, and then, "Here I am, Gael."

"Darling, hello."

"Delores?" Mother said. "You can hang up now, I've got it."

Delores put down the receiver. She and Cora finished their meals, but when it came time to clear, Delores looked at her Mother's plate, a few potatoes missing, maybe two bites from the patty. She knew Mother wouldn't eat another bite, but she left the plate on the table, just in case.

She straightened the kitchen while Cora drank her beer and read.

Once she had washed the plates and straightened the kitchen, Delores said, "I guess I should pack."

"You're going to miss it," Cora said.

"Yeah. I'm going to miss it."

"Packing won't take long," Cora said. "You want to take a walk to the beach? I'll win you a teddy bear on the pier."

Delores laughed. "Sure, why not?" Cora stood, and Delores went to her and put her arms about Cora's waist. The two of them stood holding each other in the stillness of the evening.

Delores Sarjeant marched across the great hall of Union Station, her heels sounding click-clack on the Spanish tiles. Beside her, Cora Fournier walked in lockstep. Their hands, clad in white gloves, showed the bulk of their wedding rings. Each had a small bag with them, but their luggage was already in the hands of the red caps, and would be waiting for them in their cabin on the train.

They were early for the 11:30 A.M. Super Chief departure — too early. But their cab came sooner than expected, traffic was light on the way, and Cora was an anxious traveler. She preferred to arrive early and be bored with the waiting than to suffer the drama of arriving too close to departure time. They left the Thunderbird with Mother so she'd have something to drive while Dad was in San Francisco. Delores almost warned her about being careful with it, but she thought Mother would probably be careful with cars for the rest of her life.

They found seats in the wide box chairs, a small lamp on a table between them. Cora had her book, so she was entertained. Delores pulled her camera from her bag, right under the plush mouse Cora had won her on the pier. She pulled off her gloves, put her knees together, and placed the camera on them to load a fresh roll of film. She stood and wondered what she could capture in this room. She took one shot to gather the grandeur and another of a little girl in a powder-blue pancake hat and matching cape-style coat who walked past, hand-in-hand with her father. The child's patent Mary Janes threw slippery highlights.

But nothing she saw thrilled her. Nothing that her eye considered compelling. There was no shot. Except, maybe, Cora. But Cora didn't like having her picture taken. Then again, she'd never get used to it if Delores didn't ever try.

Delores kneeled in front of Cora.

"Put your book down and smile."

Cora peered over the cover.

"No."

"You're the most interesting thing in this room."

"No."

Delores took a picture of Cora reading, pulling sharp focus on her nose.

"Hey," Cora said. "I said no."

"You said no to putting the book down. But on second thought, maybe it's a better shot with you distracted."

Delores snapped another, then moved to get more of Cora's body in. She was overdressed, as usual, in tailored wear. A salmon knee-length skirt and jacket. A white blouse with a knobby texture. A blue-green scarf tie. Her hair wavy and worn back.

"I am not your subject, Delores. You may not shoot me."

"I may. In fact, I will."

"Why are you so obstinate?"

"Why are you so afraid?"

"Here. Let me read you a quote from this book. 'When I'm up to something I find it very hard to realize that I probably look no different from the way I look on other occasions.' Well, dear, you do look different when you're up to something. You have a little smirk on your face."

They shared a momentary stare-down, in which Cora projected the air of an annoyed superior, but Delores made her eyes big and pursed her lips in mockery of that seriousness.

"You win," Cora said. She put down the book and smiled, a bit tight in the lips, but a smile nonetheless. Delores took the picture. And another.

"I'm going to take a lot more pictures of you," Delores said.

"What if I don't want you to?"

"Then I'll do it when you're not paying attention. You're too good a subject. You're too beautiful."

"That's sweet and all, Delores, but you know as well as I do that I'm not photogenic."

"You leave that part to me. I'll change your mind on it."

"If this is a price of your company," Cora said, "then I shall work on resigning myself. But don't expect everything to change just because you're suddenly bold about it." Cora picked up the book again. Delores watched her. Cora smiled when she felt Delores's eyes on her. "I adore you, you know," she said, without looking up from the page.

"How could you not?" Delores said. Then she settled back in her own chair, and after looking at the dark, strong grid work of beams above her, she shut her eyes.

She remembered that waft of eucalyptus from her first day, that brine-filled breeze from the ocean, those gents in summer-weight wool and ladies all proper and waiting to be seen.

She opened her eyes and saw a woman, a bottle blonde in the Marilyn style, but leaning more toward Jayne Mansfield. She was wearing a sweater too small and unbuttoned too far, and a pencil skirt hugged her wide hips and hobbled her step. She swung her feet as she walked, and in her wake a sea of male eyes turned to watch her pass, the woman now a starring attraction on a hundred mental movie screens.

A man tipped his hat to her as she passed him, and as she turned to smile, Delores saw uneven teeth. Her bombastic hair, false lashes, and outfit compensated for a rather plain natural look. Even her bust, high and drawn in great detail, wasn't much larger than Sammi's modest one, it was just featured more acutely. In comparison, Sammi was truly beautiful: a symmetrical face that shone without makeup, and that came alive with it. Sammi had health and vitality, whereas this lady had clever marketing.

But Delores was still quite taken with her. She stood and went out to the walkway.

"Where are you going?" Cora said, but Delores stepped briskly away. She popped her viewfinder open and put herself directly behind the woman in the center of the walkway, its converging lines ending in those grand doors.

She dropped to one knee and, with that, Delores caught one last picture in Los Angeles: That woman walking away from her, the stocking seam going into her Cuban heel, one foot placed in a line in front of the other to give the pendulum of her hips more string and swing. Also in frame: the backs of men in suits and hats watching her pass, the ones closer to Delores just slacks and penny loafers, like a thin forest of trees and woody roots, and to one side a janitor in gray coveralls leaning on a mop, just watching her saunter by. Delores caught her with her hip at the apex of one step, as pronounced as if in a stage musical when the heroine bumps aside a man with some attitude.

And just for those few seconds, before the woman was gone and the men went back to their walking or waiting or mopping, Delores fell in love with that woman and her brash assurance. Her heart fluttered in her chest, and in that moment of ache was the nugget of the future, and the standard a model would have to reach before Delores would hire her.

As soon as she got back to New York she'd place an ad, and as she held her auditions she knew she'd be looking for only one thing in a model: she'd be looking to fall in love.

1999 – Tarzana

POSTSCRIPT

PICTURES OF the woman were for sale everywhere
in the convention hall, but in the flesh she walked by as a ghost might,
unseen. She approached one poster-sized image in one of the larger
booths, a collectibles business with a dominating hand-painted sign.
The picture was perched on a stained and polished wooden easel that
held it fast on four sides. Framed under glass, matted triple thick, a
nude.

She remembered posing, standing on the beach in Santa Monica
that cool day, without a stitch, arms akimbo, the pier dominant behind
her. In this image, with the pier soft and blurred, she was crisp and
perfectly focused. The picture showed her from her toes, curled in the
sand, to the top of her head, a few hairs caught by the wind. Her smile
was wide. The shot, she was learning, was very popular. She had already
seen many reproductions, in other booths around the hall, at smaller
scale.

She reached to touch it, that version of herself forty-five years past.

Why did she pose like that, naked on the beach? What was she feeling that day?

"Hey, lady!" Behind a table sat a man with long wavy graying hair and a goatee. A T-shirt rode his gut, and on it was a picture of her face, an illustration. And not a very good one — the logo for the convention, her face hovering over bold sign-painter style script that read *SammiCon*. They gave them out at the door, and Sammi, in fact, had one tucked into her swag bag. "Are you interested? If not, don't touch."

"What's the price?" she said.

"That one? Twenty-four-hundred dollars."

"Are you joking?"

"Look, it's signed by Delores Sarjeant. Very rare. She never signs prints for sale. And that's a top-notch framing job. All acid free, museum glass, the whole thing. Those don't come cheap."

"Where would somebody put something like this? You can't put it in your living room."

"Put it in your closet, for all I care. Not my problem."

The dealer must have found her a sight. This heavy seventy-something woman, with a buoyant halo of gray frizzy hair and round face, and made to look mad — in the mad scientist way — by her scar: a vertical line from the forehead on the left side of her face, across her eye and her cheek, to her chin. Her glass eye calm and normal looking, of course. The maddest part, she imagined, was her one good eye that was always roving, never still. She certainly didn't look like a model anymore. And she didn't dress much like one, either. A gray college sweatshirt, some jeans from Costco. White sneakers.

She entertained the fantasy of taking a Sharpie and signing the picture. She wondered how much it would be worth if she did. She had never signed a single autograph. If the photographer's scribble was worth so much because she rarely signed, what was the model's worth? She realized just how much she had missed out, and that made her angry. If she had a pen she might just have broken the glass on the goddamn thing and signed it. Marked it up good. But then, he'd probably just sell it for fifteen times the price, once he found out who his vandal really was.

She went to the booth next door and flipped through the images in a bin with her name on the front in hand-drawn cartoon letters, and next to them a little line drawing of her face (looking like Betty from the Archie comics). It was like going through record album bins. Each in a plastic sleeve with a price sticker on it, cardboard keeping the package stiff. Most of them 8 x 10 reproductions of photos Delores took, but some were copies of Gael's paintings. Even some original ephemera, little calendars with the name of some printing business or service station letter-pressed under her pin-up image, all with excited little stickers gussying up the sale. *Original! Vintage! Rare! Collectible! Mint! Unopened! Unused!*

She paused at a painting reproduced on a card that showed her lying on a bearskin rug. Had a sense memory of how that thing smelled, dusty, sneezy. Had a memory of Gael and how he played opera while they worked. How he used to tell her to stay still, then tell jokes to make her laugh. How all he really wanted was someone to spend time with. How much she missed him after she left Los Angeles.

She found a seat, at the edge of the hall, near a snack vendor. She got a Diet Pepsi and some garlic fries, and sat to watch as she sipped and ate.

Sammi certainly was odd in comparison to the rest of the crowd. There were young faux rockabilly men, tattoos on their arms, who wore leather and chains, wallets attached to their belt loops; young women in tight and quite revealing vintage-style fashion (but much too tight, much too low cut, and more consistently made than real vintage, which was usually made by hand from patterns), also with tattoos.

Models — wearing seamed stockings, panty girdles, pointed bras — posed in some booths. They signed autographs and posed for pictures with fellows wearing Sammi's illustrated face on their T-shirts. One booth had a bunch of porn stars, if you could believe it, where a slob could pay to get a picture with one of them hanging on him.

There were workshops where you could get dressed up just the way Sammi used to dress, to have somebody fix your hair and makeup so that they looked like her hair and makeup used to look. Where you could get people to take pictures of you like Delores used to take of her. Apparently there was a contest going on that night to find a young lady who looked the most like Sammi, which gobsmacked her, especially after glancing at the length of the sign-up list, filled with the looping flowered bubblegum writing of modern young women.

It was an industry born out of worshiping her, and only just then was she realizing how large it was, and how much others had profited from her likeness while she had been nearly destitute for years. God was trying to show her something, and she was listening as hard as her wandering mind would allow.

She placed her trash on top of a bin, already overflowing, licked her fingers and then wiped them on her pants as she walked to get in line. She should have brought a book. She saw this might take a while. She stopped at a booth she'd seen earlier, where a hardback was featured.

"How much?" Sammi said.

"Twenty-five," said the man behind a folding card table. He didn't look up. He was signing his name on the first pages. "The author will sign it for five dollars."

"Are you the author?"

"In fact I am, yes," he said, and then he blew on the wet ink.

Sammi counted out twenty-five dollars and put it on the table. "I don't want your autograph," she said. She carried the book to the forming line that snaked through a set of double doors, and she opened to the title page.

THE INFAMOUS SAMMI BRILL
*The unauthorized biography of America's mysterious
pin-up sweetheart*
BY
Stockton Powell
AUTHOR OF
*"Gams and Stems, the Leg Lovers of Golden Age Hollywood" and
"On the Heels of Despair, the Foot Lickers and Shoe Makers of the
Silver Screen"*

She'd reached the second chapter — this fellow apparently talked to many people from her early life and still managed to get everything wrong — when the line started moving. The doors led to a short hallway, and then they opened into a modest room where, at another folding table, sat Delores Sarjeant. Behind her, as if transported across time with a finger snap, for it was in absolutely perfect shape, sat that baby-blue Thunderbird.

Delores was old, of course, but she looked healthy. Her hair was awful, barely styled, short, flat, and gray. She wore obscenely bold eyeglasses and a kind of men's bowling shirt, which was red with a white vertical stripe that capped over her breast in a circle that itself highlighted an embroidered monogram, *DS*.

Every person in line got a smile and a sign, and if they wanted, they could come around and get a picture with her. Delores gamely grinned wide for each fan.

When Sammi was about ten people away from the front, Delores stood and stretched, and looked down the line. She looked right past Sammi, but then something must have snagged her, for she looked back and her eyes went wide. She dropped her pen, and her hand went to her mouth.

"My god," she said. Everybody in line turned to see what had caught Delores's attention. Sammi, feeling awkward, held up a hand and waved.

Delores moved toward her, with a slowed gait, her torso bent as if she had spinal trouble. She made her way to Sammi and stood in front of her, pulled herself up as straight as she could, and said it again. "My god."

And then her fingers went to Sammi's face, to her cheek, and she traced the scar with a delicate touch.

"I made it," she said to Delores. "Thank you for inviting me."

"I was hoping you'd come," she said.

"That's Sammi!" said a man in line. "That's the real Sammi Brill, right here, in line!"

People moved in closer. One woman, in pigtail braids, brought a camera to her face and snapped shots in rapid succession.

Delores pulled Sammi close as if to protect her, then whispered in her ear: "Let's get the hell out of here."

Delores took her hand and led her out of the line, to the Thunderbird. She opened the passenger door for Sammi, and then closed it behind her as might a perfect gentleman. She walked around to the other side of the car, waving away a confused young man wearing an earpiece and a microphone, who came to inquire as to her actions.

She shut the door. "You may want to wear a seatbelt," she said to Sammi, and then she rolled down the window and called out, "Open those doors, will you?"

The people in line murmured and talked to one another, moving closer to the car, breaking the line. Delores turned the key, and the Thunderbird hopped to life, the tacka-tacka-tacka purr of the motor echoing off the hard-walled interior.

Sammi watched as Delores pushed on the accelerator, but her other foot had the clutch down, so the engine roared and increased in loudness and pitch. Black exhaust poured from the back of the car. The people closest to them stepped back, turned, and coughed, waving their hands in front of their faces.

The engine was alive, a lion's cry containing a crackling fire, a rocket ship roar. It grew louder, more intense, the car shaking and vibrating around Sammi. She put her hands on the seat, grasping until her knuckles were white, burning gasoline and exhaust bitter in her mouth and nose.

In front of them, one young man had opened a series of conjoined doors and made just room enough for the car to squeeze through.

Delores pushed the gear shift into second and popped the clutch, and the wheels spun, not catching on the polished floor of the convention center. They whirled, squealed, and spit smoke and chalked melted rubber onto the floor.

Then they caught, and Sammi was thrown back against the seat as the vintage car propelled them forward. They went straight for the doors. Delores steered left and right to compensate for the fishtailing, and kept them true.

Sammi let out a cry of surprise, fear, and delight as the car rocketed toward the opening, the blinding sunlight making a pure white exit from the convention center. They cleared the doors with inches on either side, and disappeared into the bright hot light of Los Angeles.

And behind them, in the convention center, were an abandoned table full of photographs, Sharpie pens, and a long line of fans trying to guess what had just happened. The waves of exhaust, smoke, and steam settled to the floor and became part of a story that each of them in turn would tell all their friends, about that time they saw Delores Sarjeant meet Sammi Brill for the first time in forty-five years, and then kidnap her from her own convention without a word to anyone in the world.

THE END

Acknowledgments

Many people were instrumental in making this book you're holding in your hands, and I'd like to take a few moments to note them in thanks.

My irreplaceable editors: Danielle McClellan and Edward Austin Hall. The talented, patient, hilarious, and intrepid Vicki Nerino. The scholar of letters, Scott Boms. Anna Rascoët-Paz helped me with some French, Matthew Baldwin and Pamela Drouin gut-checked Pal's bad lesbian jokes.

For writing advice and generosity of spirit: Maria Semple, Kelley Eskridge, Nicola Griffith, Robin Sloan, Jack Cheng, and Kent Beeson. My early readers: Rahawa Haile and Charisse Flynn.

At Kickstarter: Maris Kreizman steered me right (and made me a staff pick!), and David Gallagher. My Kickstarter preview advice squad: André Mora, Matt Haughey, Max Temkin, and Sandor Weisz.

♥ My wife Christine, and son Lionel, for their patience, kindness, love, humor, and guidance. ♥

And, of course, my Kickstarter backers, without whom this book simply wouldn't exist (listed alphabetically by first name):

A.M. Santos, Aaron Edwards, Adam Lisagor, Aimee Herndon Bullock, Al Olson, Al Robertson, Albert McMurry, Allie Paige Craswell, Ame Lewis, Amy Duncan, Amy Lang, Amy McClellan, Andrea Inge, Andrew Bemis, André Mora, Andy Boyle, Anna Rascouët-Paz, Anne Van Wagener, Anthony Baker, Ari, Ashley Costanzo, Ashley Wells, Ashlie Tuhkanen, Barry Neufeld, Ben Tesch, Ben Trujillo, Beth Graham Budke, Bill Bowdish, Bill Couch, Bradford deCaussin, Brent Lanford, Brian Covey, Brian Phillips, Carl Collins, Celeste Thayer, Celia Wu, Chad Royal, Chelan Kelly, Chelsee, Chip Rea, Chris Darden, Chris Drackett, Chris Maly, Chris Neal, Chris Pugh, Chris Smith, Christian Metts, Christine Larsen, Christopher Osolin, Christopher Wilkins, Chrys, Cindy Bauleke, Colleen MacDonald, Constance Kwinn, Craig Saila, Damon, Dan Lantz, Daniel G. Harmann, Danielle McClellan & Charles Wheeler, Dave and Suzy Gerber, Dave Foote, Dave Olmsted, David B Wright, David Ballantine, David Gallagher, David Wright, Dennis Lee, Derrick Schultz, Devin Loudon, Dylan McCord, Edward Lukman, Elizabeth, Eric Anderson, Eric Schuh, Eric Wayne Norlander, Erik Nelson, Erik Nilsson, Erin Watson, Eugenia Chang, Evann, Fred Birchman, Gabriel Nanda, Gabriel White, George, Gina Collazo Zayas, Ginevra Kirkland, Ginger Adams, Gregory Bowers, Gretchen Bell, Hayley Lawrence, Heather, Heather Lindsley, Heaven, Hilary Lachoff, Imelda Loei, Isaac Dansicker, Jack C, Jack Cheng, Jack Large, Jacquelyn Krones, James Callan, James Dunigan, Janice Tsai, Jason Quinlan, Javaun Moradi, Jay Goldman, Jay Haskins, Jeff Scott, Jen Matson, Jeni Craswell, Jenni Prokopy, Jennifer Haupt, Jennifer Larson, Jennifer Leung, Jessica Bloom, Jessica Edelstein, Jez Burrows, Jim Cox, Jim Hardesty, Jim Ray, Jim Sykes, Jimmy Lovaas, JoAnne Kennedy, Joe Brown, Joe Hagerty, Joelle Calton, John Bennett, John Gruber, John Jacecko, John Nick, John Postlethwait, John Zagula, John Young, Josh Belzman, Julia Hensley, Julie White, Junichi Tsuneoka, Justin Henderson, Kane Jamison, Kate Bergman, Kathleen VanDerAa, Kathleen Warren, Kelly Lattin, Ken Brocx, Kenny Meyers, Kent M. Beeson, Kevin, Kevin Wilson, Kirk Loudon, Kitt Hodsden, Konny Kindlund, Kriss Chaumont, Kären Engelbrecht, Laina Vereschagin, Lance Anderson, Laura Aschenbrener, Laura Kelso, Lauren, Lauren Isaacson, Lauren McCullough, Leah Silbert, Leila Boujnane, Lela Davidson, Libby Gerber, Linda Morgan, Lisa Holmes Elkihel, Lisa Matson, Lisa Sholley,

Lisa Wilkins, Liz Townsdin, Lucas McNelly, Lucy Drury, Luke Dorny, Margie Kimberley, Marguerite Cottrell, Maria, Marie Zervantian, Marilyn McClellan, Marina Gordon, Maris Kreizman, Marisa, Mark Bixby, Mark Owen, Mary Agnes Krell, Mary Kay Feather, Mary Schile, Matt Haughey, Matt Mansfield, Matt Markoff, Matthew Anderson, Matthew Baldwin, Matthew Brown, Max Fenton, Max Temkin, Maya Gadley, Megan McGilvray, Melissa Dahl, Melvin Rivera, Michael B. Johnson, Michelle Wynne, Mike Dodge, Mike La Fon, Mike Meyer, Mike Servais, Miranda Mulligan, Molly Jackson, Molly Larsen, Morgan Engle, Nancy Van Westbroek, Naz Hamid, Nic Barajas, Nick Robinson, Nicola Griffith, Nina Frenkel, Paige, Pamela Drouin, Patricia Auburn, Patrick B. Gibson, Patrick Kelley, Patrick Williamson, Paul Constant, Paul F Rogers, Paul M. Rodriguez, Paullette Gaudet, Peter Norton, Peter Symuleski, Phil Zepeda, Pius Uzamere, PJ Macklin, Rachel Dodge, Rachel Purpel, Rachelle Pulkkila, Rahawa Haile, Raymond Irvin, Reid Bannecker, Richard W Mockler, Rob Skinner, Robert Occhialini, Roberta Larsen, Robin Forman, Robin Sloan, Robynne Raye, Roya Naini, Royal Stuart, Russell E Shaw, Ruth Schemmel, Ryan Osborn, Ryan Smith, S. Soma, Sally Hallow, Sandi Vincent, Sandor Weisz, Sara, Sara Bennett, Sarah Penn, Scott and Mary Lou Reed, Scott Boms, Scott Robbin, Sharry Nyberg, Shawn Eiferman, Shezad Morani, Spencer Sass, Stacey Bennetts, Stephanie Clary, Steve Carlson, Suresh, Susan and Robert McGinty, Susan Porter, Tammy Robacker, Tanya Korpi Macleod, Teresa Lynch, Teresa Tonai, Tessa Wizon, Thomas Brew, Thomas J Auflick, Tieg Zaharia, Tiff Doyle, Tiff Fehr, Todd Alcott, Todd Reidy, Todd Wallar, Tom Carmony, Tonia Boyle, Tracy Kincheloe, Treena Colby, Tricia McDermott, Tyler Adams, Valerie Hunting, Vicki Nerino, Victoria Ostrovskaya, Vinca Swanson, Vincent Dean, and Zoya Ali

A note on the type

This book is typeset, with minor exception, in the Harriet Series, a type family from Okay Type, designed by Jackson Cavanaugh. It takes its inspiration from Baskerville, but manages to declare itself as decidedly modern. There are surprises across the entire weight range, from playful ornate bolds, to slender and elegant light weights. You can find out more at THEHARRIETSERIES.COM

A note on equality

Same-sex marriage was legalized throughout the United States during the production of this book. Despite this, many young LGBTQ youths will still encounter serious struggles, ranging from identity issues to lack of familial support, and too often, violence. Please consider supporting a charity near you, such as Seattle's Lambert House: a drop-in center for LGBTQ youth. Find out more at LAMBERTHOUSE.ORG.

About the author

Martin McClellan is a designer and writer. He is Senior UX Designer for Breaking News (BREAKINGNEWS.COM), and co-founded The Seattle Review of Books (SEATTLEREVIEWOFBOOKS.COM). He lives with his wife Christine and son Lionel in Seattle.

Find out more at MARTINMCCLELLAN.COM.

Follow him on Twitter: @HELLBOX.

California Four O'Clock is his first novel.